A COMPLETE FICTION

A COMPLETE FICTION

A NOVEL

R. L. MAIZES

New York, NY

Copyright © 2025 by R. L. Maizes.
All rights reserved.

This is a work of fiction. Names, characters, businesses, places, events and incidents are either the products of the author's imagination or used in a fictitious manner. Any resemblance to actual persons, living or dead, or actual events is purely coincidental.

Ig Publishing, Inc.
Box 2547
New York, NY 10163
www.igpub.com

ISBN: 978-1-63246-21-14

MORE ADVANCE PRAISE FOR *A COMPLETE FICTION*

"I can't gush enough about R.L. Maizes's *A Complete Fiction*—one of the most fabulously complex, interesting, and hilarious novels I've read in years. As two protagonists fight (and fight dirty) over their respective truths, Maizes asks hard questions about cancel culture, power, politics, sexual abuse, and narrative that make me interrogate my own values. Maizes's sensitivity in tackling difficult topics further underscores the bravery and badassery of this un-put-downable book. Read it, read it! And then talk to me, because I can't stop thinking about it."—**Erika Krouse**, author of *Tell Me Everything: The Story of a Private Investigation*, Winner of 2023 Edgar Award

"*A Complete Fiction* checks all of the boxes for an incredible read that sits at the intersection of cancel culture and #metoo. It's packed full of contemporary anxiety, it's hilarious in moments, and it's a page-turner where readers will get a true joy out of being a fly on the wall to the conversations between characters. Maizes surfaces the absurdity of modern life, but in the way your smartest and most empathetic friend would. This novel is a beach read for people who also care about the cultural zeitgeist."
—**Wendy J. Fox**, author of *What If We Were Somewhere Else* and *If the Ice Had Held*

"The question of who has a right to tell a story fuels *A Complete Fiction* with righteous anger and verve. But R.L. Maizes turns the battles roiling publishing and society into a nuanced and humorous portrait of two flawed writers struggling to be heard. Through a twisting plot, revealing the complexity behind impulsive social media posts, we end up having empathy for the accused and the accuser. It's a difficult feat that Maizes pulls off beautifully."—**Arsen Kashkashian**, Head Buyer and General Manager, Boulder Bookstore

For the writers, published and unpublished.

CHAPTER ONE

Passengers would sometimes share intimate details of their lives with P.J. as she shuttled them from one place to another. Affairs. Costly mistakes at work. But when a rider named Franklin said, apropos of nothing and with an air of resignation, "I killed my wife," it was a first.

P.J. glanced in the rearview mirror. Franklin had feathered hair and a pale wide forehead she would have liked to doodle on. He seemed no more homicidal than her other passengers. "Shoot her or stab her?"

"Neither." He tapped his fingers on the door handle as if he might bolt, though P.J. was currently chasing a series of synchronized green lights through Denver's downtown.

"Splash of antifreeze in her iced tea?"

"I didn't kill her intentionally."

"Manslaughter, then."

"I guess," he said. "She asked me to drive her to the supermarket, but I said I was busy. She never liked driving. I told her to order one of your cars, but she decided to ride her bike. I'd just bought her a basket for it, and the market was only a mile away. She thought she'd have enough time to make it back before she had to get the girls from the preschool around the corner. She was almost home."

He paused and P.J. reflected that "almost" was possibly the saddest word in the English language.

"Driver said he never even saw her. If I'd taken her, she'd be alive." He shrugged off his jacket and touched the tip of a Band-Aid that poked out of the pocket of his gray short-sleeved shirt. "They're making me see a therapist, but it won't help."

P.J. wondered what the bandage was for. "Who're 'they'?"

"My brothers." Franklin smoothed his pressed black pants. "You don't have to say anything. What's there to say? I have to live with it."

"Not your fault."

"That's what everyone tells me. But if I'd driven her, she'd be alive. She never asked for much. Then, the one time she asks, I tell her, no."

"Yeah. Not your fault."

Franklin took the Band-Aid out of his pocket, sniffed it as if it were a wine cork, and put it back. "Ever since it happened, I've been afraid to drive. Afraid I might hurt someone. Do you know how much force is involved when a two-thousand-pound car hits a bike? And the blind spot on these cars is bigger than an airplane hangar."

P.J. checked her mirrors. "Definitely not your fault."

"A cyclist doesn't stand a chance," he said, as if he hadn't heard her. But then he leaned forward. "How do you figure?"

"Everything had to line up. Your wife's choice to live in the city, the fact that she met you, had kids, didn't like driving, and on and on. It all had to happen just that way to put her in front of the car. And everything in the driver's life had to line up, too. His decision to go out that afternoon, to linger over whatever he was doing earlier or to hurry, the fact that he didn't see her. It all had to happen. Don't you see? Maybe we should arrest the driver's boss, if the driver was on his way to a meeting. Or the woman who gave birth to the driver because without her there's no accident. Or the preschool administrator whose schedule made your wife hurry. Or whoever designed the street to be too wide or too narrow to allow your wife to ride safely. It's too big for you to take the blame."

Franklin seemed skeptical. "What do you do when you're not driving?"

"I write books."

"About what?"

"The latest one is a novel about sexual assault," P.J. said.

"A comedy."

"Yeah."

A text came in for P.J., but she ignored it. Ride With Me had made them watch clips of gruesome accidents caused by distracted driving. In one, a man described from his hospital bed how he'd veered off the road while scrolling through Crave. The message would be there after she dropped her passenger off.

Franklin was quiet, and P.J.'s mind drifted to Sloane, her agent, and the three books P.J. had entrusted to her to sell, the latest making the rounds of editors at small presses after being rejected by all the large presses Sloane had sent it to. Maybe she needed a different agent. Metal charms hung from P.J.'s rearview mirror: a four-leaf clover, a dream catcher, a horn of plenty, and a prosperity cat. She added one each time she finished writing a book, two with the last one, but they hadn't done her any good.

She wasn't asking to be rich, though she wouldn't have turned up her nose at one of those seven-figure advances that landed like giant *Publishers Clearing House* checks on a few stunned writers. What she really wanted was to be published. To call herself an author. To feel justified having spent twelve years bent over a laptop rather than having the two children Vlad, her ex-husband, had wanted, that he now had with someone else.

Her mind elsewhere, P.J. cruised past the therapist's office, despite the rideshare app announcing they'd arrived.

"This is me," Franklin said.

A block north of the address, she braked hard. Charms clinked and the horn of plenty beat the cat. "You want me to go back?"

"Don't bother."

"You shouldn't tell people you killed your wife," P.J. said.

"Why not?"

"They might believe you."

"Good luck with your book," he said.

After Franklin got out, P.J. read the text. It was from Sloane, asking her to call. Her agent never texted. Had her novel finally sold? She imagined a rhapsodic quote from Margaret Atwood splashed across the dust jacket. A front-page review in the Times read by a certain relative who'd given her an LSAT prep course last Christmas. And paying off Sisyphean student loans, her neck muscles relaxing for the first time since she'd received her repayment notice.

She filed away the encounter with Franklin for use in a future book, one of the few perks of the job, and called Sloane.

Bella, her agent's assistant, picked up. "She's in a meeting."

"What did she want to talk to me about?"

"She'll tell you. I'll let her know you called."

"Did someone make an offer on my book?"

"She'll talk to you about it," Bella said.

"Was she singing?" Sloane sang when she was happy, screwing up the lyrics of pop songs and Broadway musicals, alike.

"She'll call you, P.J.," Bella said.

A passenger had requested P.J.'s car, and Ride With Me penalized drivers who turned down jobs. If P.J. didn't hear from

Sloane in a few hours, she'd browbeat Bella into telling her the news.

She hit *accept* on the app and drove to a large, stuccoed Tudor home, the kind of place people bought as trophies or as tax havens for their excessive wealth. If she ever had enough money to buy a house, if she ever needed that much space, P.J. would get something sustainable, built with solar panels and a system for rain water collection. As she waited for her passenger, P.J. checked her phone, but there was nothing more from her agent. Franklin had given her five stars and a twenty-five percent tip. He seemed like a nice guy, someone she might consider dating if he ever stopped torturing himself. Not that he'd shown the slightest romantic interest in her. And he *had* killed his wife. She wished she'd asked what the Band-Aid was for. Not knowing was going to bug her all day.

What was taking her passenger so long? She was probably checking for the umpteenth time that she'd packed her new Colleen Hoover novel, while P.J.'s life dripped away like the water that greened the home's stadium-sized lawn.

A woman sporting a towering decades-old hairstyle emerged from the house, yanking a suitcase behind her. P.J. met her at the end of a flagstone walk.

"Who are you here for?" the woman asked, presumably having read about the recent kidnapping of a Ride With Me passenger by someone impersonating a driver.

"Margaret Smalls," P.J. said.

"That's me," the passenger chirped, and she surrendered the suitcase.

P.J. rolled it to the open trunk and hefted it in.

"Can't be too careful," Margaret said, once P.J. was behind the wheel.

"Psychopaths don't drive electric cars," P.J. said. "They drive gas-guzzling SUVs. But I suppose it can't hurt to be careful."

"Oh, yes. Just think about that poor girl." The woman began to describe in detail the condition of the victim's body, which had been found wrapped in a tarp in a canoe.

P.J. regretted the second donut she'd eaten on the way. "Yeah, yeah, okay. I read about it, too."

"Naturally, the casket was closed at the wake. There's only so much a mortuary can do. And you don't want to scare children. I was at a funeral once—"

P.J. turned on the radio.

Margaret shouted something about children fainting in a chapel.

"Where are you headed?" P.J. said, changing the subject.

"I'm going to visit my grandchildren."

"Nice."

"Do you have children?" the woman asked.

"Not yet."

"Are you married?"

P.J. shook her head and sped up, hoping to deliver Margaret to the airport a little sooner.

"It's none of my business," the woman said, "but maybe if you wore a little makeup, grew your hair out, dressed in something a little more flattering, you might meet a gentleman while you're driving."

P.J. glanced down at her oversized *Save the Tigers* race T-shirt, her frayed cargo pants. Was that all it would take? Spackle concealer over freckles that spattered like hot grease across her nose and cheeks every spring, pour herself into spandex tights, and men would flood her with proposals from the backseat. Dan Jones would publish her story—"How an

Utterly Annoying Passenger Helped Me Find My Soulmate"—in his *Modern Love* column.

"You could meet a pilot heading to the airport or a salesman on his way to a conference," Margaret said. "You do like men, don't you? It's fine if you don't. Everything goes nowadays, doesn't it? One of my daughters married a girl she played volleyball with. Do you play volleyball?"

P.J. pretended she hadn't heard.

After pulling up at Departures, she got Margaret's suitcase out. "Have a safe flight," she said, because she'd read somewhere that it could improve her driver rating and it was better than saying, "cheers," as she had been, which made it sound like she was drinking. P.J. chauffeured her next passenger to a five-star hotel and shut off the car. Waving at a green-uniformed attendant, she dashed to the bathroom. With its luxurious stalls, free tampons, and lavender skin lotion, it was as close as she would ever come to visiting a spa.

Still waiting to hear back from her agent, she squeezed in three more rides, all while her battery indicator flashed "very low," then drove to a charging station. A passenger in a Stetson bigger than a hot tub had commented recently on the foolishness of driving a car with limited range for a living. "Nice hat," she'd replied because there was no convincing him that his enormous pickup was turning the environment into a charred wasteland, or that her car was cheaper to drive, or that she enjoyed stopping for a charge because it gave her time to write. The one time she'd tried, she hadn't gotten a tip.

She brought up Sloan's number on her phone, but before calling rummaged in her glovebox for a pen and a small notebook. If it was finally happening, if after all the disappointments and near-misses a publisher had finally made an offer on her book, she wanted to remember every detail. She wondered which publisher it was and how large an advance they'd offered. What lovely things they'd said about the novel and her writing. Or maybe more than one publisher wanted to buy it and there'd be an auction, driving up the price. On a blank page, P.J. sketched a champagne flute, bubbles popping around the rim.

She imagined telling her friend Marissa the news. Never one to hold back, Marissa would scream. She wasn't a writer, thank God, so her joy wouldn't be adulterated with all that messy, complicated envy, a feeling P.J. knew all too well. Next, P.J. would tell her mother, who'd offer to take her shopping because that's how her mother's happiness expressed itself. She would post a nibble about the book deal on Crave. For as long as P.J. had been on the app, she'd fantasized about that.

Through her open window, she breathed in the spring air, refusing for once to let a plume of truck exhaust crush her spirit. She gave the prosperity cat a squeeze. In her coffee cup, all that was left were the dregs. She wished she'd stopped at a drive through. No matter. She would treat herself to a celebratory cup after the call, and not the cheap kind she got every morning, either.

Bella put her right through.

"I'm glad you called," Sloane said.

Next to the champagne flute, P.J. doodled a party hat. "Good news, I hope."

"I'm afraid not. I can't sell your book. I've sent it to every publisher I can think of who might be interested. The market is saturated with #metoo novels."

P.J. felt a giant bookcase fall on her, smother her beneath the uncountable words of rival authors.

"I'm sorry," Sloane said. "I know this is hard to hear."

Outside the car, a line of chargers blurred. P.J. wiped her eyes with the rag she used to clean her backup camera. Could you call yourself a writer if publishers repeatedly rejected your work? It seemed ridiculous to keep at it. She was thirty-five, broke, and no closer to reaching her goal than when she'd written the first draft of her first novel on the clunky laptop her father had been about to throw out after buying a sleek new one for himself.

She waited for Sloane to end their relationship. To tell her it was hopeless, that she didn't need an agent because she would never publish a book. P.J. wouldn't blame her.

"P.J.? Are you there?"

She supposed she could look for a new agent, but who would want to take on a three-time loser?

"You're not driving, are you?" Sloane said. "If you are, maybe you should pull over."

"I'm parked," P.J. muttered.

"Good, good. Have you written anything new? In a few years, the market might be more open to this one, and we'll try again."

P.J. raised her voice to be heard over the shrill beeping of a forklift. "You're not firing me as a client?"

"God, no. You're a good writer. I don't know why your books haven't sold except it happens that way sometimes. You hit the market at the wrong time. Or your books don't fit the zeitgeist. I wouldn't say this unless I believed it. You'll sell a book. Eventually."

Eventually. P.J. tossed her pen onto the passenger seat and it rolled over the side into car purgatory. She hated everything she'd written lately, none of it as good as the novel Sloane had just said she couldn't sell. Maybe she'd never write a novel that good again. Tipping back her cup, she got a mouthful of bitter grounds.

After Sloane hung up, P.J. grabbed another donut from the box in her backpack. Glaze coated her fingers as she bit into the moist sugary cake. Crumbs tumbled onto her shirt, the seat, and the floor, the soiled interior of her car matching the unwashed exterior. Passengers gave drivers of immaculate cars higher ratings, but P.J. couldn't bring herself to waste water so her car would look like she'd just driven it out of a showroom. She wasn't willing to deplete the planet's dwindling store of energy vacuuming it. At the end of each day, she collected plastic water bottles riders had left behind and recycled them, threw away their protein bar wrappers and used tissues, but that was it. She wasn't a maid.

As if she hadn't gotten enough bad news for one day, while P.J. was unplugging her car, Marissa texted that a book similar to P.J.'s had sold for a million dollars. P.J. assumed Marissa meant her #metoo novel, rather than her earlier books, which were lighter, and which P.J. had once hoped would make her as famous as the Shopaholic books had made Sophie Kinsella. Her most recent novel was dark and political, loosely based on the sexual assault of her sister, Mia, by the state senator she'd interned for while in college. For years after the assault, Mia would start drinking as early as breakfast. In her late twenties, she got sober, but the sisters were no longer close.

P.J. looked up the sale in *Publishers Marketplace* and read a one-sentence description of a book titled *Up the Hill* that could easily have been a description of her book, *Halls of Power*, if you changed the gender of the main character.

Don't Sweat the Small Stuff read a neon blue banner in a clothing store window. "Fuck off," P.J. said. There was nothing small about this. She reread the description of the book. It was maddening. She had known her novel was good. Yet every publisher had rejected it, saying things like, "The writing is beautiful," and even, "It's an important book." Then adding words to the effect of, "But there have been a lot of #metoo books." Not that many, apparently, as long as the #metoo book was written by a man.

"WTF!!!!!!!!" P.J. texted back.

"Right?"

P.J. called her friend. "We sent the author, George Dunn, my novel a year and a half ago."

"Why would you do that?" Marissa said.

"He's an acquiring editor at a small publisher."

"No way."

"Way." *Make It a Great Day* read another window banner, and P.J. wished for something hard to throw through the plate glass. "He rejected it. But in his email, he had a lot of nice things to say about the book."

P.J. could hear Marissa thumping the phone against her chin, as she did when she was excited. "I bet he did. I bet he had all kinds of nice things to say about it."

Had she saved the email? She usually held on to anything that complimented her writing, rereading it when despair crept up on her.

"I have to go," Marissa said. "My biology class is starting. If I leave the little hoodlums alone, they add X-rated features to my cell diagrams."

P.J. turned the Ride With Me app back on. She couldn't stop thinking about Dunn. Had he really gotten the idea for his book after reading hers? What else had he stolen from her manuscript? It was hard enough to write a book without a shady editor plagiarizing it.

Searching through old emails on her phone, she found the one from Dunn that Sloane had forwarded. He'd been as enthusiastic as she remembered. But it was the fourth line that stopped her. "I really like the way you tell the story from the point of view of the woman who was victimized and also the point of view of the sexual abuser, which wasn't an obvious choice," he'd written. *Publishers Marketplace* had described Dunn's book as told from the points of view of a Senate page and the senator who sexually assaults him. *Bingo.*

A passenger requested her car. P.J. knew she should accept the job, but she couldn't stop staring at the description of the book. A book that was hers but not hers. A book that had made another writer rich, while she struggled to pay rent on a four-hundred-square-foot studio apartment. It would be read by everyone, establishing the reputation and career of a writer, but that writer would be Dunn rather than her. Yet another novel written by a man that received accolades, while those written by women were labelled "chick lit," as if a fluffy infant bird had wandered across a keyboard randomly pecking at letters. It was misogyny, pure and simple.

P.J. opened Crave, rage exploding through her thumbs, and drafted a nibble:

> Hey @GeorgeDunn congratulations on the sale of UP THE HILL. Your book sounds a lot like my book, HALLS OF POWER, which my agent sent you. Not good enough to publish but good enough to steal?

She attached a screenshot of the incriminating email and the description of Dunn's book from *Publishers Marketplace*. Then she paused. She knew she should call Sloane before she did anything else and certainly before she made the kind of public accusation she was about to make. But her agent would want to "look into the matter," as she always did when P.J. proposed taking action. P.J. didn't want to wait. Couldn't wait, as worked up as she was. Doubting it would matter because she had barely four hundred diners on the app, she pressed *serve*.

CHAPTER TWO

George Dunn sat in his cubicle at Peapod Press, a space small enough that if he stretched his long arms, he could nearly touch the fabric walls on either side. His pole vault legs had never fit properly under the laminate desk, and he had to contort himself to avoid bruises on his knees. He'd spent much of the last hour working on edits to *Up the Hill*, though he should have been attending to the manuscripts piled two feet high on his desk and three feet on the floor.

When it came to reading submissions, George was old-fashioned, preferring printouts to electronic copies, even as he regretted the harm to the environment. He was also slow. Too slow, he'd been told numerous times by Ryan, Peapod's publisher and editor-in-chief, and it was true. A tide of manuscripts flooded Peapod's offices, and George gave each one too many chances to win him over. If the opening chapter didn't succeed, he waited to see if the second one would. If the characters were flat, he thought of ways to make them compelling. He hesitated to reject them (though that was overwhelmingly what he had to do), because as a writer himself he knew what had gone into even the weakest manuscripts and how much hope was riding on them.

His phone chimed and a Crave notification appeared on the screen. It looked like someone was congratulating him on his success. Janelle, his agent, had posted the announcement that his book had sold on all her social media channels that morning.

He supposed he should do the same, but he had mixed feelings about sharing the news. It felt like bragging, though everyone did it. At Peapod, he expected his writers to promote their work that way.

He tapped his phone and read P.J. Larkin's nibble, then read it again, hoping it didn't say what he thought it said. From the back of his chair, he grabbed a shapeless blue track jacket and pulled it on before reading the nibble again.

George remembered Larkin's novel precisely because, like his book, it was about a politician who sexually assaults a subordinate, though that's where the similarities ended. He'd admired Larkin's choice to tell the story in part from the villain's point of view, and it had inspired him to add a few chapters to Up the Hill in the abuser's voice. That wasn't plagiarism. Authors borrowed techniques from one another all the time. George emailed a copy of the nibble to Mary Chu, the editor at Saturn Books who'd bought his novel. "I read this woman's manuscript," he wrote, "but I already had a complete draft of mine. Other than both being #metoo books they're quite different." He didn't tell her about the change Larkin's novel had inspired him to make.

The nibble had no munches. No one had nibbled back, either. Maybe no one would.

Join the meal—munch the nibble to show your approval or nibble back with thoughts of your own! the app prompted. George could almost hear the annoying sound the app made when you munched, that loud crunch like someone eating potato chips in a movie theater when you were trying to hear the dialog.

He clicked on P.J. Larkin's bio and discovered that she drove for Ride With Me. He'd have to remember to use a different rideshare company. She wasn't popular on Crave. He closed the app, then silenced his phone so he could focus on work.

On his desk, a jar labeled Best Value Olives held pens famous authors had recommended in an article about book signings. George picked out a thin Sharpie favored by a National Book Award winner and uncapped it. Flipping over the title page of a manuscript he was about to reject, he practiced the new, dramatic signature he was working on for signing copies of *Up the Hill*. When the page was covered with his name, he turned over the table of contents and filled that, too, before depositing the manuscript in the recycle bin.

Within the hour, Mary emailed back. "Don't worry. Her agent submitted her book to us, too. It's very different from yours."

He supposed a claim like Larkin's was just part of his new life as the author of a Big Book. His agent had assured him *Up the Hill* would be a Big Book because of the huge advance the publisher had offered. They'd need to sell an enormous number of copies to recoup their investment, and they'd throw the weight of the company and its powerful marketing division behind the novel to make that happen.

George could hardly believe his success. For the past thirteen years, he'd toiled in obscurity, editor for a small New York publisher whose books were purchased by a few hundred readers and then disappeared. He'd done everything there: read manuscripts, wrote cover blurbs, copyedited, proofread, checked layouts, sent out promotional copy. The advance was like winning the lottery. He'd signed the Saturn contract earlier that day, ten times thicker than the ones Peapod offered its authors and full of dense legal jargon, but the advance was straightforward enough: a million dollars. A sum he associated with sports figures and investment bankers, not writers.

He'd woken at two o'clock that morning sure he'd gotten the number wrong or dreamed the deal entirely, but when he checked his desk, the contract was there and inside it that elephantine sum. Yet even as he'd held the document, squinting at it in the dim light of his desk lamp, he craved assurance that it wasn't a mistake, a misprint in the amount or in his name, a miracle meant for someone else. But he couldn't ask his agent or Mary for reassurance. He had to act as if he deserved the money. He had to pretend the book was worthy of acclaim, though he wasn't sure if it was any good at all. He just knew he wanted people to read it. And to be heard, to make up for the time when he hadn't been, when it had actually mattered.

From the alley behind Peapod's offices, he video-called his wife Kiara. "What are you doing?"

"Working?"

"Can you talk? For a minute?"

"Where are you?" she said.

"Outside." Where the brick building met the asphalt, the usual detritus had collected: a Milky Way wrapper, an empty Bud Light bottle, a thick patch of lipsticked cigarette butts, as if someone had planted and watered them and their crop had finally come in.

"Hold on." Kiara got up and closed her door. "What's wrong?"

"The sale of my book was announced in *Publishers Marketplace* today. I'm famous. Kind of."

"We'll celebrate tonight."

"We already celebrated," George said.

"We'll celebrate again." Kiara wore a peach suit, a color that had been in style for less than a minute five years before. It didn't matter. It wasn't her clothes you remembered after meeting her, but rather the kindness that enlarged her russet eyes and smoothed the worry lines etched between them.

"A woman accused me of stealing her book. On Crave."

"That's weird."

"Her agent sent it to Peapod a while back, and I read it, and we turned it down. It was about sexual assault."

"Like your book," Kiara said.

"Not really. It's a big subject."

"She must be mad you rejected it."

"Funny thing is, I really liked it. I liked the voice. I cared about the characters. It made me cry." In the sunless alley, he shivered, wishing for something warmer than the thin track jacket.

"Why didn't you publish it?"

"We felt there were too many books like it." Which wasn't exactly true. He'd liked the novel enough to recommend to Ryan that Peapod publish it, and the editor-in-chief had read it and agreed. George had typed up an email to Larkin's agent lavishly praising the novel's straightforward prose and how well she captured the psychology of victim and abuser and the political climate of Washington, D.C. But then, reading the email over, he became afraid that if they published her book there would be less room for his own #metoo novel when the time came. Larkin's book deserved an audience. Readers would identify with the protagonist and it would help them process their own #metoo trauma. The fact that it had been sent to Peapod meant Larkin's agent was running out of options. George wasn't planning to publish *Up the Hill* at a small publisher like Peapod. He had bigger hopes for it even then. But if his hopes didn't pan out, if large publishers had moved past #metoo, or if they rejected his book for reasons that had nothing to do with its quality but because certain tastemakers had decided novels that year should be set exclusively on volcanic islands or written entirely without possessive pronouns, then he liked the idea of his book having somewhere soft to land. He deleted the offer in the last sentence of the email and replaced it with a rejection, writing that the market was saturated with #metoo books. He knew it meant Larkin's novel might never be published, the years she'd spent writing it wasted.

"Did you nibble back?" Kiara said.

"Mary said to ignore it."

"Probably best. Sorry that happened on your big day."

***

George had worked on *Up the Hill* for a decade. After staring at other writers' manuscripts all day, he'd come home and prepare dinner with Kiara: some one-pot recipe they'd found in the paper that never looked quite like the picture when it was done. At seven or eight, after swallowing an energy shot that as often as not gave him heart palpitations, he'd finally sit down in front of his laptop. How many times had he revised the book? Twenty? Thirty? He'd lost count. He was stuck at one point. A few drafts made the book worse. It was only after he added the sexual abuser's voice that he thought he had it right.

He sent it to well-known agents who'd submitted books to him at Peapod. Despite the personal connection, they passed with the same platitudes he'd written himself: "There was a lot to admire here." "We appreciated the chance to consider it." "Ours is just one opinion." He contacted little-known agents and received rejections from them, too. Hoping to keep George from the despair he felt at each new rebuff, Kiara insisted on locking up his phone and computer during their brief time-share-company-sponsored vacation in Cancún.

The email arrived on a Sunday night. George barely remembered querying Janelle Park, a young agent who did editing on the side. She wanted him to know how much his book had meant to her, even if she didn't end up representing him, but she hoped she would. She admired his beautifully crafted sentences and said she could see how much care had gone into the manuscript.

The message was a flint in a dark forest.

Janelle had sold only three books: a mystery and two romance novels. Nothing like George's book. She wasn't the right agent for him, but she was the only one who wanted to represent him. On Monday morning, he called and accepted her offer. At a restaurant that night, he ordered a bottle of cheap sparkling wine and told the server he'd just gotten an agent for his book, Kiara adding, "He did," as if otherwise no one would believe him.

"I have a good feeling about your novel," Janelle had said. "It has #metoo elements, but the victim is male. That's unique and will make it more marketable." It turned out, she was right. Mainstream publishers liked the idea of portraying a man as the injured party. At an auction, nine publishers bid on the book. George's future blazed.

CHAPTER THREE

A slight girl named Rayne climbed into P.J.'s car. She could have been thirteen or fourteen, though everyone looked young to P.J. these days. Islands of pink flesh appeared through holes in the girl's pricey jeans.

P.J. wasn't supposed to pick up unaccompanied minors, but certain parents ordered rides for their kids because it was easier than chauffeuring them. Many of those kids had the rideshare app on their own phones. She wasn't going to leave them stranded because at least with her they were safe. Besides, by the time she realized her passenger was a kid, she'd already used some of her precious charge to reach them.

The girl was headed to an upscale department store. P.J. imagined her buying an entire summer wardrobe without giving a thought to how much CO_2 manufacturing a single pair of shorts belched into the environment. If P.J. were rich—like George Dunn would be once he received his advance—she'd continue to buy used clothing. But she'd drive a top-of-the-line electric car and charge it in the garage of her new townhome. She might shell out a few thousand dollars for a matchmaker. Between driving and writing, she found it hard to muster the energy to date, and when she did, she met few men who could understand her disdain for the luxury electronics on which they spent half of their salaries and then deposited in landfills as soon as newer models came out. "Have you considered that the problem might not be the men?" Marissa had said when P.J. complained.

She wondered what was happening with her nibble. Was there still time to purge it? Dunn had probably seen it by now. If that was the case, she hoped it had at least a few munches. Even if they were just from friends. She was dying to check her phone but had turned off Crave notifications so she wouldn't be tempted.

"I like your car," Rayne said.

P.J. patted the steering wheel. "Zero emissions."

"Nice. I told my parents to get an electric car, but they think climate change is a liberal hoax."

If she ever had kids, P.J. imagined they would be enlightened like her passenger. "At least you tried."

"Right? That's all you can do."

The girl was texting. Probably telling her friends about the awesome driver she'd met. Not like the one passenger who, after being subjected to one of P.J.'s environmental lectures, said, "Why do you care? You'll probably die before the apocalypse." How old had he thought she was?

P.J. said to Rayne, "After you get your license, maybe you'll get an electric car."

The girl didn't look up. "I can get anything I want."

"That's what I figured. So maybe you'll get an EV."

"Yeah. I don't know."

"What don't you know?" P.J. said.

"I just don't know."

"You don't know if you should try to save the planet?"

"I just don't know. My brother has a classic Hummer that's pretty sweet."

"Pretty sweet? Pretty *sweet*? How about rising temperatures, are they pretty sweet? Is the polar ice melting pretty sweet? And so many species being wiped out, some that haven't even been discovered yet?" P.J. twisted in her seat to face Rayne. The girl looked surprised, maybe even a little frightened, but P.J. couldn't stop. "Are rising oceans *pretty sweet*? What about wildfires? And floods? Also *pretty sweet*? And extinction of species?"

"You said that already," Rayne said softly. "About the species."

P.J. turned back toward the road. Fuck kids. The planet was overpopulated.

"I mean, it's good that you have an electric car. Since you drive a lot," the girl said.

When it came to the environment, P.J. was used to adults being stupid, but she expected more from kids, who would have to live with the worst effects of climate change. According to her GPS, they'd arrive at the department store in five minutes. Then she could pull over and see if anyone had nibbled back at her.

"Hey!" Rayne said. "Watch out!"

P.J. jerked the wheel, narrowly avoiding a motorcycle that had swerved into her lane. "You're not going to give me a bad rating, are you?"

"I probably won't rate you at all. I have a lot of shopping to do. Plus, I'm meeting my friends. I'll probably forget you as soon as I get out of the car."

When Rayne started texting again, P.J. hit the brake, tossing the girl from her seat.

***

Opening Crave, P.J. nearly dropped her phone. Her nibble had been re-served more than two thousand times, the number climbing as she watched. Jacqueline Overtree, editor of *Women's Work*, a magazine for professional women, had weighed in on P.J.'s side to her ten million diners. Listed as popular menu items on the app were the hashtags #CancelGeorgeDunn and

#UnpaidLiteraryLabor. People were inviting Saturn Books and Peapod Press to join the meal.

P.J. reread the one-sentence description of Dunn's book. How alike were their novels? She didn't really know. Yet it couldn't be a coincidence that an editor who'd admired her book came out with one that sounded so similar a year and a half later.

She'd been served hundreds of private meals, including one from Lysistrata, a feminist press. They wanted to see her novel and might be interested in publishing it. Sloane had sent the manuscript to Lysistrata and had never heard back. P.J. forwarded the publisher's message to her agent.

A minute later, Sloan called. "You definitely stirred things up," she said.

"Is that good or bad?"

"It depends."

"What does that mean?" P.J. said.

"If people think you were victimized by Dunn that could be good," Sloane said. "We might sell your book on the strength of public curiosity alone. But if people think your accusation is sour grapes because his book sold for a lot of money and yours didn't sell at all, that could be bad. Do you want me to try to get a copy of the book from his publisher, so we can see what's what?"

"Sure," P.J. said, though she was anything but. What if the books turned out to be wildly different? Would she have to apologize?

Even if Dunn hadn't stolen her book, the playing field was far from level. Big publishers came out with more books by men, and men's books were reviewed more. Maybe stirring things up was what a woman had to do.

The nibbles weren't all in P.J.'s favor.

"Dunn's book isn't out yet. Has Larkin even read it? How

can she claim plagiarism if she hasn't compared the book to hers?" nibbled a female literature professor.

"Why are you sticking up for a plagiarizer?" @WomynsRites nibbled back.

"You're a traitor to your gender," nibbled back @BeaNeedsAnAgent.

And from @On_Your_Left: "What matters is that Dunn read HER book and stole HER ideas."

"Send in the cavalry! A Caucasian dude almost slipped by publishing's gatekeepers!"nibbled@SantaIsWhiteandJesusIsToo. "String him up before his western ideas corrupt your children! #draintheswamp #maga #AmericaFirst #caucasianrights"

P.J. called Marissa. "Have you seen Crave?"

"I've been with kids all morning. I'm looking," she said. "Oh my God, you're famous. But this is good, right? You don't want him to get away with stealing your book."

"The thing is, how do I know he really stole it? Maybe he just wrote a similar book?"

"Men are always stealing from women," Marissa said. "Eunice Foote discovered the greenhouse effect three years before John Tyndall, but who do you think got the credit? Chien-Shiung Wu proved a theory in particle physics but did she share in the Nobel Prize her male colleagues won? Nope. No prize for Wu. Here's a chance to even things out. You can't back down now, anyway. Think about how ridiculous you'll look." Marissa had earned her principal's license, but in more than a year of looking, she hadn't found a position in administration. P.J. knew some of the jobs Marissa had applied for had gone to other women. But it was also true, as Marissa never tired of reminding her, that the higher you looked in education, the more men you found.

***

At home that night, while P.J. fried a black bean burger for dinner, someone knocked on her front door. She wasn't expecting anyone. She looked through the peephole and saw her sister, Mia, tugging on the lifeguard whistle she always wore around her neck though she hadn't been swimming in years. P.J. opened the door and the fruity smell of drugstore shampoo wafted toward her.

Mia blinked rapidly. "I'm on Crave, you know."

"I know." The truth was she'd forgotten. She stepped away from the door, allowing Mia to enter.

Mia followed her to the far side of the studio where a white stove, a chest-high black refrigerator, and a sink that was beginning to rust lined the wall. "Did you write a book about me?"

"It's fiction." P.J. flipped the burger.

"Is it about an intern who was sexually assaulted by a state representative?"

"You want some dinner?" P.J. took two plates from the cabinet.

"Did you write about what happened to me?" Mia tapped the whistle against her lips, and P.J. was afraid she would blow it.

"The character in the book is a junior staffer, not an intern, older than you were, and she's assaulted by the chief of staff in a Congressional office in Washington, D.C., not a state senator in Colorado." P.J. had thought the nation's capital would be a more marketable backdrop.

"Does the junior staffer develop a drinking problem?" Mia said.

"No."

"No?"

"A drug problem." P.J. slid the burger onto a plate and turned off the burner, one of two that worked. She dropped slices of bread into the toaster. "Did you eat?"

"You told me your novel was about politics."

"It is."

"You can't do this. It was bad enough living through it once. I don't want to live through it again. Not to mention how humiliating it would be for people to read it."

P.J. spread margarine on the toast. "It's not you. I changed everything. And anyway, it's not published, so no one has seen it. If you don't want this, I'm going to eat it."

"That editor saw it. The one you mentioned. Anyway, who gave you permission to write about my life? Write about your own life. Or write about the environment, since you're obsessed with it."

"My life is boring. And I once tried to write about the environment. I showed my agent the first hundred pages. She said no one wanted to read a lecture pretending to be a novel."

"Not my problem," Mia said.

P.J. set the food on an oak table she'd found on the street, its only flaws half a dozen water rings and a leg that didn't quite reach the floor. The leg wasn't a problem as long she remembered not to fill her coffee mug more than halfway. What was wrong with people, throwing away perfectly good furniture? She rolled her desk chair to the table for Mia and sat on a metal folding chair. Her sister remained standing.

She'd meant to talk to Mia about the book while she was writing it. But as the novel had evolved, becoming less and less about Mia and more about characters and a plot P.J. invented, she wondered if she needed to. She convinced herself it would be better not to worry her sister before the book was finished and she could read it and see it wasn't about her. When it seemed the book would never be published, P.J. had thought, why worry Mia at all?

"I want to see the book," Mia said.

"It's not your story," P.J. said, her mouth full. "It's more violent. Are you sure it won't upset you?"

"I'm sure it will upset me. Email it to me."

"Maybe it would be better if you didn't read it."

"Better for who?" Mia opened a cabinet and took out a glass.

"Both of us?"

"Send it to me." She filled the glass with water. "If it's not about me, like you say, I'll be relieved."

"Okay." P.J. had changed nearly all of the details. She'd created an entirely new story inspired by what had happened to her sister, but different. Before she'd written a single word, she'd researched sexual assault and the many ways it could impact victims, so she'd have more than just her sister's experience in mind while she wrote it. And yet. There were a few things Mia had told her, certain things that had happened and how Mia had felt, that she'd incorporated. They gave the book its authenticity.

CHAPTER FOUR

As George rode the subway home to his Queens apartment, he scrolled through nibbles demanding Peapod fire him, Saturn cancel his book deal, Larkin sue him for copyright infringement, the Authors Union cancel his membership. In the rattle of the car, he thought he could hear the shattering of his reputation as a careful editor, an up-and-coming author, and a progressive who cared about social justice and women's rights.

There was a terrible irony in the allegation that he'd plagiarized Larkin's book. *Up the Hill* had actually been inspired by the events of his own life. But he hadn't told anyone other than his parents that he'd been sexually assaulted as a Senate page when he was sixteen. Neither his agent nor his editor knew. He hadn't even told Kiara. They knew he'd been a page, that was all.

As a young man, George had wanted nothing more than to go into politics. His father, Cyrus, a D.C. lawyer, had contacted one of their senators who helped George with his page application. When George received the appointment, he was convinced he was on his way. Pages had gone on to hold lofty public offices, including Senate seats, and in the case of Spiro Agnew—which admittedly had ended badly—the vice presidency.

During George's first week at the Capitol, Wilma Sands, senator from Tennessee, called him into her office. Nothing unusual about that. As a page appointed by the Democratic party, he was expected to work for all the Democratic senators.

He sat before her mammoth, glass-topped desk, trying to quell the shaking in his hands. He'd heard she was cruel to her staff, shouting and throwing briefing books at them. Though at six feet he was probably taller than her, she seemed enormous, square gold glasses framing a jowly face, linebacker shoulders rising beneath an algae-colored suit. "Congratulations," she said, revealing a mouth full of large, perfect teeth. "These are difficult jobs to secure."

"Thank you," he said.

"You should be proud of yourself."

"Thank you," he said, again, and then felt ridiculous for repeating himself.

She pushed a bowl of foil-wrapped chocolates toward him, a fancy Swiss variety he'd never seen before. He took the first one his fingers touched. He didn't know if he was expected to eat it in front of her or save it. He was wearing the page uniform, and if he put it in the pocket of the navy blue suit jacket it might melt, and he couldn't remember the dry cleaning schedule. "Thank you," he said for the third time, sounding like a robot or a person who spoke limited English.

"You're very polite," she said, laughing. "Go ahead and eat it."

He didn't dare say "thank you" again. Instead, he unwrapped the giant confection and put it in his mouth. He thought he'd never finish chewing, his mouth too dry to swallow. She watched him and smiled, but he couldn't say the smile was friendly, he couldn't say what it was.

She picked up a glass of water from the desk and held it out to him. "If you don't mind sharing with me."

He sipped from it gratefully.

"I read the essay you included with your page application,"

she said. "Someone on my staff sent it to me. They thought I would like it, and they were right. The writing was elegant, advanced for a young man your age." She stood and took a book of essays from a shelf and handed it to him. "For you. Montaigne is thought of as the father of the modern essay. I think you'll enjoy his work, since you're gifted in the form." George blushed. "Read them, then come back and tell me what you think."

"I will," George said, a drop of brown spit flying from his mouth onto the desk where he and the senator could see it.

The senator pulled out a handkerchief and wiped the desk. "Someone like you, destined for great things, shouldn't worry about a small thing like spit," she said. "I've got a meeting that I have to prepare for, but I enjoyed our chat."

George waited for her to give him legislative papers or a message to deliver to another official, his usual work as a page, and was surprised when she didn't. Though she'd summoned him, she didn't seem to have a task for him.

As he walked away from the office, he savored her kindness. How wrong people were to malign her! George had been homesick since he'd arrived at the Capitol. Though his parents were only a few miles away, he was living in the page dorm. His father had prohibited him from coming home before Thanksgiving to encourage George to find friends among his new peers. He hadn't. He'd never made friends easily, not at school or in scouts. The other boys in the page program talked effortlessly about football, flirted with girls before disappearing with them down Pennsylvania Avenue. But George never knew how to inject himself into a conversation, his nerves lighting up when he tried.

A few days later the senator sent for him again. "How are you settling in?" she said. "Making friends? Enjoying your time in the program?"

"It's exciting. Seeing how the Senate works," he said.

"Yes, that's the perfect word for it. Exciting. I've been a senator for fifteen years and it's still exciting. I imagine you're thinking of a career in politics." They discussed the first essay in the Montaigne, which he'd read twice.

Her gaze was uncomfortably direct. He wondered if he had something in his nose. Not knowing where to look, he examined the items on her desk, including a pad imprinted with her name and title. She nodded toward it. "Take it," she said. "As a memento."

"I was just looking—"

"I have a drawerful," she said. "Paid for by the taxpayer. Please, I'd like you to have it."

That was the way it went. One day a pad, the next a pen, books, a ticket she couldn't use to a performance at the Kennedy Center. And always the chocolates, which he learned to take with him and eat later, as sweet as any he'd ever tasted.

Six weeks into his appointment, a member of her staff called and said the senator wanted to see him. He thought little of it, he was so used to their visits by then.

"Close the door behind you," she said when he arrived.

They usually kept the door open, but George wasn't alarmed. He imagined she had something private to share.

"Come around," she said, as he was about to sit opposite her desk.

Around? She motioned for him to join her on her side of the desk. Maybe he had a spot on his tie. A bit of his breakfast. It was hard to eat in the page uniform. Looking down, he didn't see anything. She motioned again, and he approached, stopping at the corner of the large, shiny desk.

"You look very handsome," she said.

"Thank you," George mumbled, because he'd been raised right.

"Come closer," she said.

He took one step and then another. He was used to listening to adults. That was how he'd managed to become a page. And she wasn't any adult. She was a senator, a person whose authority was recognized everywhere. She'd been good to him. Presenting him with gifts, easing his loneliness, making him feel like a standout among the pages.

He could smell her herbal face cream, like the one his mother used.

She swiveled her chair around and faced him. "You seem nervous."

He was. Sweat dampened the underarms of his white button-down shirt. Whatever this was, it made him tremble.

Spray held her gunmetal gray hair an inch from her scalp. He looked down at her desk, covered with bills and other important papers. She stood up and brushed his frizzy, honey-colored bangs from his forehead. "I bet you're a lady-killer at school."

The touch of her fingers stopped time, stopped his breath, filled his lungs with cotton. He didn't say anything. She leaned her face toward his neck, sniffed his skin, and pressed her lips to the side of his Adam's apple.

He pissed himself.

He'd gulped down three glasses of orange juice at breakfast and now it all flowed out of him. He closed his eyes, wishing he were a camp counselor like his cousin Allen, who he'd always outshone. When he looked at his feet, the senator's eyes followed. She jumped back from the puddle that was forming.

She pointed to the bathroom attached to her office. "Go

clean yourself up," she said in a voice he'd never heard before, one as brittle as slate.

By the time he came out, she was gone. He told the director of the page program he felt sick and had to go back to the dormitory. The man didn't seem surprised.

The senator never talked to him again.

He didn't tell anyone in the program what had happened. To speak of it was to speak of his own humiliation. He knew what she'd done was wrong, but also that she had the dual advantages of age and power. Who would believe him? Telling would hurt him more than it hurt her.

He had no intention of telling his parents, either. It would just upset his mother and anger his father. But when he returned home for Thanksgiving, the truth spilled out even before he brought his suitcase upstairs. As his father shut his eyes to consider the senator's behavior, George felt safe for the first time in weeks. His father would know what to do. He would protect George and others like him. Cyrus was a man of authority. A man who by profession knew the rules and followed them, insisting others do the same. He wasn't afraid of Wilma Sands.

Faith, his mother, had prepared a pot roast because it was George's favorite. He could smell the savory juices and something else, something sweet, perhaps a pumpkin bread. His stomach cheered, the sound like gears turning. A red cotton throw he'd napped under as a young boy hung over the back of the couch. It felt good to be home.

"You can't make an accusation like that without thinking about the repercussions," Cyrus said.

It took George a minute to comprehend that his father was taking a position opposite his own. That Cyrus had offered a reprimand in place of the help George needed. As young as he was, George understood his father meant repercussions to himself and his law practice. The damage both would sustain if Cyrus—or George—tried to undermine a prominent Democratic senator. A political institution.

His mother hung onto the banister. She looked like she wanted to say something, but before she could, Cyrus flung a series of questions at George, the kind he would direct at a hostile witness whose testimony he wished to cast in doubt. "You're sure this isn't just a fantasy of yours? An older woman coming on to you?" ("No," George said.) "Why would a U.S. Senator put her career in jeopardy like that?" ("I don't know," George said.) "Maybe she was just being nice? Or making a joke? I've seen her be quite funny." ("No," George said again.)

What kind of joke could it have been? Bombarded by his father's questions, George began to doubt his own memory. Had he imagined it? Or misinterpreted the senator's intentions? He didn't think so, but he could no longer be sure.

For the second time that fall, young George's landscape shifted, revealing hidden dangers. People he thought he knew behaved as strangers. His father retreated to his study. His mother stood between George and the study door, as if unsure to whom she owed a greater allegiance. Alone, George climbed the elegant wood staircase to his bedroom.

He still thought he wanted a career in politics. He'd worked on campaigns every summer since he was twelve. If he publicly accused Senator Sands, he would lose all that. And if his parents didn't believe him, who would? He convinced himself that what the senator had done was trivial. But it wasn't. He didn't know that until he was writing *Up the Hill*.

He lost fifteen pounds at the Capitol. When his page

appointment ended and he returned home, his mother took him to his pediatrician who ran tests that came up negative. He finished his junior and senior years of high school, tried to forget what had happened, and thought he had succeeded. He never participated in politics again. In college, he majored in English literature.

He began writing a novel, a political thriller. A tall Senate page as the hero. But that wasn't the story he was meant to tell, no matter how hard he tried. It wasn't until he started writing a #metoo novel that his words came alive. He set the story in the present, changed the state the senator was from, her appearance, and the committees she headed, so no one would suspect who had inspired the character.

***

When he returned from work, Kiara was sitting on the couch, hooking a black rug. It would end up at the back of their bedroom closet atop a waist-high stack of other bleak, monochromatic rugs.

"Is that a new project?" he said. "I like it."

"Thanks."

She'd taken up the hobby two years before. At the time, he'd suggested that she incorporate a design. "Something pastoral or a cityscape. A bit of color."

"Maybe," she'd said, without looking up from the brown rug on her lap.

"You might enjoy working on it more if it was livelier."

"I enjoy working on it this way."

"It was just a suggestion," George said.

She paused in her labor. "Here's a suggestion: Why don't you write about baby bunnies? Or kittens, or—"

"I got it."

He was grateful she didn't want to hang them.

Kiara set the black yarn and the latch on the coffee table and made room on the couch for George. "That woman is a jerk, and her nibble is ridiculous."

He sat next to her and squeezed her hand. She was a foot shorter than him and equally pasty from a life lived too much inside. A twist-tie secured her ponytail. He could imagine her grabbing it in the kitchen, the first thing she saw, so she could get on with her project.

"I watched you write that book. We both know you didn't steal it. I'm sure this will blow over." Kiara managed afterschool programs for an educational nonprofit. She had no literary aspirations, for which he was generally grateful—why should they both be unhappy?—but which also meant she didn't understand that literary scandals came with their own supply of oxygen, which was writers' love of a good story, true or not.

"Maybe it will blow over and maybe it won't," George said.

"What did Mary say?"

"She said not to worry about it, but that was before it went viral."

"Saturn offered a million dollars for your book," Kiara said. "They're not going to abandon it or you."

"I hope you're right." George remembered a literary organization withdrawing a novel it had selected for its book club, One Nation Reads, after the author was accused of defrauding a company he'd worked for. Even after they learned the charge was fabricated by a rival author who hoped his book would be selected instead (it wasn't), they refused to reinstate the novel.

Kiara shoved the rug into a plastic bag. "Let's go out for

sushi. That will cheer you up."

Since the sale of *Up the Hill*, neither had rushed to buy a new car or cell phone. They hadn't swapped their department store wedding bands for something grander. George was waiting to get the advance to repay his parents two thousand dollars they'd lent him to replace the timing belt on his ancient Subaru. His agent had given him the names of an accountant and a financial planner, but George hadn't called them yet. Their only concession to luxury had been to start going to restaurants they'd once reserved for anniversaries and birthdays. "Let's get the sixty-piece platter," George said, relishing the extravagance of ordering something they'd never finish, that they'd end up throwing away, as if that could make up for years of eating stale leftovers.

As they were getting ready to leave for dinner, Mary called. "Saturn will have to make a statement," she said.

"What kind of statement?"

"Something to the effect of us standing by the book. That it's a book you worked on for ten years. That you entered it in contests five years ago before you ever set eyes on Larkin's novel. That reading her book was part of your job. She submitted it, and you read it. That's what you do as an editor. But it has nothing to do with yours. We'll work out the details with P.R. Come in first thing."

George emailed Ryan to tell him he would need to take the morning off.

Looking around his garden-level apartment—such a misleading name for a place that was half buried—George knew if he ever had the chance to leave, he wouldn't miss it. What little light entered from the small windows just above his head couldn't dispel the feeling that night was about to fall, even in the middle of the day. When he left the windows open, the sound of trucks backfiring startled him and the rage of the couple next door, whose fights often spilled into the street, made him cringe. George felt arguments should be hidden, like sex, but that never stopped him from pausing in whatever he was doing to listen.

He and Kiara had filled the living room with discount furniture: a rough fabric sofa, a particle board desk and bookshelves, and a metal floor lamp with an adjustable neck. They wouldn't take any of it when they left. The only objects in the room he cared about were their wedding photo, shot at the city clerk's office, and two small paintings of crows, a gift from the artist after George had edited her website. He supposed he also had to take the eleven-volume *Story of Civilization* that overwhelmed the room, sent by his father for their most recent anniversary though neither he nor Kiara had expressed any interest in it.

When George had announced his intention to become a writer, Cyrus had discouraged him. They were at a dinner celebrating his college graduation. "What are you going to write about?" Cyrus had said, cutting into a filet mignon, blood pooling below his knife. "The trauma of getting braces? The pain of acne outbreaks? Leave writing to the people who have experienced something remarkable in their lives. Like Nelson Mandela. Or to historians. Or scientists. Like that guy in a wheelchair who wrote about the cosmos."

"Stephen Hawking," George had said. "And it's not really relevant that he was in a wheelchair." A waiter in a black vest refilled George's wine glass. George buttered a piece of bread. His fourth. "Anyway, I write fiction. I make stuff up. So it doesn't matter if I had a happy childhood." Though George protested, the criticism stung. He wondered if his father was right, forgetting his own history at the Capitol. Even when he remembered it, he questioned whether it was enough. How much did one have to suffer to become a writer? How much truth should one's fiction contain? Thinking about Cyrus never failed to stir up George's formidable self-doubt.

***

At Saturn Books the next morning, the receptionist frowned sympathetically when she saw George. Did everyone know? He waited in the lobby while she buzzed Mary. On the wall behind her desk was a giant image of Jamie Queen's new horror novel, *Unexpected Company*, an axe poised above a sleeping head on the cover. Janelle arrived and kissed him on both cheeks, though she was from Cincinnati not Paris. She wore a black suit and black pumps, and while that was classic Manhattan fashion, George couldn't help but feel she'd dressed for his funeral.

Mary strode into the lobby a minute later and reached up to clap him on the back. Small and powerful, she reminded him of a jet fighter. "Don't worry. This is just a hiccup. In a year, you'll laugh thinking back on it. I hope you're not worrying. If you knew how often we had to put out statements about one thing or another. It keeps Annette—our P.R. person, you'll meet her—employed. Seriously, there's nothing to worry about."

Every time his editor said the word "worry," George's stomach dropped a bit further. He'd always known the book deal was too good to be true. That somehow his story wouldn't have a fairytale ending. "Could you stop staying 'worry'?"

"Did I say 'worry'?" Mary said.

"Three times."

"Are you sure?" Mary said. "I don't think I did. Anyway, I meant don't be concerned. At all. We'll get this scandal under control."

"It's a scandal now?" George said.

"No, no, not a scandal. Just a charge. A baseless plagiarism charge. Hate to even use that word. Let's just say the P word. Or better yet. Let's not say anything. Let's just talk to Annette." She wheeled around and started back toward Saturn's inner offices. George and Janelle hurried to catch up.

In her office, Annette sat behind three giant computer screens. George imagined media coverage of Saturn's books splashed across each one. He wondered if she had a tab open to Crave. Annette stood and offered George her hand, her fingers covered in so many silver rings shaking it felt like grabbing a chain link fence. "I hope this hasn't got you too upset," she said.

"I've been better," George said.

"Yes, but you should know things like this happen all the time," Annette said. "There are only so many stories out there. It's not surprising if there are some similarities. And some people are always going to feel cheated if they don't get a deal. I read your book when we acquired it. It's terrific, by the way. And last night I read P.J. Larkin's manuscript. They're obviously quite different. I didn't find any similar passages. Not that I thought I would."

She had compared the books. It was the smart thing to do. He understood that. Yet somehow it stung.

Annette asked how he'd come to read Larkin's book, why Peapod had turned it down, and the timeline over which he'd written *Up the Hill*. Then she turned to her computer and typed for a while, while George, Janelle, and Mary stared at their phones. George couldn't help scrolling through Crave where the hashtag #publishPJinstead was now also a popular menu item.

"Okay," Annette said, picking up a statement from the printer. "Take a look at this. If you're good with it, we'll run it by the higher ups and then issue it later today. I'm going to send it over to Peapod, too, so we're all on the same page."

They were verifying his story. George felt like a crime suspect, his word no longer good without corroboration.

STATEMENT BY SATURN BOOKS AND PEAPOD PRESS REGARDING *UP THE HILL*

George Dunn worked on his novel, *Up the Hill*, for ten years, long before he had heard of P.J. Larkin or read her manuscript titled, *Halls of Power*. Dunn's novel won an honorable mention in the John Updike Debut Novel Contest five years before Ms. Larkin submitted her book to Dunn at Peapod Press. While Dunn thought Larkin's novel was a fine book, many works of fiction and nonfiction covering similar territory had recently been released, so Peapod declined to publish it. Anyone who reads both books, as we have, will immediately see that *Up the Hill* doesn't borrow from *Halls of Power*, and that the two books have little in common other than certain timeless themes. Saturn stands behind Dunn's remarkable debut and can't wait to bring it to readers everywhere.

The statement was signed by the heads of Saturn and Peapod, put up on both publisher's websites, and posted on all of their social media channels. It was sent as part of a press release to major news outlets.

Annette advised George not to respond individually and to stay off Crave. He was more than happy to take the first part of the advice but the second part was all but impossible. He had a nearly physical urge to see what people were nibbling about him, and when he did, it wasn't good. The joint statement did little to quell the uproar.

A middle-aged lawyer who shared his views regularly on TV nibbled to his seven hundred thousand followers: "If the charge is true, George Dunn has victimized P.J. Larkin a second time by stealing her story." The nibble was re-served fifteen hundred times, no one paying any attention to the "if" at the start or the fact that P.J.'s book was fiction. She never claimed to have been victimized by anyone.

Throughout the day, a conservative TV news station advertised the teaser, "White Men Under Attack on Crave—Again. Tune in at 9." When they finally aired the story, the mustached host started out chuckling. "We probably shouldn't be running this segment. I mean, white men under attack is hardly news, is it? It would be news if we *weren't* under attack."

His guest nodded vigorously. "Yeah, but you gotta love it when liberals eat their own. I did a little research on this guy George Dunn. Turns out he wrote an op-ed in his campus newspaper, arguing that men should be required to take courses in"—he formed air quotes—"feminist studies."

The host rolled his eyes. "How do you like them feminaaaz—feminists, now, George?"

The clip went viral after a Republican Congressman who thought the slip was hilarious served it, tagging George.

CHAPTER FIVE

P.J. and Mia sat opposite each other at their parents' dining room table, Lawrence and Dina at either end. Sunday brunch was a family tradition. When P.J. was married, her ex-husband, Vlad, had joined them. Each week, he'd stood before the pictures of P.J.'s and Mia's christenings that hung above the fireplace and commented as if he'd just thought of it, "Have there ever been two cuter babies? Where do I go to get two as adorable as these?"

During Mia's time in rehab, the family had continued to gather at one in the afternoon every Sunday to eat, their conversations skirting awkwardly around her absence. Years having passed since then, the family usually pretended it had never happened, neither the assault nor all the rest, distracting themselves with the latest political scandal to grip the country, how the Rockies or Broncos were faring, or one of the warmhearted stories Dina brought home from the birthing center where she worked as a nurse.

As children, P.J. and Mia couldn't have been more different. Their mother was always reminding P.J. not to shout, Mia to speak up. P.J. had so many friends, her mother started calling them all Dear, and it wasn't until P.J. was in high school that she realized her mother didn't know their names. Mia preferred to spend her time at the back of her mother's small walk-in closet with a book. When they visited the library every Friday, Mia borrowed three books for every one of P.J.'s, and after Mia finished her own, she read P.J.'s neglected ones. That P.J. became a writer was partly due to the influence the girls had on each other.

Despite their differences, the sisters had been close. When P.J. was eleven and Mia was ten, they played on the same Little League team. After Mia struck out nine times over three games, the other girls began to call her "The Choker."

"Give her a chance!" P.J. shouted, and when that failed to stop them, "Shut the fuck up!" which got her benched for two games.

After the season ended, P.J. took Mia to a nearby park, carrying an orange bucket with half a dozen balls in it. She pitched to Mia, underhanded and slow, doing her best to make contact with her sister's bat. "That bat is not a book. Don't look at it!" P.J. yelled.

Mia missed every pitch and when the bucket was empty slammed the bat into the patchy grass. "I hate this game!" she shouted, but P.J. knew it was a lie. They were wearing matching Triple-A Zephyrs T-shirts their uncle Simon had bought out of a guy's trunk before the start of a game he'd taken them to. Mia didn't hate Little League. She just hated playing badly. P.J. ignored her and gathered the balls. She picked up the bat and handed it back to her sister.

Their second time out, Mia hit a weak ground ball to P.J., who cheered as if she'd hit a home run. By the third week, Mia was hitting one in four pitches, and half got by her sister. P.J. stopped pitching the ball easy.

At the start of the next season, Mia had hit a triple her first time at bat, and no one had ever called her "The Choker" again.

Looking at Mia over a platter of bagels, P.J wondered if her sister had told their parents about the book. Dina poured a mixture of orange juice and lemon-lime soda, her idea of a virgin mimosa, into each of their glasses. None of them liked it. Her mother thought it showed support for Mia's sobriety but hated the calories. It made Mia miss what she couldn't have, and Lawrence what he couldn't have when his daughter was in the house. P.J. could tell by the way he pushed his glass away, his large fingers leaving smudges, that he wanted something else. Preferably, something aged and amber. P.J. didn't understand why they didn't drink something healthy, like lemon water or tomato juice.

"Eli tells me you're famous," Lawrence said, pointing his fork at P.J. "Something about someone plagiarizing your book?" Eli was a professor in the English department at the small college where Lawrence taught philosophy. They had sung together in the faculty acapella group until Lawrence left the group three years before.

Copies of baroque paintings, Rembrandt's "The Night Watch" and Caravaggio's "David and Goliath," gave the living room a claustrophobic feel. P.J.'s neck grew warm. "How does Eli know about it?"

"He read about it on a literary website. So give us the story." Her father speared a piece of smoked salmon and laid it on his bagel.

"Not much of a story. My agent submitted the book to an editor at a small press and he plagiarized it." Asking questions was as natural to Lawrence as wearing tweed. P.J. steeled herself.

"How did you find out?" he said.

"I read a description of his book and it sounded just like mine. His sold for seven figures. I'm surprised he thought he could get away with it."

"You haven't read the book?"

"It's not out yet, so I couldn't actually read it. My agent is getting a copy for me." P.J. reached for the tub of vegan cream cheese.

"That isn't much evidence on which to make such a serious charge." He was giving her a hard look, the gray in his gray-green eyes, pronounced.

"I'm sure P.J. wouldn't say something like that unless it was true," Dina said.

"The description was exactly like my book." A bit of an exaggeration, but P.J. hoped it would end the discussion.

"What is the book about? You never showed it to us." Lawrence took a sip of the mimosa, grunted, then slid it away.

"You never asked to see it."

"We didn't want to pressure you," her mother said. "We figured you'd offer if you wanted us to read it. We're very proud of you, you know. Writing a whole book."

"I've written several books."

"And we're proud of each one," Dina said.

P.J. scowled at her mother.

"So what's the book about?" Lawrence said.

With her knife, P.J. carved a frowny face in the cream cheese.

"Would you like a pen and paper?" Dina got up and went into the kitchen.

"Politics," P.J. said.

An onion protruded from his sandwich, and Lawrence tucked it back in. "That's a pretty broad subject. Anything more specific?"

"Just tell them," Mia said.

"Tell us what?" Dina handed P.J. a dull pencil and a pad illustrated with a too-bright, smiling sun.

P.J. shook her head, but there was no stopping Mia. "The book is about me."

"It's not about her," P.J. said. "It's a fictionalized account of a woman who is sexually assaulted by someone she works for." She set the pad and pencil next to her plate.

"Oh." Dina flushed, the color of her cheeks briefly matching the sliced tomato on her plate.

"And the someone who assaults her happens to work in politics," Mia said.

Lawrence set down his sandwich.

"And then the fictionalized me develops substance abuse problems."

"Oh," Dina said again.

"She's making it sound worse than it is. I changed almost everything," P.J. said.

"Did you ask your sister's permission?" Lawrence said.

"I didn't ask Mia's permission because I didn't want to upset her," P.J. said. "Since it's not about her."

"Woo-hoo! I'm right here," Mia said, waving her hands. "It never occurred to you to say, 'Hey, I'm writing a novel about sexual assault'? That isn't something you thought I'd be interested in?"

"I was planning to talk to you about it before it was published."

Lawrence got up, found a fresh glass, and filled it with Scotch. "Do the woman's parents appear in the book?"

"Her mother's dead," P.J. said.

"You killed me?" Dina said.

"I didn't kill *you*. I killed the character's mother."

Lawrence sipped his Scotch. "And the father?"

"What about him?" P.J. said.

"Is he dead, too?"

"No. The father's not dead."

Dina patted her lips with a napkin. "I just don't understand why you had to kill me."

"What's his name?" Lawrence said.

"His name?"

"The father's name. What is it?"

P.J. hesitated. "His name is Lorrie," she said. "But I meant to change it. I can still change it."

"I see," her father said.

***

P.J. had just returned to her apartment when she received a call from a *Publishers Weekly* reporter. He was writing a short piece about the controversy and wanted to know if she had anything to add to what she had served on Crave.

"It's time women stopped getting the short end of the stick in publishing," P.J. said. What about the fact that she hadn't read George Dunn's book? the reporter asked. Her agent was getting a copy for her, P.J. said. But it couldn't be a coincidence that the editor who read her manuscript came out with a remarkably similar book, a #metoo story set on Capitol Hill and told from the points of view of victim and abuser.

The story ran on Monday. The reporter had included part of Saturn's statement. Dunn was quoted, too: "It's total bullshit. By the time I read P.J. Larkin's book, I had a complete manuscript. I had written dozens of drafts. And can someone please explain to me how you can make a plagiarism claim about a book you haven't read? I would ask what I ever did to P.J. Larkin, but I guess I know the answer. I rejected her book."

If anyone in the publishing world had missed the scandal earlier, they knew about it now. A *Guardian* reporter left a message on P.J.'s phone, but she didn't call back. She got dozens of emails from other journalists wanting to talk, including reporters from *The New York Times* and *The Washington Post*. #CancelGeorgeDunn was still a popular menu item on Crave. Period, a group that advocated for women in publishing, weighed in with a statement of its own. "While we can't say at this juncture how close the two books are, or if Dunn borrowed from Larkin, the fact that he read her book in a professional capacity and that his covers similar ground should be cause for concern and further inquiry."

An editor from Lysistrata Press called P.J.'s agent. They were interested in acquiring P.J.'s book. "It's so well written and heartbreaking. It's almost hard to believe it's fiction," the editor said.

P.J. remembered the afternoon Mia had told her what happened. It was the beginning of June, and P.J. had just returned from Michigan where she'd graduated from college. Mia came into P.J.'s bedroom and closed the door. Her sister was moving slowly, as if she'd aged unnaturally since P.J. had last seen her. She wore a turtleneck and wool pants, clothes that were too warm for the season. Her lips were dry and cracked.

P.J. imagined Mia had met a guy and they'd broken up. She prepared to tell her sister she'd meet other men. That she was beautiful and funny and anyone would be lucky to date her. As she waited for Mia to say something, P.J. looked at her high school lacrosse trophy, picturing how she and Mia and the rest of the team had celebrated at a pizzeria when they'd reached the semi-finals. She wondered if she should take the theater posters from August Wilson's *Fences* and Peter Shaffer's *Equus* with her when she got a place of her own. At the time, she was trying to decide whether to become a celebrated playwright or a best-selling novelist.

When Mia sat on the bed, P.J. squeezed her sister's knee. "Whatever it is, you can tell me."

Mia picked at her lips. "He touched me."

"Who?" P.J. said. It wasn't the kind of thing you would say about a boyfriend.

"Allen Blackwell," Mia whispered, as if she was ashamed or afraid someone would hear, or both. Blackwell was their state representative. Mia had interned for him during the spring semester.

"Touched you *how*?"

Mia began to cry, her back bent under the weight of what had happened.

P.J. held on to her, alert to a calamity that might have already sabotaged Mia's future. "Touched you how?"

"He invited me to dinner."

"Okay." She gently removed Mia's hand from her lip which was starting to bleed.

"He said he wanted to talk about opportunities in the office during my senior year. I was flattered." On P.J.'s wall, the second hand of a Wolverines clock seemed to slow down. "We went to a Mexican restaurant and he ordered a pitcher of margaritas. Fiesta banners hung on the wall. I remember thinking they were like smiles.

"He said what a terrific job I was doing. That I had a promising future. That there were positions in the office for me, paid positions that would be a great way to start my career. A mariachi band was playing. He kept refilling my glass, telling me stories about the other senators and laughing."

The pain in Mia's eyes was like a cut from a dull saw, raw and torn. Mia's hand was back at her lips. P.J. pulled it away and held on to it.

"When the pitcher was empty, he ordered a car for me. I was still eating, but he seemed in a hurry all of a sudden. Standing up, I had to grab the back of my chair to keep from falling. He put his arm around my waist, and I figured he was just helping me walk. I was surprised when he got into the car with me." Mia looked around P.J.'s room as if remembering where she was. She stood up and paced the length of the bed, then shook her head, part of an argument she was having with herself.

When she continued, her voice was ragged and angry. "We got to my apartment building, and he followed me upstairs. My roommates weren't home. I wanted him to go, but he sat on the couch. He said he wanted to make sure I was okay. He said to get ready for bed, and he would just make sure I was okay.

"I was in my bedroom. Without knocking, he opened the door. He said, 'I'm just making sure you're okay.' I was in my underwear. I said, 'I just need to go to sleep.' He was my boss. And I was so out of it. He came closer and said, 'Why don't you sit down?' The room was spinning, so I sat. He put his hand inside my bra.

"I don't know why I didn't scream."

Mia's forehead was damp. P.J. waited for her to continue, hoping she wouldn't. Hoping what she'd already said was the worst of it. An ice cream truck's familiar tune grew louder outside. Kids screamed to one another. People were having a normal evening.

"He put his fingers inside my underwear," Mia said softly. The air around the sisters thickened. "I froze. He said, 'you're wet.' I said, 'I just want to go to bed. Please.' He said, 'I've wanted to do this since the first time I saw you. I can't help it. You're so beautiful.' He was moving his fingers inside me. I said, 'Please stop.' He unzipped his pants and took himself out.

He kept touching me until he came on my thigh. Then he left. The next day and for the rest of the semester, he would always compliment my work, to me and to the rest of the staff, but he never looked at me or acknowledged what happened." Mia sat, grasping the bedspread with her fist, her head low.

"What did you do?" P.J. said.

"What could I do?"

"I'm so sorry," P.J. said. "Did you tell Mom and Dad?"

"I can't."

"You have to. Not right now. But when you're ready."

They sat together for a long time, Mia telling P.J. about having to pretend it had never happened. Maneuvering as best she could so she was never alone with Blackwell again. Never going to any of the social events she was invited to, saying she was too tired or had a headache, which was usually true. She described the new clothing she had bought: the modest collars and the pants with buttons that were difficult to undo. Every day, she went back to her apartment and drank a bottle of wine, then slept it off, so she could show up for class and the internship again. Her roommates had tried to get her to go out with them, but she was afraid of running into Blackwell at a restaurant or bar.

Mia wouldn't be ready to tell their parents for five years, not until she entered rehab. P.J. wasn't there when she told them, but Dina said Lawrence was so angry, he bent his cell phone. They went to the police, but the district attorney said there wasn't enough evidence to file charges. Lawrence wanted Mia to go public, but she was trying to put it behind her. Instead, he hired a lawyer who approached the senator. It wasn't the first time there had been a complaint of that nature against him. Blackwell agreed to resign, claiming it was because of his health.

In *Halls of Power*, P.J. had completely changed the details of the assault. Yet people who knew their family might remember that Mia had worked for a politician. A few might know that her sister had been to rehab.

Though P.J. had been inspired by her sister's story, could a story ever belong to anyone? They weren't close anymore. It wasn't like when they were growing up and shared clothes and a love for baseball and lacrosse. After Mia dropped out of college, she struggled to keep a job. She lived with P.J. for a time, sharing P.J.'s only bed, barely eating, and overwhelming the recycling bin with empty bottles. P.J. would have let her little sister live with her forever. Each day she opened her eyes hoping Mia would figure out how to turn her life around. Until the afternoon P.J. came home and found Mia unconscious on the floor.

When Mia got out of rehab, P.J. invited her to live with her again, but Mia said she preferred to live with people who were sober and could understand what she was going through.

CHAPTER SIX

Monday afternoon, Ryan summoned George into his office, where the editor-in-chief was doing bicep curls. To show off his build, Ryan wore clothes a size too small. His quads pressed like cables against his khaki pants. His biceps strained against the sleeves of a lemon yellow polo shirt, gray chest hair snaking above the collar. Next to his desk he kept a mini-stepper with resistance bands that he hopped on during calls with irate or weeping authors, times when a normal editor would have squeezed a stress ball or raked a Zen garden.

"Hey buddy," Ryan said, a bad start considering he'd never called George that before. "It's too distracting having you in the office right now. Several agents have told me they won't send us submissions as long as you're here."

"Which agents? The ones whose books I didn't acquire?"

"Does it matter?" Ryan said, watching a dumbbell rise.

"It matters to me."

Ryan lifted a weight above his head. "Anyway, we're going to have to make today your last day."

"Very funny."

"Not joking."

George grabbed the dumbbells from Ryan's hands and dropped them with a clank against the nearest wall, ignoring the stand that held the rest of the set. "You're firing me because an unhappy writer fabricated a story about me?"

Ryan sat at his desk and motioned for George to sit opposite him. "Not just any unhappy writer. One who sent us her novel. A novel that bears some similarity to your novel."

George sat. He'd barely had time to enjoy his success, to savor the idea of being a published author rather than a poseur who struggled to support his family. His achievement threatened to evaporate as if it had never existed at all, his path a straight line from obscurity to notoriety. "I've been here thirteen years."

"Look, I'm sorry it worked out this way." Ryan plucked a mechanical pencil from a cup.

"It will validate what they're saying, that I stole her book."

The editor-in-chief looked up. "Did you? I know I signed Saturn's statement, but you told them we thought there was a glut of #metoo books, when actually we had decided to publish Larkin's book. Before you unilaterally changed your mind. You never did tell me why you changed your mind."

"Jesus Christ."

"And you never showed me your novel. But I'm sure you had a good reason." Ryan touched the tip of the pencil to his finger.

"You want to read it?" George said. "I'm happy to send you a copy."

"I'd like to, yes. I want to see what kind of book gets a million-dollar advance. And if it's as different from Larkin's as you say, I'll be able to defend you better and to defend the company better."

"Fine." On the desk was a perfectly ordered Rubik's cube that Ryan didn't allow anyone else in the office to so much as breathe on. "You really want me out of here today?"

"By end of day. Just hand off whatever you're working on to me. I'll take care of it. Do it myself or parcel it out to the others. And it's not what I want," Ryan said. "It's what's best for the company. We'll just say you decided to write full-time."

"Is this Sandy's idea?" The managing editor had never liked him.

"Nope. Sandy thought we ought to wait until it was clear whether the allegation was true. Though I guess I can tell you now that she never wanted me to hire you in the first place. She was pushing for another applicant, a woman with more publishing experience. But you went to my alma mater."

It was hard to believe so much time had passed since then. The offices looked much the same as they had the day of his interview. Cubicles for everyone except Ryan and Sandy. Peapod had advertised for an assistant editor. Although George had earned an English degree three years before, he'd been working nights as a bartender and writing fiction during the day. All he had to show for his efforts were a few publications in literary journals no one read. He told himself a career in publishing would give him more satisfaction than mixing mint drinks, and would allow him to shepherd good literature into the world, even if it wasn't his. He wasn't giving up his dream, but he was hedging his bets. He read a grammar handbook in preparation for the interview. When he arrived at Peapod, Sandy stuck him in a dusty cubicle. He took a copyediting test on a computer, sitting on a chair with a back that collapsed if he put the least bit of pressure on it. He wasn't sure how he'd done.

When Sandy interviewed him, she asked whether he was aware of any systemic problems in publishing. He managed to stammer something about racial bias. Not having worked in the industry, he'd never given it much thought. She seemed skeptical that his experience in a bar prepared him for a position where no one had time to hold his hand or train him, and where his mistakes would be visible to readers who never hesitated to email and nibble about every spelling and usage error they found. After the interview, she walked him to Ryan's office, sighing as she introduced him. "He did better than I would have expected on the test, but tests aren't everything, as I'm sure you would agree, Mr. Dunn," she said, forcing him to weigh in against himself.

George resigned himself to not getting the job. At least the chair he was offered in Ryan's office wasn't broken. He unbuttoned his corduroy sport jacket and squeezed a balled-up tissue in the pocket. He hoped the interview would end quickly.

"Don't mind Sandy. She can get a bit pissy when she doesn't get her way," Ryan said, when the managing editor was gone. He asked George whether Professor Black still spiked his Coke with so much gin it was the color of ginger ale, and if Professor Lilly still called male students, "Champ," and female ones, "Doll," and whether the cafeteria still served a meatloaf that gave you the runs for a week. The only question related to publishing was what were George's favorite books. At the end of the interview, Ryan hired him. The dusty cubicle became his, a year passing before there was money in the budget to replace the broken chair.

After Saturn agreed to buy *Up the Hill*, George had considered quitting. He'd pictured the party they would throw for him on his last day: his book title written on a cake; the required joke about how he would become so famous he'd forget them all; and a present they'd all chipped in on—tickets to a hot Broadway show or a gift certificate to a trendy SoHo restaurant. He imagined Sandy saying, "I'm sorry we never got to know each other better. Ryan was right about you. You're a great editor."

He'd decided to hold on to the job because selling one book was no guarantee he'd sell another. He'd never foreseen he'd be let go, a claim of theft all anyone would remember.

George scrubbed his computer of personal information and

backed up his contacts on a thumb drive. Pulling up the email he'd sent P.J. Larkin, he reread it, stopping where he'd complimented her for including the point of view of the victimizer, his finger poised to delete the message. In the end he left it, convinced he hadn't done anything wrong. He secured the manuscripts he'd been working on with rubber bands and carried them to Ryan's office, dropping them outside the door. The office was empty. He walked to the desk and picked up the Rubik's cube. What would he get out of scrambling it? A moment's revenge? A story he might tell years from now, after the shame of his current situation had worn off? Ryan had once given him a chance, despite George's lack of experience. He'd promoted George from assistant to associate to senior editor. For years, they'd worked well together. Why burn a bridge he might need? But then he remembered Ryan asking if he'd plagiarized Larkin's book and he tightened his grip on the puzzle and twisted, one turn for each year of his life he'd given Peapod.

In the supply closet, he found a cardboard box and packed up his belongings, wrapping in cover proofs a photograph he'd taken with Kiara at the Grand Canyon. He'd approached the edge of the canyon for the photo but quickly stepped away. Now he wondered if there were other kinds of falls, less lethal, but nearly as impossible to recover from. He shoved a copy of the Saturn contract into his briefcase, the joy it had given him gone. He gathered the pens recommended by famous authors. He'd once thought they would bring him luck. Then he thought they had. Now he viewed them as ordinary pens without the power to save him. He packed a tin of cookies that an agent had sent to congratulate him on the sale of *Up the Hill*. It had arrived the morning after Larkin's post. Ordinarily, he would have shared the cookies with his colleagues in the break room, basking in their good wishes, but under the circumstances he'd preferred to hide in his cubicle. He pocketed a Swiss Army knife sent to him by an author whose manuscript he'd cut by a third. He grabbed grammar and punctuation guides he'd brought into the office thirteen years ago and still occasionally referred to, and his university diploma and certificate from Big Brothers that he'd propped on a shelf, lacking solid walls on which to hang them.

He still spent time with his Little Brother in the program, though at sixteen Seth wasn't little anymore. George took him to Knicks games and helped him write essays for English class. For Seth's last birthday, George had bought tickets to a WWE match, Seth keeping it a secret from his mother and George telling Kiara they'd gone to the theatre. What would Seth believe if he learned about the scandal? When Seth had been suspended for cheating in his first year of high school, George had told him there were other, better ways to succeed. Hard work, preparation. What would Seth think of his advice now?

***

From the landing inside his front door, George could hear Kiara riding the exercise bicycle, the TV tuned to CNN. The warm smell of her sweat filled the apartment. He carried the box of personal items down the stairs and into the living room. "I got fired."

Kiara stopped pedaling. "Seriously?"

"After thirteen years. Because of the whole P.J. Larkin thing. Ryan asked for a copy of my book. Can you believe that? He thinks I stole her novel."

"Are you going to send it to him?"

"Why wouldn't I?" He dropped the box on the coffee table and turned off the TV. "He didn't offer to pay me severance."

"I guess they figure since you're going to be rich, you don't need it. And on the bright side, it's true."

He sat on the couch. "That's not the point. And we haven't gotten the advance yet."

"But we will. And in the meantime, you can finish the edits to *Up the Hill*."

"They *fired* me. Do you know how bad that makes me look? Really bad. Like I'm guilty of something." George checked Crave. Word had already gotten out that he no longer worked at Peapod. How was that possible? He continued to scroll until he came to the screenshot someone had served of Peapod's staff page, his photo and bio conspicuously absent. The administrative assistant must have made the changes as soon as George left the office. They would probably advertise the open position tomorrow. It made George sick.

@On_Your_Left nibbled: "Looks like @PeapodPress got rid of plagiarist George Dunn. Now you, @SaturnBooks."

George closed the app. "I need to tell you something."

Kiara climbed off the bike. "What is it?"

"The book isn't entirely fictional," he said.

"I know. You were a page."

"That's not what I'm talking about."

Lifting the bottom of her baggy T-shirt, Kiara wiped her forehead, then the rest of her face. "What *are* you talking about?"

His eyelid began to twitch. If he told her, she would see him the way he saw himself, as someone weak, not fully a man. But he couldn't hide it from her any longer. Not with everything that was going on. "One of the senators I was working for came on to me. When I was at the Capitol. We were alone in her office and she kissed me. She might have gone further, but we kind of got interrupted."

Kiara rarely got angry, but now the brightness drained from her face and her jaw tightened. "That's horrible. Did you tell anyone?"

"I told my parents. My father didn't believe me. He thought it was some kind of fantasy. Or a way to get attention. Or that I misunderstood what happened. That the senator was just being nice. He didn't think women *could* sexually assault men. He thought that was something only men could do."

"What about your mother?"

"I don't know what she thought."

"I'm sorry." Kiara sat next to him. She wiped her face again though the sweat had dried.

"Thanks," George said.

"For what?"

"For believing me."

"You don't have to thank me for that."

George let out a breath, relieved to have the pressure of his secret released and that she hadn't dismissed what had happened as trivial. "Let's order dinner and watch a movie. I just want to forget this day."

She didn't answer immediately.

"Korean barbecue?" George said.

"Why didn't you tell me?" she said, her voice gentle.

"I told you now."

"Yes, but before."

"I was ashamed."

"You're not the one who should be ashamed."

"Thanks," he said.

"Did you ever see anyone? After it happened?"

"I lost weight and my mom was worried. She took me to a bunch of doctors."

"A therapist?" Kiara said.

George shifted the box of personal belongings to his lap and rummaged through it, unsure of what he was looking for. "No." He unwrapped the picture of the two of them at the Grand Canyon. "Do you think I should? See someone?"

"Maybe." Kiara took the picture.

"It was a long time ago," George said.

"The photo or what happened?"

"Both. It still gives me vertigo." The tenant above them began to practice scales on his trumpet. "It makes certain things difficult." Like sex, which he'd come to dread. He avoided it when he could. On anniversaries and birthdays, he smoked weed to get through it.

Kiara set the photo down. "I noticed."

"You have?"

She nodded.

"Sorry," he said.

"I thought it was me. That you didn't find me attractive anymore. I wondered if there was someone else. A writer, maybe. Someone who could understand what you were going through with the book."

"No. No. No. I would never—I can't relax."

"I get it now," Kiara said.

"I should probably see a therapist."

"That would be good."

Was anyone happy with him? Just as he was? He couldn't blame Kiara. She was entitled to more than he gave her. It had been different when they were dating, after years of loneliness had stoked his libido. In the early years of their marriage, afraid Kiara would discover he was damaged, he'd feigned sexual interest, always making the first move because it allowed him a measure of control.

"Do you want to tell me more about what happened with the senator?" Kiara said.

"No."

She got up. "Send Ryan your book. I'm going to take a shower and then we'll order dinner. Tomorrow you'll wake up and begin your life as a full-time writer. We'll find you a therapist. The scandal will blow over as soon as more people compare the books. The problem is hardly anyone has been able to do that. You, Mary, that P.R. woman from Saturn. Once Ryan reads your book, he'll come to your defense."

"Don't you think if he was going to do that, he would have waited to fire me?"

***

After he sent Ryan a copy of *Up the Hill*, George opened the manuscript, figuring he'd get in a few minutes of editing while Kiara showered. Despite everything, he felt the surge of excitement that always accompanied his own pages materializing before him. The vastness of possibility and a receptivity toward whatever the universe and his own psyche had in store for the narrative.

He was proud of the book, which he'd spent a quarter of his life writing. Ninety thousand words in the end, but he must have written more than a million through all the drafts. The characters were products of his imagination. If they had started out as the senator and himself, by the end they were something else entirely. They bore no resemblance at all to the characters in Larkin's book. Never had.

It had been difficult to write about sexual assault. Overwhelming at times. During the darkest scenes, he'd walked away from his desk over and over, Kiara poking her head out of the bedroom to ask if he was okay. He'd nodded and reminded himself he was no longer sixteen, reality soothing him as it did when he woke from a nightmare.

George opened a tab to an animal shelter website. If he was going to write full time, he should adopt a dog. He'd never owned one. Never had any pet, his father of the opinion that time spent with animals was wasted time. George imagined a pup lying quietly at his feet as he worked and walking calmly beside him when he went out for air. Chasing a Frisbee in the park, leaping and catching it to the delight of children. When he returned from his book tour, the dog wouldn't be able to contain its joy. And when George stayed home, the animal would wag approvingly at him each time their eyes met. Serving photos with the rescued dog on Crave would show a softer side of him, countering the image of him as a monster that Larkin and others were trying to create. George scrolled through pictures of the available animals until he came to a yellow Labrador retriever. Hadn't he read somewhere that Labs were loyal?

In the bathroom, he shouted to Kiara above the sound of the spray, "I have an idea."

"What's that?" she said, shutting the water.

George handed her a towel. "Let's adopt a dog. To keep me company at home."

"You sure you want to add something to the mix right now?"

"There's this yellow Lab at the shelter. She looks really friendly."

"Dogs are work. You know that, right?" She toweled her hair, then wrapped it, forming one of those turbans that never failed to impress George with its stability.

"I know. I mean, you have to walk them."

"Yes, you have to give them exercise. Feed them. Clean up after them. If they need to go out, you can't ignore them because you want to finish editing a page or because it happens to be the middle of the night. Some need training."

"You don't think I'm capable of taking care of a dog?"

"I didn't say that."

***

At the shelter, an exuberant volunteer led them into a fenced yard.

"She's a great dog," the woman said. "I thought about adopting her myself."

Before George could ask why she hadn't, she was off to fetch the animal. If grass had ever grown in the yard, it had long since died, and in the hard ground hopeful human and animal prints had been preserved. An empty water dish lay next to the chain-link fence.

A clipboard in the pocket of her green "Make My Day, Adopt Today" vest, the volunteer returned with a yellow lab named Cheese. "Here you go," she said, unclipping the dog's leash. An inch-long scar that hadn't been obvious in the photo snagged the crown of the dog's head. Her right ear was torn. Half flopped forward and half back, like petals on opposite sides of a flower. Though mostly tan, she had three white feet. The volunteer bent and exchanged kisses with the dog. She whispered something into the animal's ear, perhaps words of encouragement, before leaving the three of them alone.

Kiara picked up a dirty tennis ball and handed it to George. He tossed it across the yard, but Cheese showed little interest.

"Try petting her," Kiara said.

When George tapped the dog on the head, she shrank from his hand.

"Like this." Kiara scratched Cheese behind the ear and the lab groaned with pleasure.

"That's what I did."

"You dribbled her head like a basketball." Growing up, Kiara had shepherds. "Scratch her under the chin."

George followed Kiara's instructions, but the dog bared her teeth. "She hates me."

"I wonder if she's had bad experiences with men."

"Great," George said.

Cheese nosed Kiara's hand and Kiara scratched her again. "Maybe we should consider a different dog." The dog licked Kiara's knuckles.

Was it true that dogs could sense a person's character? George desired nothing more in that moment than for Cheese to affirm the goodness in him. The dog lay on her back. "We tired her out."

"She's showing submission. Rub her belly."

He ran his fingers along the dog's abdomen, but whether Cheese enjoyed it or merely tolerated it, he couldn't say.

"She's great, right?" the volunteer said, bouncing back into the enclosure.

"Is she afraid of men?" Kiara said.

The volunteer pulled out the clipboard and examined the questionnaire the dog's prior owner had filled out upon surrendering her. "Doesn't say anything about that."

"Maybe we'll look at another dog," Kiara said. "Just to be safe."

"Too bad," the volunteer said. "I was hoping it would work out. She's been here a while."

George looked at Cheese. "How long?"

"About six months."

For the second time, George wondered how the dog got her injuries. "How long do you keep them? Before, you know."

The volunteer didn't answer.

At the shelter store, they spent a small fortune on premium dog food, salmon treats, stainless steel bowls, a soft oval bed, a plush snake that squeaked, a hard rubber bone, a collar and leash. Kiara rode next to Cheese in the back seat, while George drove them home.

"What do you think of her name?" Kiara said.

In the rearview mirror, George saw the dog rest her muzzle on Kiara's lap.

"It's fine, I guess."

"We could change it," Kiara said. "Give her a new start."

"Sure. Let's call her Gorgonzola."

"I'm serious."

"Fine. How about Blue?" George said.

"Too sad. How about Mozzarella? We could call her Mutt for short. What do you think about that, huh, Mutt?" The dog whapped the Subaru's torn fabric seat with her tail. "She likes it."

"It's you she likes." He turned on the radio.

At home, they squeezed Mutt's bed next to George's desk in the living room, but the dog made herself at home on the couch. When George sat next to her, she climbed off. He tossed a pillow in her direction, regretting it when she cowered.

He checked his email and groaned. Saturn had sent a revised contract.

"What is it?" Kiara said.

"I got an email from Janelle. Saturn beefed up the plagiarism language in the contract."

Mutt rubbed against Kiara's legs. "Can they do that?"

"They hadn't signed the contract yet. It was in a pile on

someone's desk. Christ. They've read both books. They know how different they are. It wasn't Mary's idea, but she alerted legal to what was going on and now they want more protection. Janelle says not to worry, just to sign the new one and send it back."

"What are you going to do?"

"Take Mutt for a walk, if she'll let me," George said.

The dog hid behind Kiara. "Maybe I'll come," she said.

CHAPTER SEVEN

Scarlet tulips bloomed in carefully tended beds alongside the entrance to Flatiron Park where P.J. met Marissa on Monday afternoon after her friend finished teaching. People sometimes mistook the women for sisters, not only because of the bleached white hair they both wore short, or their stature, two to three inches below average for women in that part of the country, but because of the way they had of looking at you, just shy of a stare. Lysistrata had offered twenty-five thousand dollars for *Halls of Power*. It seemed like a fortune until P.J. thought of how much George Dunn had received for *Up the Hill*. Sloane said they shouldn't accept the offer yet. Several other publishers had asked to see the book, including two that had turned it down in the past. Sloane had given them a one-week deadline.

"How are we going to spend your newfound wealth?" Marissa said, as the women set off on a run. "I know. Let's go to Costa Rica. Or Prague—isn't that where all the writers hang out now? Or, even better, Mermaids of America."

P.J. looked at her friend. "*Mermaids of America?*"

"It's a theme park in Florida. I've wanted to go since I was a kid."

"As much as I'd like to fulfill your childhood dream, I have a dream of my own that involves paying off my student loans one day," P.J. said, breathing hard. "And I'm going to give my sister part of the advance." Mia earned even less than P.J. did, sometimes visiting food pantries to make ends meet.

"Help your sister and with what's left, let's go to Costa Rica. I'll nuzzle a three-toed sloth. You'll hook up with a forest ranger and live happily ever after above the canopy, never having to see another smokestack or combustion engine. Your next novel will chronicle the adventures of a brilliant, under-appreciated high school teacher in an interspecies relationship with a sloth and the struggles of their sloth-human babies."

"And my loans?"

"We'll be in the rain forest. The bank will never find us."

P.J. wiped her nose against her sleeve. "I see. We'll be on the run like Thelma and Louise."

"Remember watching that in the student union freshman year? You cried when they went over the cliff."

"We both cried."

They'd first met earlier that day in the cafeteria line. P.J. had been complaining about the lack of organic food, and the server, who was also a student, had waved a large spoon and said, "All I do is shovel it."

Turning to the woman next to her, P.J. said, "It's ridiculous, right?"

"Organic food would be *sick*," Marissa said. "And how about more flavors in the ice cream bar, like chamomile and raspberry and hemp." She rolled her eyes. When she'd set her lunch tray next to P.J.'s at an otherwise empty table, P.J. had been surprised.

Marissa's running shoes thumped the earthen path. "It was snowing after the movie. You made us watch the flakes for like an hour, even though you grew up in Colorado."

"I wanted to see if Michigan snow was different. Also, I was stoned."

Alongside the trail, aspen and elm trees were waking up after the long winter. A creek burbled, water from melting glaciers caressing rocks and exposed roots.

"It's not the way I imagined selling a novel," P.J. said. "I'm afraid they only want it because of the George Dunn thing."

"Nothing is ever exactly the way we want it," Marissa said.

"I guess."

"You'll be published, and you'll have exposed Dunn."

"He was fired," P.J. said.

"I saw." Marissa sipped from a water bottle.

P.J. was still waiting for Sloane to send her a copy of Dunn's book. She wished she'd read it already and confirmed her suspicions. Vlad had always encouraged her to sleep on angry emails before sending them, knowing she'd reconsider and delete them in the morning. Maybe she should have done that before serving the nibble? "You think he'll be okay?"

"I don't think he'll kill himself, if that's what you mean." Marissa offered the water to P.J.

"God. I hadn't thought of that."

"Aren't writers used to getting bad news?" Marissa said. "You got plenty over the years."

"You generally get the bad news in private. You're not humiliated in front of the whole world. Not that he doesn't deserve it." P.J. tipped back the bottle.

While looking at his phone, a runner veered into Marissa's path. She jumped out of his way, nearly falling into the creek. "Hey!"

He looked back. "Sorry!"

"I accept your apology," she shouted, though he'd rounded a bend. She turned toward P.J. "Dunn's website says he's married. Married men live longer. Their wives take care of them."

"Everything's moving so fast," P.J. said.

"Digital age, baby!" Marissa quickened her pace. "How

about we meet tonight at Baxter's to toast your status as a soon-to-be-published author?"

P.J. struggled to keep up. "What if I run into Alex?" She'd spent the night with him a month before, breaking her rule against sleeping with other writers. A relationship, she believed, couldn't survive the neediness of two writers. It could barely survive the neediness of one. She hadn't seen Alex since.

"It's time you two made up," Marissa said.

"We're not fighting, exactly." But it was rare for P.J. and Alex to go this long without speaking. They'd both been married when they met. He'd been Vlad's friend until P.J. attended a fiction workshop with him. Alex's comments about other writers' stories had been kind and smart, setting him apart in an environment that often resembled a slaughterhouse, writers hanging gray and lifeless on hooks, blood soaking their manuscripts below. Occasionally, P.J. had been the one wielding a cleaver, she was ashamed to remember.

After the workshop, she and Alex continued to read each other's work. They celebrated together when they found agents. During her divorce, P.J. had worried that like their bedroom set, Alex would go to Vlad, but he remained her friend. She was attracted to his skinny-girl physique and the doggedness with which he pursued his literary aspirations, and despite her rule, she couldn't help wondering what it would be like to date someone with whom she had so much in common. Nevertheless, she'd always discouraged his romantic overtures. That is, until she ran into him at Baxter's four weeks ago, right after receiving yet another rejection on her novel, making it seem all but certain the book would suffer the fate of her earlier ones.

He'd bought her two beers and told her how talented she was and that her gifts were sure to be recognized. Unusual pillow talk, but exactly what she longed to hear. He was on his second glass of Scotch when she led him to an empty booth in a corner of the room where she unbuttoned the denim shirt she wore over a gray tank top. The clamor of the bar receded. He pressed his forehead to hers and teased her lips. Her neglected beer slowly went flat. If people stared, she didn't notice.

But the next morning, with her legs still draped over his and her small breasts holding the memory of his tongue, he read a text from his agent and launched into a forty-five minute diatribe about the man, ignoring the intimacy they'd shared the night before and that P.J. was hoping to repeat. She rolled away from him and thought of her rule. She couldn't see a future with Alex, a writer's life, rife with uncertainty, doubled.

When he'd texted later that day to ask her out, she hadn't replied. She'd sent his call to voicemail.

"Don't you want to tell him how many publishers are interested in your book?" Marissa said.

"I don't want to make him feel bad."

"It will give him hope for his own novel."

P.J. doubted it. Writers' brains favored the catastrophic and damning over the optimistic and encouraging. The writers she knew, anyway.

"At the very least, he'll be impressed," Marissa said.

P.J. imagined telling Alex about the offer on her book as they stood in front of a row of fruit-infused vodkas, and him saying, *You deserve it. You've worked so hard.*

***

At Baxter's, voices crashed off the walls and ceiling, settled in half empty beer steins and atop fried shrimp. P.J. wore a flowing black silk top and a choker with a mother earth medal. She needed to start dressing better now that she was going to be a published author. You never knew who you might meet, who you might run into that needed to hear your exciting news.

Autographed photos of Colorado athletes lined the walls: John Elway, Terrell Davis, Patrick Roy, Joe Sakic, Payton Manning, Shannon Sharpe. Would women ever find their way onto the wall? Where was Missy Franklin, Mikaela Shiffrin, or Lindsay Vonn? At the bar, Marissa ordered two Negra Modelos, while P.J. scanned the crowd, looking for Alex's square head and rectangular glasses. She hoped there were no hard feelings. She spotted him at a booth with his friend Len.

"If it isn't the star of publishing's biggest scandal," Len said, as they walked up. He bit the top off a shrimp and licked his stubby fingers. A financial planner, Len wore a navy suit and fashionable tortoiseshell glasses. "You're a popular menu item on Crave."

Alex stared at a bowl of peanut sauce, and P.J. wondered what he thought of her newly acquired fame. Len slid over to make room for Marissa.

"That editor read her book before writing his own," Marissa said.

P.J. hovered over Alex, who didn't seem inclined to move.

"Do you actually know when he wrote his book?" Len said.

"I know he liked mine enough to send my agent a gushing email. And then miraculously he sold a similar one a year and a half later." P.J. swigged her beer.

"Move over," Marissa said to Alex. Reluctantly, he did, and P.J. sat next to him. "Is it really that surprising to find a man taking credit for a woman's work?" Marissa said to Len. She tapped her phone excitedly against her chin.

"Here it comes," Len said.

"Does the name Rosalind Franklin mean anything to you?" Marissa said. "Of course, it doesn't. She only discovered the double helix that Watson and Crick got a Nobel Prize for."

"I'm guessing the nibble was your idea," Len said to Marissa.

"As a matter of fact, it wasn't," she said.

"If you would all shut up for a minute, I have news," P.J. said. "Lysistrata made an offer on my novel."

"Congratulations." Alex said, without enthusiasm. He tipped his empty beer bottle toward her.

"I'll get some Champagne," P.J. said, though she wasn't sure whether she had enough room on her credit card. She wandered back to the bar and asked a bartender who looked like he was still in high school to send over a bottle and four glasses, resisting the urge to request only three and let Len buy his own drinks.

When the Champagne came, Marissa raised her glass. "To my friend. Nice to see effort rewarded. And having skimmed the book, I think I can say, it's terrific."

"You *skimmed* it?" P.J. said.

Marissa shrugged. "You know I don't read fiction."

P.J. sometimes felt that as a writer she spent her days making some awful medicine, like castor oil, that at best people held their noses before taking.

"Congrats," Len said. "It's tough out there."

Alex touched his glass to P.J.'s, then downed his Champagne.

"I'm sure we'll be toasting you soon," P.J. said.

"I wish my agent were as sure. He's had my latest opus since Christmas. That's almost four months, but who's counting. Anyway, let's celebrate you. It really is a wonderful book. I'm surprised it took publishers so long to embrace it."

The compliment delighted P.J. briefly, then embarrassed her once she remembered the reason for the publishers' sudden interest. The sale of her book would always be tainted. Like those *New York Times* bestsellers marked with tiny daggers to indicate irregularities were responsible for their success.

They finished off Len's shrimp, and P.J. ordered fries and onion rings for the table.

"Seriously, it's a great book, an important one even," said Alex, on his second glass of Champagne.

"Thank you," P.J. said, her face warming. "How's work?"

"Oh, you know. Coming up with ad campaigns for women's stockings that the client will reject. Fantastic. How's driving?"

"Tiring," P.J. said.

"We should all switch jobs for a day," Marissa said. "I can lose a lot of money in the market, and Len you can try to get a class of tenth graders to care about natural selection."

"Or we could all shut the fuck up about jobs we chose, jobs we should quit if they make us miserable. How about that?" Len said.

They were quiet. For once, Len was right.

A server delivered their order. Marissa grabbed a fry and dipped it in mayonnaise. When the bottle of Champagne was empty, they switched back to beer.

On one of the many large TV screens above the bar the Rockies scored, and the room shook with cheers and claps and fists banging on tables. Marissa and Len were arguing the virtues of onion rings versus fries. "Limp," Marissa said, pinching a soggy onion ring between her fingers.

"Scrawny," Len said, holding up a fry half the size of his pinkie before dunking it in ketchup and eating it.

"At least the fry is firm," Marissa said.

"Firmness is important," Len said. "I'll give you that. But you want it to be big, don't you?"

"I've had some pretty fine small ones." Marissa smiled as if remembering.

"The real question"—Len lowered his glasses to the tip of his nose—"is which lasts longer?"

P.J.'s phone buzzed. It was a text from Mia: "Where's the book?"

Before replying, P.J. finished her beer. She couldn't hide the novel from Mia forever, especially now that it was going to be published. "I'll send it."

"You said that last week."

"I'll send it when I get home," P.J. texted.

"If it's not about me, you would have sent it already."

P.J. wasn't only concerned about Mia recognizing herself in the novel. Any book about sexual assault might trigger her sister's PTSD. How solid was Mia's sobriety? Years had gone by without Mia slipping up, and P.J. had stopped worrying about it for the most part. But now she wasn't so sure.

She set her phone on the table and said to Alex, "Sorry for not answering your texts."

"Don't worry about it." Absorbed in his small screen, Alex swiped left.

Was he on Bumble? It was a shitty thing to do in front of her even if they weren't dating. She leaned toward him, but he turned his phone away before she could see what he was looking at. "I should have explained why I didn't want to go out," she said.

His phone chimed and he read the message. As he typed a reply, he said, "I know your rule about not getting involved with writers. I'm beginning to agree with it."

P.J. wished he would look at her. "You are?"

Another chime. Whatever Alex read made him laugh, and

he smiled while replying.

"What's so funny?" P.J. said.

"What?"

"What are you laughing at?"

"Nothing." He laid his phone face down on the table. "Anyway, I'm not mad. You made the right call. We shouldn't date each other. We wouldn't be good together, although that night was very nice." He looked up, his eyes and mouth softening, a ring of black hair trapped behind the lens of his glasses. "Really nice."

She reached over and slipped the hair out. "It was, wasn't it?" She thought he might kiss her then. Perhaps she wanted him to. What would be the harm in sleeping together just once more? To celebrate her good news. It didn't have to mean anything. But then his phone chimed again.

***

Along one wall of P.J.'s apartment books packed metal shelves, arranged according to categories that once had seemed reasonable but that she could no longer remember. Opposite the shelves stood an old-fashioned card catalog a library had been giving away. When P.J. lent a book, she noted on a card who borrowed it. Unlike the shelves, the cards were arranged alphabetically by author, allowing her to identify a borrower quickly. She rarely hurried anyone. Some of her books had been out for years. But she liked knowing where they were because there were times when she felt an urgent need to be re-immersed in a particular story. It had happened with Isabel Allende's *The House of Spirits* after a health scare, and with Jennifer Egan's *A Visit from the Goon Squad* when she'd forgotten to file her taxes, and she couldn't predict when it might happen again.

To reduce the number of trees killed by the book industry, P.J. bought only used books. She couldn't bear e-readers because they didn't let her press a copy into a friend's hand, saying, "You have read this," and they had no smell and certainly not that loamy paper odor she had come to associate with beauty and comfort and adventure.

When her own book came out, she would encourage people to buy new copies, as many as possible. For once, she would put the environment second. She didn't feel good about it, but she'd do it. She had to if she wanted to be a success.

After she signed a contract with a publisher, she would add "author" and the title of her novel to her social media bios. She would no longer be afraid to nibble other writers on Crave. The successful ones who knew what they were talking about. She might even become friends with some of them. Well, she would if she lived in Brooklyn. But there were a few authors in Colorado, too. When she introduced herself, she would casually drop the release date of her first novel. Her first, implying there would be others.

She opened her laptop and composed an email to Mia, explaining how helpless she'd felt when Mia had told her about the assault. How she'd wondered if she could have done anything to prevent it, even going so far as to ask herself whether she should have stayed in Colorado for college. She said she'd written the book hoping to protect other women from similar attacks, and the last thing she wanted was to hurt Mia.

She proofread the email, fixed typos and an autocorrect error, and attached *Halls of Power*. Maybe it would be all right. Maybe Mia would see the value in the book.

Her finger hovering over send, she remembered Vlad's advice. Though this wasn't an angry email, perhaps she should wait a day. Or two. Enough time to look at *Halls of Power* again, the parts that might upset Mia. She contemplated rewriting them, but she had an offer on the book and didn't know if the publisher would allow that or even if she wanted to. After she slept on it, she would have a clearer idea of what to do. She saved the email and closed her laptop.

CHAPTER EIGHT

Their first morning together, George tried to take Mutt for a walk. Clipping on a leash with reflective striping that had cost the alarming sum of forty-five dollars, he tugged her toward the stairs.

"Offer her a biscuit," Kiara coached, while attempting to leave for work.

George held out a cookie, but the dog flattened herself on the carpet. "It's a dog skin rug," George said. Kiara didn't laugh. She exchanged her briefcase for the leash, Mutt prancing out of the apartment alongside her mistress without the necessity of a bribe.

After fifteen minutes, they returned, Kiara late for work and annoyed with George, though it was the dog that had caused all the trouble. Hurrying out again, Kiara failed to wish him good luck with his writing but managed to bestow several kisses on Mutt's brow.

In the otherwise quiet apartment, the sound of George's bacon popping was as loud as fireworks. The dog's kibble rattled like a maraca as it hit the metal bowl. He poured a cup of coffee and had taken no more than a sip when Mutt's bowl was empty again. She did look skinny. He replenished her food and turned on the radio, tuning it to a news station whose reports of war and famine and environmental disaster put his own troubles in perspective. The dog stared at him as he ate but ignored the piece of bacon George held out in the hope of winning her over. After breakfast, Mutt retired to a corner of the bedroom, the plush bed next to George's desk in the living room remaining empty.

Promptly at nine George sat before his laptop and set his fingers on the keyboard. He was determined to treat writing as a job. But as he was about to begin editing *Up the Hill*, he noticed a fine coating of dust on his stapler, on the covered ceramic bowl that held paperclips, and on his laptop monitor. He found a rag and wiped them, then settled back into his seat, ready to start. Except that his museum wall calendar still showed March. He flipped it to April, only to have the tack that secured it to the wall pop out and the calendar flap to the floor. After retrieving them, he wondered if he might see the art better if the calendar were higher or lower. He tried several locations, leaving pinpricks behind on the wall, until he settled once again on the original spot.

He sat down and cracked his knuckles. He was finally ready to begin. More than ready. Excited. Though it was no longer nine o'clock—it was, in fact, nearly ten—he had all day.

He rested his hand on his Bluetooth mouse and moved it, but the cursor didn't respond. He tried the mouse again. The battery was dead. He could have used the laptop's trackpad, but it wasn't ergonomic, and he didn't want to end up with a stiff neck. While he rummaged through kitchen drawers looking for a charging cable, he noticed the dishes in the sink and washed them, then started a load of laundry because it seemed silly not to. He was paying the electric bill when he caught the dog staring at him from the bedroom doorway, but when he held out the plush snake they'd bought for her, she retreated. Not long after, she began to snore, the sound oddly comforting.

It was late morning and George still hadn't started when Ryan called. "I'm a third of the way through, and I have to say, your book is very different from Larkin's. There are some structural similarities and they're both set in Washington, but really, other than that, they have little in common. It's very well written. Yours, I mean. Hers, too. Anyway, I'm not surprised you got a monster deal."

"I accept your apology," George said. "But I'm not coming back. I'll just do my edits for Saturn."

"I wasn't offering to rehire you. It would just stir the pot. People would think we don't support women."

George crushed the toy snake under his heel and it squeaked, startling him.

"When both books come out, you'll be vindicated and so will Peapod," Ryan said. He was breathing hard, and George pictured him lifting.

"What do you mean, when *both* books come out?"

"Yours will be released by Saturn, and Larkin's will be published by…us or someone else."

"You made an offer on that woman's book?"

"We're planning to."

"*Why?*" Mutt poked her head into the room.

"It's a good book, and Larkin is less likely to sue us if we're her publisher. I still don't understand why you turned it down. It's a moving story that has something to add to the #metoo conversation. All the attention won't hurt sales. Not to mention that it will make people feel like we're on the right side."

"The side of someone who makes false accusations?" George heard Ryan's mini-stepper creak. He wanted to wrap a resistance band around the editor-in-chief's neck.

"The side of women," Ryan said. "Who apparently still face barriers in publishing, or so Sandy is always telling me. We'll have to make a pretty attractive offer. I'm not talking your league but big for us. Sandy heard Larkin has a lot of interest."

"Could you not mention her again?" George said.

Ryan grunted. "Larkin? Or Sandy?"

"Either one."

"I'm beginning to think," the editor-in-chief puffed, "that you have a problem with strong women."

After Ryan hung up, George opened Crave. Nothing new from Larkin, but the story continued to churn. Every writer whose manuscript he'd rejected seemed to have nibbled about it. They speculated he'd plagiarized their books, too, in smaller, less obvious ways, then sent a rejection to cover his tracks. George sighed. No one ever thought their book wasn't good enough for publication.

@JusticeInPrint had served a link to its statistical analysis of the books Peapod had published during the past twenty-five years, including the finding that ninety-two percent of Peapod's authors were White. George refused to believe it was that bad, until he examined their underlying data. He could remember advocating for a certain Black author's book, but how adamant had he been? Had he too easily accepted Ryan's excuse that the audience for the man's books would be too small, never acknowledging the role they played in keeping it small by choosing to read and publish the work of people whose lives mirrored their own? He hadn't fought as hard for Black authors after that, thinking he already knew Ryan's answer. Peapod's record was probably no worse than that of many other publishing houses, but it was hard to make the argument that they were no more racist than anyone else.

George opened the new contract Saturn had sent and read the plagiarism language. A single paragraph had swelled like a malignant tumor into two pages. He groaned when he read the phrases: "wasn't influenced in any way by Larkin's manuscript" and "didn't borrow any language, technique, or idea from Larkin." Saturn had to know writers found inspiration in one another's work all the time without committing plagiarism. What the publisher was asking for was unreasonable. Who knew what influenced a writer? In one way or another, everything George read influenced him.

He managed to revise only a page that morning. Concerned that Mutt might have to pee, he tried again to take her out. When she refused to go, he left the apartment alone. Rain stung his cheeks, defeating him after a single step. He hurried into the grocery store across the street. Otto, the owner, greeted him with a nod. The man's face was gray or maybe it was the poor lighting in the place.

"The usual," George said.

Otto poured a black coffee.

George had bought coffee and *The New York Times* at the store every weekday morning for as long as he'd lived in the apartment.

"Thought you were sick or something. When I didn't see you," Otto said, sliding the paper cup across the counter.

"Working from home today."

"Must be nice. Break from the office."

"I suppose."

"Lot of customers disappear. They want the coffee with the heart on top." The owner handed George a cellophane-wrapped Danish covered in white icing, the kind that hurt George's teeth. "No charge." The man's knuckles were swollen and red. It had been a long time since he'd had help in the store.

George tucked a newspaper under his arm and, touched by the owner's predicament, grabbed a Twix for Kiara.

Returning to his apartment, he went into the bedroom to check on Mutt and stepped in a large spongy spot on the carpet. He wet paper towels, got on his knees, and rubbed, the towels dissolving into hundreds of curdled specs against which the vacuum, in addition to frightening Mutt, proved useless. He gave up. Sitting on the couch, he sipped his coffee and tore open the pastry.

The crinkle of the cellophane brought Mutt running. "*This is what you like?*" He tore off a piece and tossed it toward the dog, who ate it and licked the carpet where it had landed. He threw another piece and Mutt ate that one, too. Delighted to have found a way to ingratiate himself with his new companion, George dismissed the question that fluttered briefly through his mind: How much sticky pastry is too much for a dog? He lobbed one chunk after another, bringing the dog ever closer, until he placed the remainder directly in front of his damp socks. Mutt lifted it gently and carried it to the bedroom. He would buy her another tomorrow. Perhaps she would take it from his hand.

He returned to his book, stopping for lunch at two. Throughout the day, thoughts died in his head because he had no one to share them with. At the office, he would dissect the latest Mets game with Raquel, Peapod's editorial assistant. He would schmooze with Ryan about books that had sold at auction for enormous sums and then failed to catch the public's imagination, conversations that had comforted him in the way of all schadenfreude, until *Up the Hill* had sold and he worried that would be its fate.

He missed serving nibbles of publishing news and observations on Crave. He hadn't been banned from the platform, but felt he had, because no matter what he served, he was trolled. He called Kiara, but she was too busy to talk. He left a message for Janelle, telling her he'd reviewed the new contract and wanted to discuss it.

In the next room, Mutt was coughing, but George didn't think much of it. He called his cousin, Lilly, who managed a bagel store. There was no one from whom she would have heard about the scandal. It wasn't the kind of thing she or her husband, Patrick, followed.

"Can you talk?" he said.

"I can never talk." In the background someone ordered a cinnamon raisin bagel with lite cream cheese. "What's up?"

"We got a dog."

"Nice! What will you do with him while you're at work?"

"I left Peapod."

"Everything okay?"

"Why wouldn't it be? It's just weird working at home on a weekday. It's too quiet. No copy machine. No phones."

"You want noise? Find a bagel shop and work there."

"That's not a bad idea."

"Seriously, it's the lunch rush. I have to go."

In the bedroom, George caught Mutt eating the last of her puke. At least he wouldn't have to clean it up.

***

George camped out at a table next to a window in a café, sipping a mocha latte and working on *Up the Hill*. He replaced words and rewrote sentences and then, in a wash of insecurity, changed them back to what he'd had before. Outside, from the safety of a high branch, a squirrel screeched at a dog. The wood chair George sat on was neither comfortable nor uncomfortable, neither handsome nor ugly, neither well-made nor shoddy, all in keeping with the character of the place which was the absence of character.

Two tables away, a man in an ill-fitting Oxford shirt pitched life insurance to a woman. She sipped her tea and snuck glances at her phone. On a couch, a man with pencil-thickened eyebrows ticked off for his friend the qualities he required in a woman ("under one hundred ten so I look hella ripped standing next to her;" "a hottie who works so I can chill;" "someone who doesn't whine about shit like gluten.")

George felt a surge of love for Kiara. Gratitude for a life spent worrying over words. Would he look back at this time and laugh, as Mary had assured him? Her suggestions for improving the novel were good, but that didn't mean she could predict the future.

Sipping his latte, he overheard two customers waiting in line.

"What a douchebag. Stealing a book that was submitted to him," said the guy, whose blue hair reached his shoulders.

His companion was texting. Her hand-shaped silver earrings gave George (and everyone else) the middle finger. "People want to be successful, but they don't want to put in the work."

"At least he was fired," Blue Hair said.

"Yeah, but his book is still being published." Earrings still hadn't looked up.

"We'll see."

The woman's thumbs stopped moving. "Did they cancel his book?"

"Not yet. Some of us are planning to protest in front of Saturn Books later today. I'll text you the deets."

George couldn't bear to hear any more. Reaching to close his laptop, he caught the edge of his drink. He grabbed the computer in time to save it, but the seven-dollar coffee waterfalled onto his khaki pants. The couple stared at him, registering only a clumsy guy who'd been eavesdropping on their conversation.

***

"They said they were going to protest," he told Kiara, as he blotted the carpet with a sponge. He'd found instructions for removing the pee stain on the internet.

"Everyone's always protesting everything," Kiara said.

"But this could make the news. If you don't know the real story, it sounds like I did something terrible. It will make Saturn look bad."

Even as he spoke, TV producers were editing the footage of picketers in front of Saturn's building, its bank of mirrored doors doubling the crowd. Men and women, young and old, milled about holding signs: *Read More Women. George Dunn is a Thief. Cancel George Dunn.* A teenager with one foot on a skateboard yelled through a megaphone, "A woman's place is on the bestseller list!" before starting a chant George couldn't make out.

He and Kiara watched it all later from their full-sized bed, wearing T-shirts with images of Saturn and its rings, gifts from Kiara's brother, Liam. Allison, Liam's wife, had probably bought them. Just as Kiara was the one who remembered the anniversaries and birthdays of their relatives, the occasions marked perennially on her calendar. What had George done before he'd met her? Forgotten them, he supposed. Embarrassed to wear the T-shirts in public, they wore them nightly when they weren't in the wash. George had considered getting a second set. For a few weeks they'd made him ridiculously happy.

A reporter was interviewing one of the protestors. "What brought you out here today?"

The woman pointed to her sign, which read, *I Support PJ.* "He stole her book! Word for word!"

"Neither book is published. Have you read them?" asked the reporter.

"Who has time to read?" the woman said.

The camera cut back to the anchor. "In this day and age, it shouldn't come as a surprise that women are demanding fair treatment."

"I'm fucked," George said.

Kiara was soon snoring, but in George's mind placards bearing his name multiplied until they filled every corner of the room. Eventually, he gave up on sleep and lost himself in Saturn's latest science fiction release, a bestseller despite evidence the male author had stolen plot points from a woman.

CHAPTER NINE

After a segment about drought in the Western United States and a few bars of "Make It Rain," the radio host segued into a story about the demonstration in front of Saturn the day before. P.J. wondered what her passenger, a woman in an off-white summer suit, thought about the scandal. "I hope she sues that editor for copyright infringement," P.J. said. Her legal name—Patricia Larkin—appeared on the driver information card fastened to the back seat, but she thought it was unlikely the woman would figure out the story was about her. Passengers never imagined she could be anything other than a driver.

The woman remained silent.

P.J. tried again. "Can you believe the editor thought the writer wouldn't figure it out?"

The woman adjusted her multi-colored scarf and set her portfolio beside her. "People do foolish things in their hunger for success. To get it or to hold on to it. Extremely foolish things."

"That's exactly it," P.J. said, but was her passenger referring to George Dunn or to P.J. Larkin? She met the woman's eyes in the rearview mirror but couldn't read them. "She really got the last word," P.J. said, turning in her seat. "The last *word*. Because they're both writers?"

The passenger's smile was polite.

On the radio, an analyst gave her view of the economy.

"Do you enjoy driving?" the woman asked.

"Not really," P.J. said. Without thinking, she added, "I do

it because it gives me time to write." She pulled over, having reached the woman's office. "Please don't give me a bad rating for saying I don't enjoy driving."

"If I were going to give you a bad rating, *P.J.*, it would be for other things."

"Oh," P.J. said.

The passenger climbed out of the car. "I said *if*."

***

P.J. pulled into a McDonald's parking lot to eat the peanut butter sandwich she'd packed for lunch. As she chewed, she saw she had two emails from Sloane. The first contained an offer on *Halls of Power* from, of all places, Peapod Press. No doubt trying to counter the terrible publicity. And perhaps to right the egregious wrong they had done. Should she let them? The money—forty thousand dollars—was good. A fortune to her and to a small publisher like Peapod. She liked the idea of making them pay.

She read the second email and struggled to swallow. Dropping her half-eaten sandwich on the passenger seat, she grabbed the prosperity cat with her free hand, kissed it, and shouted—slugs of whole wheat bread, peanut butter, and saliva strafing the windshield—"Good kitty!" Black Bear Press, a major publishing house, had offered three hundred fifty thousand dollars for her book.

When P.J. called Sloane, the agent picked up on the first ring. "This is unbelievable," P.J. said.

"Believe it. The editor, Babette Aller, wants to talk to you. It's totally routine. She just wants to make sure she can work with you before signing."

"When? When does she want to talk?"

"Tomorrow at ten."

"Oh. I told my friend I'd go to an appointment with her," P.J. said.

"Cancel it! Tell her something urgent came up!"

P.J. wanted to cancel it. But she wouldn't because she knew Marissa was afraid of what she'd learn at the ultrasound appointment that had been scheduled after her mammogram detected an abnormality. Marissa's mother had died of breast cancer. "I can't. How about tomorrow afternoon?"

"Let me check." Sloane sounded annoyed, but it couldn't be helped. "I'll call you right back."

P.J. fantasized about how she'd spend the money, whatever was left after Sloane took fifteen percent, and the government siphoned off nearly twice that in taxes. After she gave Mia enough to make a difference in her life. Perhaps she'd put a down payment on one of the net-zero condos that had just gone up on the outskirts of Denver. She pictured a place with a mountain view and a gym where guys doing crunches debated the best screen adaptation of *Pride and Prejudice*, sweat glistening on their six-packs.

She imagined receiving fan mail from women who said the book had changed their lives, feminist organizations sponsoring luncheons in her honor, and Fortune 500 companies inviting her to speak, her fee larger than what she earned in a month driving. She'd replace her old drip coffee maker with a Keurig and sign up for a subscription of recyclable pods.

Her phone rang. "How about 2 p.m.?" Sloane said.

"That's perfect." Marissa's appointment would be over by then. P.J. grabbed a notebook and pen. "What does the editor want to talk about?"

"She just wants to say hi. Tell you how much she loved the

book. She might have a few edits she wants to discuss," Sloane said.

"What kind of edits? I thought you said she loved the book?"

"She loves the book. She just sees some ways to improve it. Don't worry. And don't bring up the whole George Dunn thing."

At the mention of Dunn, P.J. doodled the Crave logo, a drooling mouth.

"And don't mention that we pitched her two years ago and she passed. As far as you know, this is the first time she's seen the book."

"Okay."

"Don't bring up anything, really, just follow Babette's lead and answer her questions."

P.J. drew a zipper over the mouth.

"Tell her how thrilled you are to have Black Bear publish your book and to work with her. Tell her how much you loved other books she's edited." Sloane named two books.

"I haven't read them," P.J. said.

"Can you read them tonight?"

"Both?"

"Just read some reviews. She's not going to quiz you."

P.J. felt her heart beating against her bra. "Okay."

"Don't be nervous. This is routine," Sloane said.

"I am nervous."

"Well, I'm excited. This is long overdue. The book is wonderful." The agent belted out: "*I thought that I felt you clapping. I thought that I heard you smile.*"

"That's not how the song goes." P.J. checked the time. Ride With Me had started paying a higher rate to more productive drivers. Until P.J. received a publishing advance, she needed to qualify for it. "I should go."

"They'll call you on this number. Circle back with me after you talk to them to let me know how it went. Hey, congratulations!"

"Thanks. I better go."

"Babette Aller is terrific to work with."

P.J. accepted a job on the Ride With Me app. "That's great. I have to—"

"Don't mention Dunn's book. Unless Babette asks you directly," Sloane said.

"Okay. I get it."

"I just want to make sure you remember."

"I'll remember. I have to pick someone up."

"Go. Go. Call me af—"

P.J. disconnected the call and raced to get the passenger, the remainder of her sandwich forgotten.

***

The women waited for the ultrasound technician, Marissa lying on a table in a blue cotton gown that fell open in front, P.J. sitting on a stiff vinyl chair.

"It's been a while since anyone's touched them," Marissa said, looking down at her chest. "Other than for the mammogram."

"You have, haven't you?" P.J. cupped her breasts through her *There Is No Planet B* T-shirt.

"Doesn't count," Marissa said.

"You want me to touch them?" P.J. said. "I'll do it right now."

Marissa shook her head. "I appreciate the offer. But no."

"You sure? I'm very good at it. Almost as good as I am at writing." P.J. circled her nipples with her fingers.

"I want to see the technician's face when she comes in and sees that."

"She'd probably appreciate it. Scanning breasts all day seems like a boring job."

"Except when she sees something bad," Marissa said.

"That won't be you."

Marissa pulled her gown closed. "Unless it is."

P.J. walked over and took her friend's hand, "I'm not through with you."

"Yeah, that's not how it works."

A woman in polka dot scrubs entered the room, *Vera* printed on her name tag. "Raise your left arm above your head," she said, after double-checking that it was the left breast she was supposed to scan. She applied a liberal amount of gel to Marissa's skin, then rolled a wand over her breast while looking at a monitor.

"What do you see?" Marissa said.

"The radiologist will come in and talk to you about it," the technician said.

"That sounds ominous."

"It's not meant that way. I'm not allowed to talk to patients about the scans." She wiped off the excess gel with a tissue and covered Marissa's breast.

Marissa tightened a bow at the top of the gown. "My mom died of breast cancer."

"I'm sorry to hear that," Vera said, tossing the soiled tissue into the trash.

"Thanks."

"Are you warm enough? I could get you a blanket."

"I'm fine."

The technician tidied up the exam room and readied fresh supplies should the radiologist want to take another look. "I'm pretty sure it's just dense breast tissue. Nothing to worry about. But I didn't tell you that. The doctor will be in soon."

"Thanks," Marissa said.

Twenty minutes later, the doctor marched in, filling the room with conviction. "You'll be happy to know it's nothing unusual," she said. "Your breasts are heterogeneously dense, which just means you have mostly dense breast tissue. It's not uncommon. We'll keep an eye on it, but for now there's nothing to worry about."

When the doctor left, P.J. kissed Marissa on the forehead.

***

Babette Aller's voice boomed out of P.J.'s phone. "We love your book! Of course it's fiction, but we believed every word! You must have done a lot of research!"

P.J. remembered how hard it had been for Mia to talk about the assault. Listening to her had been a kind of research, she supposed, but she'd done other kinds, too. She'd talked to district attorneys and police officers; interviewed women who'd been sexually assaulted, some who'd reported the crime and many who hadn't; read countless survivor memoirs. She clenched the phone. "I'm glad it came across as authentic."

"Oh, yes, very authentic. We love the writing, too. The voice is unique. A bit desperate, a bit unpredictable, but very believable. The main character is definitely someone the reader would want to help if not be friends with. We did have one or two ideas."

P.J. clicked open a pen. "Ideas?"

"Nothing major. Nothing to be worried about."

"Like what?"

"Let's start with the title, *Halls of Power*."

"What's wrong with the title?"

"There's nothing wrong with it, not exactly. But it's a bit masculine, a bit cigars and whiskey, don't you think? How about something like *Girl Is in the House*. Marketing loves it."

P.J. scribbled the new title followed by a dozen question marks.

"For the cover we could do a stylized image of the Capitol with a silhouette of a girl in a window. Incorporate some nice pastel colors. And maybe you could beef up the plot a bit. But honestly, the book is perfect."

"Beef up the plot?" P.J. drew a steer's head, horns poised to pierce someone. It probably wasn't the time to tell her new editor she was vegan.

"I can tell you're not sure. Don't worry about that now. We'll send you our notes. Shouldn't be more than a few pages. Did I tell you how excited we are about the book? It's perfect and we have such high hopes for it."

"You told me."

After she talked to the editor, P.J. called Sloane. "Did you know about the title change?"

"They mentioned it."

P.J. surfed Crave as they talked. "*Girl Is in the House*? It's ridiculous." She munched two nibbles, her phone emitting a ridiculously satisfying crunch each time, like the sound of celery being eaten, while a pair of fat lips popped up. When a diner attacked her, she shut their menu, so she'd never again have to see what they nibbled.

"It's not unusual for the publisher to change the title. The thing now is to get the book under contract. This is just a little disappointment." The agent crooned: "*It's like raiiiiin when you're already there.*"

"Not how the song goes," P.J. said.

"I'm pretty sure it is. But whatever you say." The agent sang again: "*It's strawberry jam, when you really like grape.*"

"Not in the song, either."

***

The next day, when P.J. finished driving, she met Marissa at a trailhead.

"You should give me a commission," Marissa said, as they started hiking up the rocky path.

"All of a sudden everyone wants to publish it."

"You're going to be rich, or at least rich enough to drive less and write more." Marissa bent to examine a mushroom.

P.J. breathed deeply, delighting in the smell of pine, the brightness of the creek that bubbled alongside the trail, and the sweet decay that was forever brewing on the forest floor. "They want to change the title to *Girl Is in the Hous*e."

"What's wrong with that?"

"For one thing my sis—I mean, my main character—isn't a girl, she's a woman."

"Jesus. Don't slip like that when Terry Gross interviews you."

"You think she will?" P.J. said.

Marissa studied the moss that covered one side of a boulder. "Why not?"

P.J. wondered what she would wear for the interview before remembering it was radio.

"She might ask about the nibble," Marissa said.

"I'm not afraid to talk about it. That's all I've been doing is talking about it." She'd spent years writing and rewriting books, thinking about them until there was no room in her head for anything else, struggling to sew their plots together so the seams didn't show. Yet all anyone seemed to care about was a nibble to which she'd given less than ten second's worth of thought.

"Thanks for coming with me yesterday," Marissa said.

"I'm your person," P.J. said.

"We're each other's people."

Marissa's father had disappeared when Marissa was eight. She was an only child. After her mother died, Marissa had worried no one was responsible for her anymore. "The hard thing about being an orphan, especially an unmarried one," she said, after everyone but P.J. had left her mother's memorial service, "is that no one is assigned to you."

P.J. straightened a folding chair. "I'm assigned to you."

She became Marissa's emergency contact on school forms and kept Marissa's spare key in case she locked herself out of her apartment, though she never did. She learned the combination to Marissa's locker at the gym, so that if Marissa got dementia before P.J. did, some thirty or forty years down the road, Marissa wouldn't be stuck in sweaty clothes without her car keys or phone. When Marissa came down with the flu, P.J. brought her chicken soup from Whole Foods, something she would never eat, then did the dishes and vacuumed Marissa's place, the appliance a stranger to P.J.'s apartment. P.J. had her mother to minister to her when she was sick, but sometimes she asked Marissa for help, so her friend would feel they relied on each other.

It was late afternoon, and a chill filled the canyon as they hiked. Blue jays called to one another.

"Heterogeneously dense," P.J. said. She liked the sound of the radiologist's words. Not just the good prognosis they implied, but the actual words themselves, the music in them, one "s" following another like air being released from a balloon.

Which would be worse, she wondered, having cancer or being shamed on Crave if it turned out she'd falsely accused Dunn? Cancer could be deadly but at least people had sympathy for you. If her charge against Dunn was mistaken, Black Bear might refuse to publish her book. P.J.'s feet left the trail and she sailed past a butterfly bush like the insect for which it was named, landing hard on her knees. "*Ow!*" After she caught her breath, she sat up and glanced behind her at the nest of roots that had snagged her hiking boot.

Marissa crouched next to her. "Are you okay?"

"I'm fine," P.J. said, wondering if the fall was a punishment.

"You sure?"

P.J. flexed her ankles and knees. "Yeah."

"I could do CPR on you. They made us get training." Marissa puckered her lips.

P.J. stood, brushing the dirt from her torn skin. "You'll have to find another victim."

"Okay, but if you stop breathing, tell me."

"You'll be the first to know." As she continued walking, P.J. tried to look where she was going, to put the George Dunn matter aside at least until she was on flat land again, which was harder than it seemed.

When they reached the top of the trail, they took in the hazy view of the city. It was rush hour below and traffic covered the roads like a rash. They snapped pictures for their social media accounts. Noticing she had service, P.J. opened Crave and served the image with the caption, "rising above it," the app emitting a clattering sound, as it did every time a diner served a nibble. Her account had grown to fifty thousand diners. They immediately began munching and re-serving the nibble with chef's kisses, each one a balm to her ego, battered by years of rejection.

"Earth to P.J.! We're on a hike! In nature! Remember, nature? One of your favorite things? Jesus, you're worse than my students! Do I have to take your phone?"

P.J. looked up, having momentarily forgotten where she was. She perched next to Marissa on a log, and they sipped from water bottles and ate the dried apricots and cashews Marissa had packed for both of them, knowing P.J. would forget.

***

P.J. pulled into the parking lot at her apartment building and with a dirty napkin wiped blood from her knees. On the passenger seat, her phone buzzed.

"What the fuck?" Mia texted. "Must be some book if you're afraid to send it."

P.J. opened the email she had drafted to Mia four days before. She hadn't looked at it or the manuscript since. Because she couldn't think of a way around it, she took a deep breath and pressed send.

She hobbled up the three stairs that led to her front door. Inside, the air was stale. She opened a window, forgetting to secure the manuscript on her desk that any stray Front Range gale might blow apart. In the refrigerator: beer, soy milk, an onion, a reusable container filled with mold that had once been eggplant with garlic sauce or possibly tofu with broccoli. She'd stopped at the supermarket after the hike to pick up something for dinner, but seeing how crowded it was, she'd left without buying anything. She filled a bowl with red and blue Smiley Oats, never having outgrown the comfort of sugar-coated carbohydrates.

CHAPTER TEN

Sitting in a hard, plastic chair in his agent's Flushing office, George rolled the new Saturn contract into a fat tube. "I'm not happy about this."

With her career taking off, Janelle had stopped accepting editing projects to supplement her income. Legions of would-be authors contacted her for representation, and she'd sold two more books, the writers so starved for recognition they ignored her instructions and nibbled about the deals before the particulars were worked out. When George called, Janelle no longer picked up. Instead, he got an answering service and had to wait for a return call that wasn't guaranteed to come the same day. She'd begun to drop high-powered editors' names and her hairstyle had gone from a bob to an asymmetrical cut. Any day, he expected her to move to Manhattan. Despite all that, she still hadn't upgraded the chairs. He shifted on the rigid surface.

"The new contract language is obnoxious," Janelle said. "But you didn't plagiarize, so you have nothing to worry about." Her email chimed and she glanced to see who the message was from, irritating George, who felt certain that when she weighed the sender's importance against his own, his fell short.

"I don't like the part about not being influenced in any way." George unrolled the contract and flattened it against Janelle's desk, but when he removed his hands, it curled up again. He tried rolling it in the opposite direction, but the paper resisted, folding instead. "Everything we read influences us," he said.

"We get ideas from other writers, we borrow techniques. That's perfectly normal and every writer does it. It's not plagiarism."

Janelle's email chimed again, and her attention flickered to her computer. "Are you thinking about something specific?"

"No." He yanked the sides of the contract. "Kind of."

Janelle's mouth slipped open, registering alarm, before she composed herself. "Tell me and we'll handle it together."

George adjusted himself in his seat. "You should get some better chairs."

"Did you borrow something? From Larkin's book?"

He set the contract on her desk. "I liked that she included scenes from the villain's point of view. He's a rapist, and you wouldn't think it would work, but it does. So I decided to incorporate the senator's point of view in my novel, as you know. My book was already written when I read Larkin's, but I changed it in that way after reading hers."

Janelle reached into her desk drawer and pulled out two candy bars. As she held one out to George, he saw Senator Sands behind the desk. "Go ahead and eat it," the senator said, smiling in that coercive way she had.

George closed his eyes. He wheezed, his throat the size of a hollow needle.

The senator held out a glass of water. "If you don't mind sharing with me."

He felt a hand on his shoulder.

"George? Everything okay?"

When he opened his eyes, Janelle was standing over him. The pressure in his head subsided. "I need a second."

Janelle returned to her chair. He considered asking her to put the candy away, but he didn't want to come across as any odder than he already had.

She tore open the wrapper and took a bite, probing her teeth with her tongue after she swallowed. "You're not going to tell anyone what you just told me. About Larkin's book." With her pinkie, she excavated a bit of candy from behind a molar and ate it. "I don't think what you did was wrong, but someone might try to make something out of it."

"It wasn't wrong," George said.

"That's what I said."

"No. You said you didn't think it was wrong. It wasn't."

"The important thing is not to mention it." She picked up the candy bar, then changed her mind and set it down. "No one knows when you added that element to the book, and no one needs to know."

"Fine," George said. "But I don't like being treated like I did something wrong."

"Okay." Janelle looked out the window at a view of beige high-rises. "I'm on your side, but I don't think we should fight the changes to the contract. We won't win, and it will look like we're hiding something."

George wondered if Janelle believed him, or if she thought he'd borrowed more from Larkin's book. "Read it."

"What?"

"Larkin's book. *Halls of Power*."

"I don't need to read it," she said, but she didn't look at him. "You should know, there have been several offers on her novel, and I wouldn't be surprised if whoever acquires it tries to come out with it at the same time as yours. They might think the controversy will drive sales. And it might."

"Just what I need, this Larkin business to follow me forever. At least people reading both books will see how little they have in common." The contract lay on the desk like an accordion's crushed bellows. George tried to smooth it out, but it was hopeless. He picked up a pen and signed it.

"Larkin's agent asked for a copy of your manuscript. I'm going to send it. I don't see as I have much choice. Maybe once Larkin reads it, she'll say she made a mistake." Janelle took another bite of candy.

"Maybe," George said, but he thought there was a better chance of the senator coming forward to say *she* had made a mistake.

CHAPTER ELEVEN

It was Saturday morning, and P.J. wasn't driving. Purple and red bruises lit up her knees. Somewhere outside of her apartment, a flicker knocked. She admired the bird's industry. She had read they drummed to establish territory, to attract a mate, and to find bugs. Whatever it was after, she hoped it succeeded.

Babette Aller had been satisfied with the call. Under other circumstances, P.J. would have immediately told her parents, a conversation she had imagined since her sophomore year of college when she announced her intention to major in English with a concentration in creative writing. ("Being a writer is quite a bit harder than you might think. It's not for everyone," her father had said, discouraging and insulting her at the same time.) She'd thought they would throw a party for her when her first book came out, with a cake made to look like the novel and non-alcoholic sparkling wine to show Mia they hadn't forgotten about her. She'd pictured them inviting all their friends and passing out postcards to remind people to order copies once they got home. But as things stood, there would probably be no celebrating with them.

Instead, when the book was released, she would host a party herself. While she made coffee, she thought about who, other than Marissa and Alex and maybe Len, she would invite. The writers she knew were spread around the country. When they saw her good news on Crave, they would munch and re-serve it with clapping emojis. They would be happy for her, and jealous, too, just as she had been each time one of them had gotten a book deal. She didn't often see the friends she had grown up with. They were busy with kids and socialized with other parents. They still sent her Christmas cards, and while she wouldn't waste paper that way, she was glad they thought of her. They would probably be eager to come to the party of a published author, a person on the precipice of fame.

But the party would come later. First, she would look at those net-zero apartments. Perhaps one on a higher floor with a soaking tub. She considered moving to Brooklyn, but the money would barely get her a parking space there. No, it was better to stay in Colorado. It might not have as many museums or theaters, but it had the Rocky Mountains, a reminder that the planet hadn't been completely paved over.

She would have to tell Mia the book had sold. But not yet. She wanted to savor her success without conflict. She hoped her sister would come around after she read it and saw the lengths to which P.J. had gone to erase the connection to Mia and their family.

Sloane had sent Dunn's book. P.J. scrolled through *Up the Hill* on her laptop, taking notes. Both were #metoo books set in Congress. In each, there was an age discrepancy and a power imbalance between the hero and the villain. They were told from similar points of view. If Dunn hadn't read and praised her book, P.J. might have considered the similarities coincidental. But he had read it. The books were different, too, in more ways than she could count, which made her pause to weigh how close two books had to be to justify the charge she had made.

***

"Do you really think he would have sent an email praising the book if he planned to steal it?" Len asked P.J. They were sitting with Alex and Marissa in a luxury box that belonged to Alex's firm, waiting for the Wednesday night Rockies game to start.

Before Len had opened his mouth, P.J. had been enjoying the classic rock blasting from speakers, pitchers warming up, her veggie hot dog and beer. She'd been successfully ignoring the expanse of manicured grass whose maintenance taxed the planet. "Maybe he didn't plan to steal it when he sent the email. Or maybe he wrote his book without realizing he was stealing mine. It happens. That's why I'm always careful not to read a book that's too similar to what I'm writing. I don't want to unintentionally copy it."

"There are a lot of #metoo books," Len said. "Sadly, sexual assault is not uncommon. Neither of your books breaks entirely new ground."

"Hardly any book *breaks entirely new ground*," P.J. said, before realizing she was making George Dunn's argument.

"Maybe you could let it go now that you have a book deal," Alex said. "Focus on your own success. Celebrate it. Forget about Dunn."

"I couldn't forget about it even if I wanted to. The thing has taken on a life of its own," P.J. said. "People I don't know are calling on Saturn to cancel Dunn's book."

"It's ironic," Len said.

"What?" P.J. licked mustard from her finger.

"You're not completely innocent, either," Len said, "when it comes to stealing someone's story. At least your sister might not think so."

P.J. turned to Alex, but he was scribbling on his scorecard. They'd discussed the ethics of writing about family. He must have told Len. She bit into her hot dog, Alex's betrayal leeching its flavor. "What happened to my sister changed my life, too," P.J. said to Len. "I've spent years thinking about it. It was natural to want to write about it. Writing is how I make sense of things, not that I could ever make sense of what happened to Mia."

"Okay," Len said. "But couldn't you have written about it without publishing what you wrote?"

"Sure, but it would be like an orchestra playing to an empty concert hall. Kind of pointless."

As the players were announced, Marissa pulled on a mitt. "We're here to watch a game, okay? To relax. So how about we drop the subject."

"Excellent idea," Alex said.

P.J. sipped her beer. Len was wrong to compare her writing process to Dunn's. Authors were inspired by actual events all the time. Jodie Picoult, one of P.J.'s favorite authors, had made a name for herself fictionalizing news stories. It was from Picoult that P.J. had gotten the idea to tell her story from multiple points of view. She supposed Len would say that was no different than Dunn getting ideas from her. But it was. Dunn was an editor to whom she'd entrusted her unpublished book. He was supposed to accept it or pass on it, not pass on it to steal from it.

A fly ball sailed over Marissa's outstretched glove. Checking the scoreboard, P.J. saw she had missed the top of the first inning.

***

When P.J. got home from the game, her sister was sitting on the steps outside of her apartment.

Mia's lifeguard whistle glimmered, reflecting the exterior lamp. "I told you those things in confidence."

P.J. held out her hand, but Mia ignored it, standing on her own.

"When did you read it?" P.J. said. "I just sent it to you a few days ago."

"I stayed up all night. It made me sick."

P.J. unlocked the door and turned on the single overhead light inside. "If you read it, you know it's not about you."

"You can bullshit other people, but this is my life. Just because you changed some details, that doesn't mean people won't know who you're writing about. *I* knew." Pain compressed Mia's voice. Crud nestled in the corners of her eyes and floated on her lashes.

While writing the book, P.J. had chosen to believe that Mia wouldn't recognize herself in the character P.J. invented, and if she did, she wouldn't mind because of the good the book might do. P.J. had been desperate to write something meaningful, something that would sell. In Mia's story, she'd thought she found both. When the book hadn't sold, she'd felt relief mixed with the terrible disappointment. At least Mia would never see it. "No one reads anymore," P.J. said, sounding pathetic even to herself.

"*That's* your defense?" Mia said. "Then why did you bother? Why have you spent your whole adult life trying to get published? Why go to the trouble of writing about what happened to me if no one reads?"

"It's an important story. And it's not what happened to you. It's fiction. The main character is older than you were. She was raised in a different city by a single father who's the head of security for a large corporation, not a professor. She has three older brothers who go on trial after exacting revenge for what happened to her. One brother flips on the other two. How much more different could I have made it?"

"I'm not the only one you're hurting. How do you think

Mom and Dad will feel when they read it?"

They would read it. Once it was published, or sooner, if Mia had forwarded a copy to them. They read everything she wrote, her mother praising it all indiscriminately, her father pointing out each book's flaws. "I sold it to Black Bear Press," P.J. said softly.

Mia sank to the carpet. "When?"

"Last week. They offered me three hundred fifty thousand dollars. It will change my life. Honestly, I can't even believe it. I'm going to share it with you." P.J. sat next to her sister. "It will change your life, too."

"I don't want your money. That's not what this is about." She lowered her head to her knees.

"I know that. I just thought I could make your life easier."

"How about not making my life harder?"

"It won't be as bad as you think. The book is a novel not a memoir. No one will connect it to you. No one will have any reason to think it's anything other than a story I made up, inspired by the bad behavior of men everywhere, from Hollywood to corporate America."

"Maybe what happened to me will come out and maybe it won't," Mia said. "But I'll worry about it all the time. I'll think about it and feel the shame. Isn't that enough? How much pain does it have to cause me before it matters?"

P.J. considered calling her agent and cancelling the deal. She wondered what it would feel like to choose her sister's peace of mind over her own dreams. Probably good for a minute and then bad for the rest of her life, once she realized she'd missed her opportunity to be published and would drive for Ride With Me until someone took her keys away when she was ninety. "I can't do that," she said, though the debate had existed only in her head.

"Can't do what?" Mia said.

"Anything. I can't do anything about it. We made a deal with the press."

Mia looked up. "You're an asshole, you know that?"

This wasn't how P.J. imagined publishing her first book would feel. "Maybe I am," she said.

***

P.J. laid a white cloth napkin on her lap. Lawrence filled everyone's glasses with virgin mimosa, while Dina passed cold chicken, cucumber salad, and the soy quiche she'd made with P.J. in mind or as Lawrence called it, the "quiche-less quiche." P.J. had arrived last, interrupting a conversation she guessed was about her, and now the dining room was unnaturally silent, and Mia was glaring at her as if P.J. were the one who had assaulted her.

"Your sister emailed us a copy of your book," Lawrence said.

"I would have sent you a copy," P.J. said. "You just had to ask."

Her father sipped the mocktail and stared at the far wall, imagining a real drink or perhaps a different set of daughters. "Nevertheless."

Nevertheless? What did that mean?

"I read the first three chapters last night," he said.

"And? What did you think? Did you like them?" P.J. said.

"Like them? They were painful."

"But as a novel, as art." Just once, P.J. wished her father would acknowledge that her work was good.

"That's hardly the point," Lawrence said. "I could see you made an effort to hide Mia's identity—our identities—but I don't think it would be impossible for someone to figure out what had inspired the book. So you mustn't publish it."

P.J. felt as trapped as the wingless, one-legged bird in the center of the table. "I'm under contract," she said, which wasn't technically true. She had a deal with Black Bear, but no paperwork had been signed.

"People get out of contracts," Lawrence said.

"I don't want to get out of it."

"I told you," Mia said.

"We're a family," Lawrence said. "We support each other. We certainly don't expose one another's secrets. Your mother and I have done a lot for you, P.J., and while we don't expect you to repay us, we do expect you to respect our wishes when it comes to the family."

"She won't listen," Mia said.

"Please, Mia." Lawrence held up a hand to silence her. "Maybe you can offer the publisher a different book," he said to P.J. "One of the funny ones you wrote."

"You didn't think they were funny," P.J. said.

"I didn't say they weren't funny. I said I thought you had it in you to be funnier."

P.J. stabbed her quiche with a fork. "Anyway, that's not how it works. You can't just give the publisher a different book."

"Have you tried?" Lawrence said.

"No, I haven't tried."

"You should at least try."

"Give me a little credit for knowing how the publishing industry works. I don't tell you how to navigate academia."

Lawrence choked on the cucumber slice he'd just put in his mouth. Dina's eyes widened. Mia looked at her plate. Despite being popular among students, Lawrence had been stuck as an associate professor for twenty-five years because he'd published only a few slim articles. He'd been writing a book since P.J. and Mia were children, writing it but never finishing it, despite devoting long hours in his home office to the task. P.J. and Mia had played outside in the coldest weather, so as not to disturb him, and had learned never to interrupt him unless there was a calamity, such as the roof caving in under heavy snow or a bear breaking into the kitchen. Even then they knew to turn to Dina first if she was home. Lawrence's stalled career was not something the family talked about, ever.

"Look, I'm sorry," P.J. said. "It's just that none of you seems to understand this could be my shot at getting published. And if the book does well, a publisher will be more interested in my next book. Or one of those old, marginally funny ones. This is my life, just like being a professor is yours." She couldn't seem to get away from the subject of his stalled academic career.

In the middle of refilling her glass, Dina forgot to stop pouring.

Mia grabbed her mother's hand, then threw a napkin on the widening stain. "This is my fault. Just forget it. Let her publish whatever she wants."

"No," Lawrence said. "That's not how this works. The assassin doesn't get to write the eulogy."

P.J. wasn't sure she understood the analogy, but she knew it was time to go. She pushed her chair back and stood.

Driving home, she was already hungry for the leftovers that any other week her mother would have insisted she take.

***

As P.J. accepted her first passenger on Monday, she was surprised to see Franklin's name appear on the screen. Three weeks had passed since he'd confessed in the back of her car, and she'd all but forgotten him. It was the same early morning hour, but repeat customers were unusual. There were so many people looking for rides, so many drivers available, and the algorithm favored new matches of passenger and driver to prevent people from getting to know one another and undercutting the service by arranging private rides.

"I kept turning down cars until yours came up," Franklin said, as he got in. He'd cut his hair too short and he looked like a monk, his forehead a blank sandwich board ready for the day's specials. "It was a long shot. I didn't know if you'd be driving, or if you'd be in the area, or how stubborn the algorithm would be about giving me a different driver. I had to turn down five cars."

"Why did you?" P.J. pulled into traffic, cutting off a black SUV that got eight miles per gallon on a good day. When Franklin clutched the grab handle, she eased off the accelerator.

"I don't really know. Maybe because it was a more interesting ride than most. So I figured I'd give you the work if I could." A crisp Band-Aid poked out of his pocket.

They were headed to his therapist, the SUV tailgating her. She would have slowed down out of spite, but she wanted to get Franklin to his appointment on time. "How are things going?"

"I'll probably have to move to another country. Too many memories here," Franklin said.

"If it were me, I'd move to Sweden. They're leaders in renewable energy. And they have universal health care." Though ten days had passed since P.J. banged up her knees, they still ached occasionally.

"I'll keep that in mind. My father's parents were Danish."

"I imagined you had some Nordic ancestry. I pictured them all skiing to therapists' offices." The tailgater turned off.

"Actually, they hired dogsleds to take them," Franklin said. "The mushers were a little odd but entertaining."

Dirt streaked P.J.'s windshield. All manner of green and black bugs had come to their final resting place on the glass. She turned a knob and biodegradable washer fluid spritzed. Wipers swirled the mess around.

Franklin watched with interest. "You ought to sign it and give it a title. How about, 'Number 15 with Antennae.'"

"Fastidiousness isn't environmentally sustainable," P.J. said.

"My wife would have agreed with you. She thought we'd become too dirt-obsessed." Talking about her in the past tense seemed to exhaust him.

P.J. opened her window. She never minded talking about her marriage in the past tense. By the end, she and Vlad couldn't be in the same room without taking shots at one another.

"What's happening with your cheerful book?" Franklin said.

"My agent sold it."

"Congratulations. What's the title? I'd like to buy a copy."

"It'll be a while before it's out." She told him about Black Bear changing the title to *Girl Is in the House*.

Franklin winced.

"It's bad. I know," P.J. said.

"Nothing you can do?"

"I'm trying to be a person who's easy to work with. It doesn't come naturally."

He laughed. "Here's a radical idea. Be yourself. The person who wrote the book. A package deal: the book and you, just as you are. If everyone was agreeable all the time, life would be boring and art wouldn't exist."

P.J. glanced in the rearview mirror to see if he was serious. He was.

"What's the worst that can happen?" he said.

It was fine in theory. Fine if you were a certain kind of man, like Franklin, issued a pass at birth that allowed you to be strong-willed and opinionated. To ask for things without apology. But for a woman? No. Still, she liked the way he thought and the quality of his attention. He wasn't preoccupied with his phone. You couldn't call him handsome—his face was too long, his skin too pale—but his steady manner had a calming effect on P.J. She was sorry when they reached his therapist's office. "Why don't you take my number?" she said. "In case you need a ride some time. That way, you won't have to turn down a bunch of cars to get me. You could pay me two thirds of what Ride With Me charges you."

He entered P.J.'s number into his phone.

CHAPTER TWELVE

It had been nearly a month since P.J. Larkin's nibble had upended George's life. If he thought the scandal would disappear on its own, he was mistaken. Forty-eight thousand people had signed a GetAngry.me petition demanding Saturn cancel *Up the Hill*. George had received an email inviting him to add his name because he'd signed their petitions in the past.

He'd been editing the book all day. His eyes itched and his back ached from hunching over his laptop. Most of the daylight had fled, leaving him to work by the glow of the screen. Mutt lay with her head in the bedroom and her tail in the living room, mooning him. When the doorbell rang, she whimpered. Because he wasn't expecting anyone, he figured it was UPS or Amazon delivering Kiara's pre-cut yarn or the candy she rained on students in her program. Had he ordered something? He couldn't remember. He stood and stretched, then climbed the stairs.

He didn't bother asking who it was. When he opened the door, it was as if the landing fell away, dropping him into a recurring nightmare.

"There better not be anything in that book about me." She wore a black suit. Absent the thick makeup that had given her an artificial radiance, her face resembled raw lumber. He'd followed the senator's career and knew she was retired. "I hope for your sake you didn't write about me," she said.

He was sixteen again, mute, his mouth dry. Though he longed to shut the door in her face, his arms hung helplessly at his sides. He pictured himself standing in her senate office, frozen, his pants and socks wet.

She stepped into the apartment. She couldn't have been more than five foot six in her heels, yet he had the sense of her towering over him. "If you've slandered me in any way, you'll regret it. Bad enough that you stole from that woman's book," she said. "Don't you dare bring me into it. I could tell you had a fantasy about me when you were a page. Some young men like to picture themselves with powerful women. Most have the good sense not to act on it."

He backed down the stairs on legs as wobbly as string cheese, his chest so tight he thought he was having a heart attack. He had to get away from her. The senator followed, her boxy shoes tapping the metal stair edging. Her age-swollen fingers gripped the banister like pincers. She paused at the bottom step, taking in the crowded particle board shelves, the scratched coffee table. "What a dump."

Reaching the living room's far wall, George found himself trapped. "It wasn't a fantasy. It was sexual assault," he said softly. But hadn't his father also said he'd imagined it? Even his mother, who always took his side against bullies, hadn't believed him. George trembled. The reality of his past dimmed and his doubts multiplied.

"Speak up! How do you expect me to hear you?"

It was the same brittle voice that had ordered him to get cleaned up after he'd soiled himself. She'd been close enough then for him to see makeup pooling in her pores. The pores were even larger now. "It was assault."

"You were so ridiculous. So inappropriate, coming around to my side of the desk, reaching out for me, saying, 'You're so beautiful,' as if that was something I could possibly want to hear from a page."

He felt a sudden urgency in his bladder from all the coffee he'd had. But he wouldn't. Not this time. "That's not what happened."

"I told my chief of staff. We laughed about it." Her lips curled into a facsimile of a smile. He'd seen the smile when he was sixteen and thought it real. "How about you?" she said "Did you tell anyone what you did?"

"I told my parents."

"I know who your father is. I bet he was too smart to believe you. Anyway, who do you think people will trust? Me? A beloved senator? Or you? A novelist accused of plagiarism who waited more than twenty years to say anything. My chief of staff said we should have someone from the page program talk to you about appropriate office behavior, but I said you were just young and wouldn't make that mistake again. I told him to leave you alone. I'm sure he remembers the conversation. He's still very loyal to me, you know."

George looked toward the bedroom, but Mutt had disappeared. Outside, the street was quiet. It was as if time had stopped, leaving only him and the senator and their unfinished business. "I gave up politics because of you."

She let out a single, bark-like laugh. "You're too weak for politics." Stepping toward him, she said, "I don't want to hear any more of your lies. You're a liar. That's what a novelist is. Someone who makes up stories. When you're not stealing them."

"I didn't steal that woman's book."

"Still getting into trouble. I can't say I'm surprised. Some people never straighten out." She glanced around the apartment again. "Never find their way out of the basement. I know all about your miserable life. Working for a publisher no one ever heard of. Who refused to stand by you. Represented by an unimpressive agent to say the least. Who do you think she'll be able to call if I sue you? You better email me a copy of your book, so I can see if I'm in there. If I am, you'll hear from my lawyers."

George looked at his wedding picture, wishing Kiara—who would know how to deal with someone like the senator—were home. A layer of dust had built up on the glass.

The senator followed his gaze. She walked to the picture and touched a finger to Kiara's dress. George half expected the cream-colored fabric to wrinkle. "Doesn't know how you behaved, I suspect," she said. "You, with your schoolboy crush. You didn't tell her what happened, did you? Why would you? She might not have married you if you had. How do you think she'll feel when she learns about it?"

"Get out of my house."

She climbed the stairs, her calves, as pale as oysters, pumping. When she reached the landing, she turned. "You think your situation can't get worse. I promise you, it can."

***

George lay on the couch shaking beneath a knit blanket.

"She's bluffing," Kiara called from the kitchen, where she was brewing chamomile tea. He'd told her about the senator's visit as soon as she got home, and she hadn't even paused to change out of her skirt and stockings before putting the water on. "She doesn't want the world to know she's the evil senator in the book. And if she did that to you, she did it to other pages. If she made a statement about what happened, some of the other pages might decide to come forward."

"What do you mean *if* she did it to me?" George said.

"I didn't mean anything."

"You don't believe me."

"It's a figure of speech." Kiara set two steaming mugs on the coffee table and sat on the armchair opposite the couch. "Of course, I believe you. That's how I know she won't come forward. It's too great a risk. Right now, she can hide behind the fact that the book is fiction. That it's set at a time when she had already retired. That you served as a page for any number of Democratic senators. If she were to come forward, she'd be admitting the book is about her. She'd be confessing to what she did."

Though he found comfort in the smell of the herbs and in Kiara's reliable good sense, he continued to tremble. Had the senator harassed other pages? He couldn't say because after what happened he went to great lengths to avoid her office. Whenever he saw her on a stairway, in a hall, or on the Senate floor, he fled. During her years as a senator, she'd had untold opportunities to prey on other people. He imagined men like himself, carrying shameful secrets. Men who'd felt their powerlessness and had abandoned dreams of political careers. Her footsteps on the apartment stairs echoed in his ears. Out of the corner of his eye, he could still see her salon-darkened hair. "Should I send her a copy?"

"Absolutely not. Pretend she was never here."

"What's wrong with me?" George said. "I'm still afraid of her."

"She traumatized you. It's not easy to get over that. Did you call Dr. Elias?"

He'd read the text Kiara had sent him with the psychologist's name three times without making the call. "Mutt hid. Some watchdog. Couldn't she have bit the woman's ankles? Or thrown up on her expensive shoes?" The dog was resting her muzzle on Kiara's lap. "Thanks for nothing," George said.

"I think she might have anxiety issues," Kiara said.

George sat up. He wrapped the blanket around his shoulders. Warmed his hands on the mug. "Should I tell Janelle?"

As Kiara pried off her shoes, a sweet and sour odor rose from her feet. "I wouldn't. Not unless you want to tell her all of it, including what the senator did when you were a page. She might feel she had to tell Saturn. It would give them another reason to be nervous about publishing the book."

"At least we know what her story would be," George said. "If it somehow came out that the book was based on what happened to me."

"She didn't become a senator by being nice."

"Or honest," George said. "I'd like to send it to her. To show her I'm not as helpless as she thinks." He imagined her reading it, rage undoing the work of injections meant to smooth out her forehead.

"Call the doctor," Kiara said.

***

The next morning, Janelle asked George to come into her office.

"I heard from Saturn," she said, when he arrived. "It's not good news."

"What do they want now? For me to swear a blood oath I didn't commit plagiarism?" George glared at the rigid office chair before sitting on it.

"They're planning to delay publication. Until the P.J. Larkin thing settles down."

George had never really believed in his good fortune or that he would be the author of a Big Book or see the kind of money they had agreed on. But that hadn't stopped him from imagining it all, from the three-bedroom house he and Kiara would buy to the tropical vacations they would take to escape it. Now he pictured growing old in his basement apartment. "Delay for how long?"

"They're not sure. Maybe six months. Maybe two years."

"Two years? Are you kidding me? Let's go back to the other publishers who bid on it. Let them know it's available." George shifted in the chair. Did Janelle *want* her writers to be uncomfortable?

"If you ask me to, I will. But I doubt any of them would touch it right now."

"Great. Will I at least get my advance?"

She poured him a glass of sparkling water from a large bottle on her desk. "That's the thing. They want to delay signing the contract, too."

"This is unbelievable. They read both books. They saw how different they are."

"Yes. But you did read her novel. And that's tricky, you know, an editor reading a writer's work and then coming out with something similar. And it's natural both being #metoo books that there are some similarities. Anyway, they don't think you plagiarized. But they want the noise to die down. They're getting a lot of pressure not to publish it at all. They don't want to cancel it, but they want to wait."

George squeezed his glass. Maybe he would shatter it, soak Janelle's desk and the manuscript of some other hapless writer, saving them from the misery that was publishing. "Who's pressuring them?"

"Scribblers for Justice. And there was that GetAngry.me petition." Janelle's computer chimed and she glanced over at it.

"Could you not do that?" George said.

"What?"

"Check your email while we're talking."

"Did I?" Janelle said.

"Every time. It bugs the shit out of me."

"You're upset," she said. "I understand."

"Do you? I don't have a job. How am I supposed to live?"

"Look for another one?"

"Who's going to hire me?" he said.

"I'm sorry. There's nothing I can do. If they had already signed the contract, it would be different."

"So, I'm back to square one. No book. No career. Because posturing on Crave makes a self-righteous mob feel better about themselves." How had it come to this? What had he done other than sacrifice his evenings and weekends, and jeopardize his and Kiara's financial well-being? He'd given up his aspiration to be a public servant. Perhaps he would have to abandon being a writer, too. Reinvent himself again. But as what? There was nothing else he wanted.

Janelle sipped her water. "There might be a way to change Saturn's mind."

"What?" George loosened his hold on the glass. "Just tell me and I'll do it."

"You're not going to like it."

"Tell me."

"If you could point to something in your own life that inspired the story. I know it's fiction, but writers often base their fiction on something that happened to them. If that was true here, things might be different."

He couldn't. The shame would be too great. And if he dared to name the senator? "I was a senate page," he said.

"Yes, I know. But I was thinking about something more than that. Some experience with harassment or sexual assault you may have had."

George thought about the senator's invasion of his home. He'd been up all night, hyperventilating, convinced he heard her in the living room, that she'd returned to steal a copy of his manuscript. "It isn't fair to ask me that. Writers have reasons for expressing themselves through fiction. It's an artistic decision but also a decision about how much we want to disclose about our own lives." The senators nails had been long, painted brown, and filed to a point—or was that last just something he'd imagined?

"I understand that, and I respect it. I'm just saying it would help if there was something similar to what happened in the book in your own life. It would help a lot. It might even allow Saturn to go forward now."

"They said that?"

"Not exactly, but they wondered whether there was something that would get public sympathy on your side and show that you were telling your own story rather than Larkin's."

"I wasn't telling Larkin's story! My book was written before I ever saw hers. I have drafts on my computer that go back ten years. Let's show Saturn those."

"We can do that. But I'm not sure it will be enough. Think about the other thing. Maybe there's something you would feel comfortable sharing. Because that might convince them."

George's ass was numb. He stood up. "You really ought to get rid of this chair."

***

"Assholes," George said to himself as he started his Subaru. He pulled out of his parking space and sped down the street. London planetrees ticked by. When he stopped for a light, he called Kiara.

"We'll survive without the money," she said. "Don't do anything you don't want to do."

"Why is this happening to me? Aren't I a good person?"

"You're a very good person. This isn't karma. It's the age we live in. Vigilante justice by nibble. You're in the crosshairs today. Tomorrow it will be someone else. We have a little savings. Maybe you'll qualify for unemployment."

The light changed and he blew past a nail salon, an electronics store, the rest of the block a blur.

"You could do some freelance editing," Kiara said.

"I suppose," George said.

"We'll figure it out."

Kiara was so well-meaning, so optimistic. Wonderful traits, to be sure, but it put him in the position of always being the pessimist, of having to weigh how dire their situation really was. Just once, he wished she would focus on the negative, so he could be the one to point out that there was still hope and a way to turn things around.

Ahead, the traffic light turned yellow. He pressed the accelerator and nearly swiped a door that opened without warning on a baby blue two-seater parked at the curb. He missed the light anyway.

A burly man in the driver's seat of the blue car shouted at George. "What's wrong with you?"

"Everything okay?" Kiara said.

"I have to go." George opened his passenger side window. "Sorry. I didn't see you."

"You almost took my door off! You shouldn't be talking on the phone while you're driving."

"I had it on speaker," George said, though the man had a hundred pounds on him.

"I could care less what the fuck you had it on."

"*Couldn't*," George said.

"What?"

"The correct phrase is '*couldn't* care less.' Not 'could.' Think about it. If you could care less, you must care a bit. It's poor English."

The trunk of the sports car popped open, and the driver jumped out and ran toward it. George didn't wait to find out what the man was retrieving. Later, the suspense would bother him, like an unresolved chord. But now, he floored the gas, dodged two cars in the intersection, and didn't slow down until he reached his apartment.

***

After he ate lunch, George took out the leash. To his surprise, Mutt's tail fluttered, a movement so subtle, he nearly missed it, and a great improvement over her habit of flattening herself into the carpet or hiding under the bed when he tried to walk her. He rewarded her with one of the treats Kiara had suggested dispensing when the dog did something right. George thought about the phone number Kiara had texted him. If Mutt, with her mysterious, troubled background, could change, maybe he could, too. It was just a phone call. If he didn't like the way the doctor sounded, he wouldn't make an appointment. For all he knew, she wasn't taking new patients.

While Mutt pooped on a manhole cover, sampled the neighborhood garbage, and allowed a poodle to hump her, George tried to imagine what therapy would be like. Every shameful secret he'd kept would be exposed, his weaknesses laid bare. He'd have to acknowledge his utter failure as a husband. He'd have to pay for all that. A fortune. With money he couldn't earn anymore.

Nevertheless, when they returned, he sat on the couch and called the doctor. He reached voicemail. "I want to schedule an appointment. It's for me," he said. He was too embarrassed to describe his problems. "I'm available all the time. I'm not working anymore. I'm a writer. Kind of." *Kind of?* What did that mean? And why was he telling her all of that? "My wife got your number from a colleague. I forgot her name. Not my wife's name. I remember her name. It's Kiara. I forgot the colleague's name. Anyway, maybe you're booked, because everyone in New York sees a shrink, right?" Was the term "shrink" offensive? Had he insulted the doctor even before they began? "I should have said therapist or doctor. I know you're a doctor, I mean, not the medical kind, or maybe you consider yourself a medical doctor? That's fine. Of course, it's fine. Anyway, you're probably booked—" A tone cut him off before he could leave his name. He redialed. "This is George Dunn. I just left you a long message. I forgot to leave my name. It's been a hard day. I'm kind of flustered. I've never seen a psychologist. Are you taking new patients? Anyway, this is George Dunn. I think I said that already." When he hung up, he realized he had still forgotten to leave his number. He dialed again.

***

"On the positive side, you weren't shot in a road rage incident," Kiara said that night. She pushed her latch hook through a canvas.

"I don't see why I should have to go public," George said, ignoring her attempt to cheer him up. "That day in the senator's office was the worst day of my life. I don't want to relive it each time another question occurs to someone in the media." He was taking screenshots of files that contained early drafts of *Up the Hill*. He emailed them to Janelle, with the message, "Happy?"

The agent replied with a fingers crossed emoji. A million dollars and his only book at stake and she couldn't be bothered to type even a few words.

In early versions of the novel, the main character was a charming and popular page, star of the weekly pick-up basketball games in the Senate gym. Always tapped first by Capitol staff for assignments. The page discovered a pay-to-play scheme in a senator's office and worked with the FBI on a sting, wearing a wire under his suit. The book was a thriller. No one in it was sexually assaulted. He'd stayed away from anything that triggered memories of Senator Sands or his experience with her. But it had been flat, and there had been little reason to care about the characters or the story. "A quarter of my life went into this book."

Kiara wrapped dark gray yarn around the hook and pulled it through. "A long time."

"Why did I bother? Why do any writers bother?" He looked at her lap. "Didn't you just make a gray rug?"

"This one is charcoal. That one was iron." In went the hook. "You chose a tough profession."

"It must be hard to be married to a writer," he said.

"Sometimes."

Despite everything, George smiled. He counted himself lucky that Kiara had stuck by him all the years when it seemed he might fail and treated him no differently when he succeeded. Not that she didn't celebrate with him, but he could tell that what she felt for him didn't require the kind of success they had briefly experienced.

They'd met because of Sandy. (Of all people!) A few years

after George started at Peapod, the managing editor had brought Kiara in to talk about volunteering to help children learn to read in afterschool programs. George had signed up for a year before moving on to Big Brothers. At the beginning, he had no idea how to teach a child to read. He couldn't remember how he'd learned. He'd been too young, perhaps as young as three, his mother having sat with him for hours over books about spotted dogs and monkeys and schoolgirls, until one day he simply grasped the way lines formed letters, and letters, words.

With his legs extended like ramps from a small wood chair, he'd asked for Kiara's help. She told him which books to give an older boy so as not to embarrass the child. "He's not a baby," she said, "though he lacks certain skills. Children also need their dignity protected." George talked to the boy differently after that. From week to week, his student sometimes forgot what they'd gone over together. When George became frustrated, Kiara reminded him the program wasn't there to make him feel good about himself, her manner so kind, he wasn't offended.

"I talked to Dr. Elias," George said.

("It's not unusual for people calling for the first time to be nervous. I'd be surprised if you weren't," the psychologist had said, giving George a taste of the radical acceptance that causes so many people to fall in love with their therapists.)

George turned off his computer. "I have an appointment with her in two weeks. Can you put up with me until then?"

"I can try," said Kiara.

CHAPTER THIRTEEN

Though she hadn't yet received the contract from Black Bear, P.J. closed on a condo in a net-zero building at the beginning of June, borrowing the down payment from Marissa until she got her advance. She didn't know which excited her more: the view of the Rocky Mountains or the electric car charging stations in the garage. Looking out the living room windows, P.J. imagined she could hear a soaring Bach chorus, soundtrack to a new life in which she would publish a book every two years and appear regularly on national talk shows, her mix of environmental and feminist advocacy irresistible.

If she had the money, which she didn't, she still would have refused to buy the distressed pine dining room set and the burl coffee table Marissa had bookmarked for her online, preferring to keep her old furniture and avoid the chronic consumption that plagued the country. Too broke to hire movers, she rented a truck and begged her friends to help her haul her belongings.

"In my line of work, we advise people not to spend money before they have it," Len said, straining under one end of a sofa.

Marissa twirled a lamp. "I'm happy to lend you money, too," she said to Len. "You've seen *The Sopranos*, right?"

P.J. dragged her desk chair into the service elevator. "My agent said it was a done deal."

In the apartment, Alex set down his end of the sofa and took in the view. "Impressive. I wouldn't mind writing with this backdrop."

"Come over any Saturday," P.J. said.

"I might do that. Maybe some of your publishing karma will rub off on me."

P.J. pictured the two of them writing together, going through two pots of coffee. Alex asking for advice on how to improve a scene. Stopping for lunch, which they'd make together: avocado toast or three bean salad. Drinking a beer because what the hell it was the weekend. One beer becoming two. Talking about their lives as they did the dishes. Laughing, elbows bumping, water splashing on Alex's shirt, which he'd strip off, revealing the dark nipples and narrow chest she'd conjured more than once since their night together. Not to be outdone, she'd pull off her own shirt, one arm briefly getting caught in the organic cotton sleeve. After she freed herself, she'd lead him to the bedroom, making the mistake of mentioning how well her book was doing. Alex's grin would evaporate, and his skinny shoulders would sag. He'd sulk because he still hadn't heard from his agent. Instead of having playful sex in her bright new bedroom, she'd wind up consoling him on the very couch he'd just set down.

They returned to the truck for boxes.

"Where do these go?" Len asked. A carton labelled *PRIVATE* had popped open, revealing zucchini- and parsnip-shaped vibrators and a jar of pistachio-flavored massage oil.

"You know people use vegetables because they don't have vibrators, right?" Marissa said to P.J.

"I like vegetables," P.J. said.

"Where do they go?" Len asked.

"You want to know where vibrators go?" Marissa said. "I suppose I could show you."

To P.J.'s surprise, Len blushed. "I was talking about the box."

Marissa grabbed the zucchini and pressed the on button. "If

you really want to know."

P.J. carried a carton of clothes into the bedroom.

"You should make an instructional video," Alex said to Marissa.

She turned the zucchini off. "The school board would love that. Hiring committees, too."

"You could use a pseudonym."

"We should do it together," Marissa said. "With your marketing background and my pedagogical know-how, it would be a hit."

"Maybe a series," Alex said. "Vibrators, strap-ons."

"I like where you're going with this. Naturally, we'd have to demonstrate them." Marissa undid the top two buttons on her jeans.

"Naturally," he said.

As Marissa lay her palm on Alex's chest, P.J. returned to the room. She looked from Marissa's half-open jeans to Alex and back to her friend.

Marissa dropped her hand. She buttoned her pants. "Just kidding around."

"Why do you care?" Alex said to P.J.

It was a good question. "There's a two-hundred pound dining table and a TV still on the truck," P.J. said.

***

The worn-out furniture made the apartment look shabbier. Notwithstanding the view, it didn't look like the home of a successful writer. Ducking into the bathroom, P.J. reread the email from Sloane confirming that Black Bear wanted the book. Then she washed her face, drying it on her dusty T-shirt because her towels were still in boxes.

She drove the truck back to the rental place and picked up her car, which she'd left there that morning. After stopping for two six-packs, she returned to the apartment. In the kitchen, Len and Marissa unpacked dishes. Alex watched baseball in the living room. She was grateful to all three for their help, especially Len, since they hadn't always gotten along. He'd surprised her by saying "sure" when she asked, not even pretending to check his calendar while he made up his mind. Though their clothes were streaked with grease from the moving van, and they smelled like sweat and cardboard, her friends breathed life into the condo, made it feel like home. She even discovered a benefit to the old furniture: She didn't mind when Alex rested his beer on the arm of the couch, where it would almost certainly get knocked over.

She ordered dinner, then joined Marissa and Len in the kitchen, rearranging the things they'd put away. By the time the fragrant dishes arrived—three orders of moo shu, dumplings, and two containers of fried rice, pork for her friends and vegetable for her—she'd managed to find everything she needed to set the table. The sun dropped behind the mountains, spraying purple and orange across the horizon. P.J. paused to watch it, inviting the others to join her. A hush fell over the room as they stood together, each satisfied for the time being to admire the sky as it dimmed from blue to gray to black.

CHAPTER FOURTEEN

Throughout May, George had mined his contacts but hadn't succeeded in finding a job. Most editors had ignored his emails, including ones who had bid unsuccessfully on his book. Editors who did respond, tried to cushion the bad news: "You're more than qualified, but given the controversy, we wouldn't feel comfortable bringing you on." "At any other time, your resume would rise to the top." "We don't want to waste your time with an interview."

He'd reached out to authors he'd published at Peapod who worked for publishing companies because they couldn't make a living from writing alone. A few commiserated, but no one had a position for him.

In June, though it pained him, he called Ryan. Kiara had set a basket of clean laundry on the couch before she left for work, and George folded while he talked. "Maybe you have some freelance work I could do." He set a pillowcase on the pile and told Ryan about Saturn delaying his book.

"I wish I could," Ryan said. "We haven't found your replacement and we're drowning. It seems no one wants to work for a publisher that steals women's work."

George wrestled with a fitted sheet. "You know I didn't."

"It doesn't matter what I know. What matters is what people think. Honestly, we're hoping everyone forgets you ever worked here."

It was oddly quiet on Ryan's end of the line, and George

wondered if he'd stopped working out. He pictured the editor-in-chief with spindly arms and a belly that pooched out, and for the first time in weeks, George smiled. "No one would have to know," he said. "You could pay Kiara. I'll copyedit or proofread."

"People have a way of finding things out. Anyway, this isn't public yet, but I'm going to step down as editor-in-chief and Sandy's going to take over. A consultant recommended the change as a way for us to rehabilitate our image. So I can't do anything for you."

George gave up on the sheet, throwing it on the couch. "Sorry."

"Me, too."

Mutt lay with her head hanging over the edge of her plush dog bed, pining for Kiara or a Danish, which Kiara had forbidden George from feeding her. As he scratched the dog behind the ear, she let out a depressed sigh.

***

The next day he received a job offer from Palm Beach Books, a conservative outfit whose titles included an anti-abortion screed and the memoir of a gun rights advocate. George hadn't contacted them, but they'd heard he was looking for work.

George was walking Mutt when Bob Carpenter, the publisher, called. "You have our sympathies," Bob said. "This is how society treats White men who don't toe the liberal line. We admire that you didn't bend to the left and publish diverse books, which we all know means books by anyone other than true Americans like you and me. Well, that's what we're here for. We give White folks a voice."

"Actually, I did try to publish diverse books." Mutt squatted on a narrow strip of ground next to a linden tree. "And I don't think White people are being denied a voice, that wasn't—"

"Maybe in addition to editing for us, you'll write a memoir about how even someone like you, who thought he was a good liberal, got cancelled. Show no White man is safe in this environment and never will be safe until we take back the country."

With her back feet, one tan and one white, Mutt shoveled bits of earth over the pile she had made. "Yeah, I don't think I'm the right—"

"I'm talking a six-figure advance for the memoir, not as much as Saturn offered you for *Up the Hill*, but enough to live on for a while, plus a job as a senior editor, and we'll double what you were making at Peapod."

They could go on vacation. Somewhere without Wi-Fi. Did a place like that exist anymore? He was tempted to ask the publisher if he kept workout equipment in his office. Ready to move on, Mutt pulled at the leash. George bent and collected her poop in a plastic bag. "I wouldn't be a good fit."

"No need to decide now," the publisher said. "Mull it over. Sleep on it. Talk to your wife. Look at your bank statement. We offer a great benefits package. And people read our books. You'd be surprised how many. There'd be speaking opportunities, too."

"I don't think so." George dropped the bag in an overflowing metal can.

When Kiara got home, he told her about the call.

"They'd be using you for their own political agenda," she said. "An agenda you hate."

"Imagine the books we could have published at Peapod if we'd had that kind of money."

"Pandering to the discontented pays well."

The next morning, George ran a slim ad in an online

magazine for writers, offering his services as an independent editor, charging it to an already overloaded credit card. The only people who responded wanted to talk about the scandal to sympathize, or, more often, to berate him.

He cast about for another line of work. He considered teaching, but after his experience volunteering in Kiara's program, he doubted he would be good at it.

Maybe his cousin Lilly would hire him at the bagel store. It wouldn't pay much, but he liked the idea of escaping the publishing industry for a while, being surrounded by the rich smell of freshly baked goods, and feeding people, such a simple, useful task. Bagels were comforting. You made them, people ate them, and you made some more. You had to pay attention so as not to burn yourself, but it wasn't the kind of attention editing required, that hyper-focused hunt for misplaced modifiers, inadvertent puns, logical fallacies. It wasn't the kind of mental work that was never finished. Bagels could endure only so much baking before they were ruined. They were universal crowd pleasers. No one ever said about a bagel, "The market for cinnamon raisin is too crowded" or "I just didn't believe in your sesame seeds." Together with lox and cream cheese and the *Times* crossword puzzle, they were what Sunday was made of for the people of his city.

If he completed his shift early, he could spend part of the day at his desk. He'd put aside the edits to *Up the Hill* to work on a new novel that excited him despite—or perhaps because of—everything that had happened. As he drafted the first chapters, he remembered what he loved about being a writer: the quiet hours of creation, breathing life into his characters' nostrils, as God had in his timeless bestseller. The surprises in the story that delighted him before shocking readers. The ironies that pressed a laugh from his belly. Years of satisfying effort before industry professionals met in committees to hazard reckless guesses about how the book would do in the market, before reviewers hoisted their giant magnifying glasses beneath a bright sun, before interviewers demanded explanations, though they might as well ask for explanations of the color red or the taste of ice cream. A writer could stammer "cold" or "sweet" or "creamy," but would that help someone who had never melted a spoonful of mint chocolate chip on his tongue? Working on the new book had restored balance to his life. Perhaps he was a glutton for punishment, but he had a good feeling about it.

Poor Mutt would be alone while George was at the bagel store. Yet he didn't see what choice he had. "I'm sorry," he said to the dog, who had squeezed under the coffee table. George found half a banana in the refrigerator and sat on the floor, feeding pieces to Mutt, the dog surprising him by licking his hand long after the fruit was gone.

***

"Bagels?" Kiara said, as she put away hamburger buns that had been on sale. There was no more sushi.

"I'd be able to bring some home. Maybe even the everything bagels you like." He unpacked frozen vegetables, rice, beans, and chickpeas, staples he had enjoyed until they began eating them most nights. He knew he should be grateful. He wasn't hungry, though the composition of his diet had shrunk.

"Bagels," Kiara said.

"It's just until Saturn signs the contract."

"And this is what you want?"

"It's a huge relief," George said. "A chance to forget about Saturn and Peapod for a while. To work on my new book."

"And Lilly was okay with this?"

"I haven't asked her yet. I wanted to talk to you first. She'd have to train me. But I'm looking forward to it."

"If you put it that way, I guess I agree. I doubt it would pay much, but we could manage."

"Okay. I'll call her."

When he reached Lily, she said she was sorry, but she had just hired someone. Though she wanted to help, she didn't have anything open.

***

On Sunday, George took Seth, the boy he mentored through the Big Brothers program, to a Mets game. He hadn't seen Seth since P.J.'s nibble. He'd put off calling, hoping to be vindicated by the time they spoke. Seth was active on Crave.

George had splurged on seats close to the field when he'd thought he was going to be rich. "How's your mom?" George asked, once they were settled with hot dogs, a soda for Seth, and a beer for him.

"Same," Seth said. "She works a lot. Everyone wants her to do their tile."

"I guess that's good," George said.

Seth sipped the soda and burped. He looked at George, and George could tell he wanted to ask him something. "What is it?" George said.

"Did you steal that lady's book?"

"No."

They stood so a family of four in blue and orange jerseys could get to their seats.

"Everyone says you did." Seth bent the straw with his teeth.

"Not everyone."

"A lot of people."

George set his beer in the cup holder. "Yeah. A lot of people." Seth waited.

"People like to repeat ugly things they read or hear or things that make them angry," George said. "It makes them feel like they're doing something, though they aren't. Not really. They don't stop to worry about what's true."

They stood again, allowing a man hugging four tubs of popcorn to pass. Seth had torn a hole in his straw, bending it back and forth. He pulled it out and took the cap off the cup.

"It's like any rumor, except it's worse online," George said. "Picture the wave spreading in a stadium a thousand times bigger than this one."

"Did you read her book?" Seth said.

"Yes. That's my job. Or it was my job."

"You got fired?"

The concern in Seth's voice touched George. "Yeah."

Seth planted his foot on the green seatback in front of him. "They believed the woman who accused you."

"Enough people believed her."

"I don't," Seth said.

George was surprised at the relief he felt. "Why is that?"

"You were always working on it. Always talking about working on it. 'I just finished the tenth draft.' 'The fifteenth draft.' 'I feel really good about the book.' 'I'm not sure about the book.' Sometimes, I wished you would shut up about it. Talk about something else. A movie you liked. A trip you went on. Anyway, you didn't need to steal her book, because you wrote one yourself."

George sipped his beer. "Thanks, I think."

"Don't mention it."

In the bullpen, the pitcher warmed up. The sunbaked afternoon, the beer, and the faith of his young friend combined to loosen George's anxiety. Seth was nearly as tall as him. He'd be graduating from high school next year and would no longer be in the program. Though George would remain in contact with him, he felt the beginnings of a loss. He and Kiara had agreed they didn't want kids, but now George questioned that decision. He imagined a clutch of children standing by him when the world turned its back. Yet he knew there was no guarantee that even children would take his side.

CHAPTER FIFTEEN

"What you said about the accident helped," Franklin said. "About it not being my fault because so many things had to happen." He and P.J. were sitting in a red leather booth in Dash's Diner, eating sandwiches and potato chips, while eggs sizzled and home fries toughened on a grill. He said the way she explained it had made sense to him because he was an engineer who was always looking at complicated environments. "I'm not saying I feel good about it."

"I wouldn't think you would," P.J. said.

Franklin wiped his lips on a paper napkin. "Every morning when I get dressed, I see her jeans folded in the closet. And the mail is always full of catalogs she liked. She used to sit at the kitchen table with her chai and point out pretty nesting bowls and stainless steel pots that wouldn't give us Alzheimer's, though she mostly shopped at Randy's, that discount store. She bought my shoes there. They never fit as well as shoes I picked out for myself, but I didn't have the heart to tell her. I just wore them and stuck bandages where they chafed." His large brown lace-ups filled one white and one black checkerboard tile. As usual, a Band-Aid nested in his pocket.

P.J. doubted a man would ever wear uncomfortable shoes for her. Vlad certainly hadn't been one to do it. When they lived together in his first year of graduate school, he woke early so he could shower before her, using up the last of the hot water. She was no better, finishing the coffee while he was at his morning class and not bothering to prepare more though she knew he'd want a cup when he returned. She wondered what their relationship would have been like if she'd just made that second pot.

"How are things going with the book?" Franklin said.

Did he know about her accusation against Dunn? He'd never mentioned it and didn't seem to live his life on Crave, unlike her and her friends. "My book? I don't really know. My publisher doesn't tell me anything. It's like the FBI over there, and I can't seem to get a security clearance. I think they're looking forward to the day when computers spit out all the books and they don't have to deal with writers at all." P.J. resented having to compete with AI. Life was hard enough with other authors breathing down her neck, trying to fill the few spots that might be open on a publisher's list. A blender whirred, and P.J. waited for it to finish. "Imagine trying to compete with programs that don't have to support themselves. That don't have to worry about hurting anyone."

Franklin sipped his coffee. "Are you worried about hurting someone?"

P.J. chewed a soggy potato chip. "My sister thinks the book is about her."

"Is it?"

"Not really."

"Is it worth alienating her? Over a book?" Franklin said.

"If it's a book I spent years writing? That will finally get published after who knows how many rejections? And I'll get paid for writing it? For writing something? Anything? Yes, it's worth it. It's not really about her, anyway." She pushed her plate away. "I'm not happy she's upset. I wish she wasn't. But is it worth it? Yes." Had he invited her to lunch just to make her feel bad?

"Sorry. Didn't mean to rain on your aspirations." With his fork, Franklin scraped together flecks of tuna and celery that had fallen from his sandwich.

What was it with her and men? P.J. blamed her father for setting a poor example. She couldn't remember the last time Lawrence bought Dina an impractical gift. Tulips and black-eyed Susans shuddered in the breeze of their kitchen fan, bouquets Dina picked up at the supermarket, laying them in her cart alongside containers of low-fat yogurt and Calcium gummies. Her mother wore silver bracelets and earrings with bits of tiger's eye or citrine she found at craft fairs, not bothering to tell Lawrence. He wouldn't have objected, but he might have delivered a short lecture about materialism. Dina worked part-time as an obstetric nurse, a profession she loved, and that Lawrence claimed to hold in high regard, except when her shifts interfered with his dinner. He ate out those nights, then complained about excess salt or fat or the high price of his bar tab. Dina sometimes called P.J. to complain while Lawrence was on campus. On the other hand, her parents hiked through pine forests in the summer. In the winter, they skied slopes they'd memorized early in their marriage. On Sunday afternoons, they attended Tony-award winning plays that travelled to Denver with lesser-known casts. The faculty dinners they hosted ended at nine-thirty sharp, when the dean's wife stood and stretched, and cleared a half-finished bottle of wine from the table. P.J. didn't think it would be enough for her, but it was more than she'd had with Vlad. She wondered whether Alex would have been the kind of partner to surprise her with a trip to Paris or whether he would have been more like her father.

Franklin cradled his cup. "I'm hardly one to give advice, considering how badly I've screwed up my own life. But I do think that as long as you keep talking to your sister, there's always hope of working things out. You're both still alive. That's something." A server cleared their plates. "You'll figure it out," Franklin said.

"When?" P.J. said.

He waved his hands over his water glass. "I see two women with white hair, one in a solar-powered wheelchair."

"Very funny." When Franklin had said he wanted to take her to lunch to thank her, P.J. had wondered if he wanted something more. She'd imagined dating him, his long arm around her shoulders, his fingers knitting her hair, as they attended an avant-garde play neither understood. They'd head to Baxter's when it was over, and she'd introduce him to her friends, who would text their approval while they were still at the bar.

"Sharon thought I'd love these shoes," Franklin said, looking down at his feet. "She was proud of what a bargain they'd been. I still wear them. I'm afraid I'll miss the chafing if I stop."

Would he ever stop talking about shoes? He was too preoccupied with Sharon to be good relationship material. And he came with children, an instant family that would interfere with her writing and with Saturday night dates that culminated in Sunday breakfasts. "They're a way of keeping her close," P.J. said. "And proof that even though in a moment of distraction you said no to her, there were many more moments when you said yes."

Franklin stared at her, grief rearranging his features. "Thanks," he said, quietly. "I never thought of it that way."

"I guess you owe me another lunch."

"And I thought 'starving artist' was just a euphemism."

Franklin paid the check, and P.J. gave him a ride back to his office free of charge. He still wasn't driving.

***

Saturday morning, P.J. prepared a tofu scramble with spinach and mushrooms. She sliced cantaloupe, washed blackberries, and brewed coffee in a French press. No one was joining her. Unwelcome at her parents' brunch, she'd decided to make her own. Her mother had sent a tablecloth and napkins made from recycled cotton as a housewarming gift, and P.J. set the table with them.

She'd invited her friends and was surprised none of them could make it. Alex had said he needed to work on his novel. Marissa was preparing her summer school classes, which was odd, because she'd taught the same courses for the past five years. Len had a date and refused to give details. Perhaps she'd crowed too much about her book deal, alienating Alex and reminding Marissa that she hadn't been invited for an interview after sending out a new round of administrator applications. Or maybe Marissa's summer school curriculum had changed. Taking Franklin's advice, she'd even called Mia. "I know we're in a rough patch, but would you like to come for brunch on Saturday? It would be nice to see you."

"What's wrong? Have you run out of material?" Mia said. "I'm afraid you'll have to suck someone else's blood."

P.J. had thought about inviting Franklin but was afraid he, too, would find an excuse to turn her down.

When was the last time she'd made such a nice meal for herself? She savored the aroma of the sautéing garlic. Took in the view of the mountain range, half bare as it threw off its snowy blanket for the summer. Sixty million years older than the Colosseum or the Western Wall. P.J. doubted she would ever tire of the scene. She hadn't been to church since Christmas, when she'd gone with her family, a tradition that failed to touch her, bored her, actually, though she managed to keep that to herself. But alone, contemplating the craggy peaks, she felt something akin to religion, humbled and outside of ordinary time.

She removed the skillet from the fire. Poured a cup of coffee and added almond milk. Settled into a calm that was one of the pleasures of living alone, a self-sufficiency that was one of the delights of being uncoupled. Moments when she yearned for neither the prince nor the kiss. She never knew how long her contentment would last, or what breeze would usher in an aching loneliness that was no less painful for itself being temporary. She spooned the scramble and fruit onto a plate. Warm spinach filled her mouth.

After the meal, she would work on a new book. The story spanned a week during a winter storm. She'd begun it after she moved in, her desk pressed against the window. It wasn't inspired by anything that happened to anyone she knew.

***

Four days later, P.J. sat in the library nibbling about her book deal, which had been announced that morning in *Publishers Marketplace*. She put her phone on vibrate to avoid bothering other patrons with the app's sounds—clatters, crunches, and horns honking when private meals were delivered.

A schedule of events hung on a corkboard: story time, French conversation, Western poets reading series. A man stood typing at a computer terminal, battered shopping bags at his feet. At a table, an artist sketched herself with colored pencils using a selfie for reference. A librarian begged a man who entered, "Please. Leave the rabbit outside."

Books lined up like dogs in an overcrowded shelter waiting

to be taken home.

As expected, writers she knew munched and re-served her nibble, joined the meal to say how happy they were for her, and served GIFs: slices of cake with twinkling sparklers and champagne bottles with popping corks. "Thank you!" she responded, over and over, adding blown kisses and hearts, hoping to prod the algorithm to share her news ever farther.

She'd been waiting forever to announce a book deal and to receive the kind of attention being lavished on her nibble. She checked whether she was a popular menu item. She wasn't. Give it time, she thought. When she saw that @evehadanalibi had tagged her in a three-course meal, she got excited. She didn't know @evehadanalibi but figured she was someone who had liked the sound of the book. One of the many strangers who were about to become fans of her work. When she became famous, a small drooling mouth—the Crave mini-logo—would pop up next to her name to show she was legit, the real P.J. Larkin. Like the ones attached to the names of all her literary heroes.

P.J. read the meal.

GIRL IS IN THE HOUSE isn't @PJLarkin's story to tell. It's the story of how my friend was raped by her employer. Larkin stole it to write a bestseller. She doesn't know anything about being sexually assaulted.

My friend is still suffering from the attack. Please contribute to the Better Day Fund I set up for her, so she can finish her college degree. To respect her privacy, I'm keeping her anonymous.

If you think @PJLarkin has no right to tell this story,

contact @BlackBearPress and tell them not to publish her book and re-serve this meal!!!

"Fuck!" P.J. said. A man looked up from his magazine. "Sorry," she said. What was @evehadanalibi trying to do? And how did she know P.J.'s book was inspired by Mia's story? The Crave account belonged to a woman named Avery Baron who lived in Denver and whose bio said, "sober warrior." P.J. googled her but didn't find much. The woman's three-course meal was taking off.

From the bathroom, P.J. called her sister. "Have you seen Crave?"

"Yeah."

"Who's Avery Baron?"

"What do you want?" Mia said.

"Make her purge the meal!"

"I can't make her do anything."

A girl came out of a stall and washed her hands. "You're not supposed to talk on your phone in the library."

P.J. turned to face the wall. "How does she know about my book?"

"She's in group therapy with me."

"Doesn't publicizing what you talk about violate the rules?"

"I won't tell if you don't tell."

On Mia's end of the line, P.J. heard the rattle of a cart. Her sister's latest job was cleaning hotel rooms. "Is there someplace quiet you could go where we could talk?" P.J. said.

"I'm working." P.J. heard a knock, and then Mia shouted, "*Housekeeping!*"

"Tell Avery to stop."

"Nope." She asked a hotel guest, "*Would you like a change of towels?*"

Courtesy is Contagious read a sign on the bathroom wall. "Please. Can't you at least take a break for a minute?"

"No."

"People will figure out it's you in the book."

"Look who's concerned about my privacy all of a sudden. Anyway, she didn't use my name."

"*I* didn't use your name. And I was always concerned about your privacy. That's why I changed all the details in the book." *Requests Work Better Than Demands* read another sign. "Please. Please, ask her to purge it. At least until we have a chance to talk."

"We just talked," Mia said, before shouting, "*I'll come back later.*" P.J. heard the cart rattle again.

The three-course meal was garnering more attention than P.J.'s announcement had.

@studyshakespeare nibbled back, "'What's past is prologue.' After accusing @GeorgeDunn of stealing her story turns out @PJLarkin's the thief. #writersbehavingbadly"

@godisgreat380 weighed in: "Thou shalt not steal, @PJLarkin! #readthebible #itsallinthere"

@DoctorofLit joined the meal: "Not surprised to see a privileged woman like @PJLarkin colonizing the experience of a sexual assault victim. Karen much?"

P.J. couldn't help but nibble back. "Privileged? I drive for a fucking rideshare company, *Doctor*!" She wished she could hear the clatter when she served it.

She caught only one nibble in her favor. "The only thing @PJLarkin is guilty of is daring to use her imagination. Quick! Send a SWAT team armed with erasers," served @aliceinnovelland.

P.J. pressed her head against the cold tile wall. "You're going to scare my publisher," she said to Mia.

"So?"

"So they might pull out of the deal."

"That's the idea," Mia said.

P.J. wanted to reach through the phone and shake her sister. Instead, she forced herself to speak softly. "This Avery person isn't helping you."

"Actually, the Better Day Fund is doing pretty well. It's up to twenty-two hundred dollars."

"How do you know she'll give you the money?" P.J. said.

"Why wouldn't she? We're close. Not everyone betrays their friends—or their sisters." Mia knocked on a guest's door.

"What you're doing is unfair. What happened to you wasn't my fault."

Everyone on Crave seemed to be joining Avery Baron's meal. The same people who had supported P.J. when she said Dunn had stolen her book were now championing Mia's cause without even knowing her name.

@BeaNeedsAnAgent served, "Not @PJLarkin's story to tell. #silencePJ"

@WomynsRites nibbled, "Sisters don't steal from sisters."

"Please," P.J. said, squeezing her phone, "tell her to say she made a mistake until we sort this out."

"*Housekeeping!*" Mia said.

***

P.J. texted Sloane from her car, and her agent video-called her. Sloane was working from home, books and manuscripts stacked high on a table behind her. On one of the piles, a yellow-headed cockatiel pranced in a circle chanting, "Great book! Great book!"

After P.J. explained the situation, Sloane opened Crave, her scowl deepening as she scrolled.

P.J. grabbed her notebook and drew a whirlpool. "Should we tell Black Bear?"

"They're tagged. I'll call them."

"Are they going to cancel the deal?"

"I doubt it." Sloane sipped from a giant mug. A drop of milky liquid rolled down the side and she caught it and licked her finger. "Who's the book about?"

To the whirlpool, P.J. added a pair of drowning hands. "It's not about anyone. I made it up. My sister, Mia, worked for a politician, a state senator in Colorado. She was sexually assaulted by him, but what happened to her is totally different from what happens in the book."

"I wish you had told me," Sloane said.

"Don't writers get inspiration from life all the time? Do they always tell you?"

"It helps when they do."

P.J. glanced at Crave. Trolls had attacked all her recent nibbles, even the most innocuous, like the one in which she condemned book bans. ("@PJLarkin's book should be banned! It's stolen!" @Freespeech2391 had nibbled back.) Afraid to become targets, the same writers who'd congratulated her earlier had fallen silent. She couldn't blame them. Under similar circumstances, she'd hidden, too.

"Black Bear will want to be sure you did a good job disguising Mia's identity and the identity of others in the book, especially the state senator," Sloane said.

"I did," P.J. said.

"Let's hope so."

"I made him a U.S. Congresswoman's chief of staff."

"Can you make him something else?" Sloane said. "Something outside of politics?"

"Not without rewriting the whole book."
"Think about it."
In one of the drowning hands, P.J. drew a pen.

CHAPTER SIXTEEN

George couldn't believe what he was reading. Had Larkin really stolen someone's story? The news made him giddy. He poured chocolate syrup into his coffee to celebrate, cackling while he stirred it. When Mutt poked her head into the kitchen to investigate the sound, George tossed her two biscuits. "Now who's a thief?" he said to her. His book deal would be back on track! Mutt wagged, delighted with the unearned snack. George called Janelle but got her answering service.

"Did you see it?" he said, when she called back two hours later.

"I saw it."

"What a joke. Tell Saturn and let's publish my book." George sipped the sweetened coffee, which had grown cold. The air around him felt lighter than it had in months.

"First of all, it's just an accusation," Janelle said.

"Are you serious? *Just an accusation*? Everything Larkin said about me was *just an accusation*."

"Second, even if it's true, and Larkin was inspired by someone else's story, that doesn't make it wrong."

George wondered if another agent would have fought harder for him, demanded that Saturn publish his book or at least pay part of the advance. Perhaps the problem was Janelle's inexperience. Not having handled many deals, maybe she was intimidated by Saturn. He considered switching agents. But who would take him in the middle of a scandal? "Call Saturn."

"I'll call them, but I can't promise it will make a difference. People can want to cancel Larkin and you at the same time. In fact, one of the arguments against Larkin, that she shouldn't have written about sexual assault because she hasn't experienced it, applies to you, too."

George groaned.

"Just wait for things to calm down," Janelle said. "People will forget. Then Saturn will publish it."

"Tell my landlord to wait. Or the utility company."

"I'm sorry. Truly, I am. But I have to go. I have a meeting."

George picked up a pricey fountain pen from his desk. He'd bought it years ago, splurging because it was recommended by an author who'd attended a prestigious writing program. He wondered what he could get for it on Craigslist.

***

Saturday morning, George lay awake, thinking about the senator. He'd been up half the night, weighing whether to tell the world what she'd done to him. Saturn hadn't been willing to move forward after Janelle showed them his ten-year-old drafts. The accusation against Larkin hadn't changed their minds, either.

Outside his bedroom window, pigeons burbled. George envied their contentment. Wishing Kiara was up, he flipped from his left side to his right, then back again, jogging the tired mattress. She stirred.

"I'm going to go public," he said.

"Good morning to you," she said, her voice mottled with sleep.

"I'm can't let her ruin my life a second time." He imagined shaming her on national television, creating a revolting coda to her legacy. People would rush to revise her Wikipedia entry.

He would do it himself if necessary. "All I'm good at is writing and editing. I won't let her or P.J. Larkin take that away. If the senator comes after me…"

"Yes?" Kiara said, her eyes open now.

"I don't know."

She wrapped herself around him, and he savored the warmth of her belly against his side, her hand on his chest. They no longer wore their Saturn T-shirts. Kiara slept naked and George wore pajama bottoms.

His therapist had them doing an exercise called Touching with Tenderness. The saccharine name alone had nearly defeated him. For fifteen minutes, three times a week, they embraced. Standing, sitting, or lying down, in different rooms of the apartment, with or without clothes. It wasn't allowed to lead to sex, which made George feel safe. He'd renamed it Hands On, and later, Calzone, for the way Kiara wrapped her body around his. He'd begun to look forward to it.

"We don't need a book deal to be happy," Kiara said.

"I need it." The book represented too much of his life. He wasn't sure when he would finish the new novel or if any other book would be as important to him as *Up the Hill*.

"She'll come after us. Reporters will want to know if you told me, and what am I going to say? Right before you went public, but not earlier in our marriage?"

He rolled away from her. "Tell them whatever you like. I can't spend my life being afraid of people like Wilma Sands and P.J. Larkin."

Kiara pulled the sheet up to her neck. "If that's what you need to do, that's what you should do. But, please, talk to your agent before you make any public announcements. And maybe a lawyer. And discuss it with Dr. Elias, too."

The window had grown brighter but the ledge was empty, the pigeons having taken their happy murmurings to someone else's apartment.

CHAPTER SEVENTEEN

"Pretty scary the way people turned against you," Alex said, fanning himself with his race bib. Seven-thirty in the morning, but it was already hot. Len and Marissa were doing sprints, loosening up for the 10K to support a local women's shelter. P.J. had always enjoyed these events, everyone coming out for a cause. Now she was just glad she was anonymous except for a race number.

Alex pinned the bib to his T-shirt. "What happens next?"

"I'm talking to Black Bear's lawyer on Monday. They want to make sure no one can sue us. People are saying I shouldn't have written about a character who was sexually assaulted since I'm not a survivor myself. I hope Black Bear doesn't agree."

"You should write about whatever you want," Len said, twisting at the waist. "The screenwriters who wrote *Titanic* never went down with a ship, and last time I checked the ones who wrote *San Andreas* didn't die in an earthquake. Anyway, by that logic, no one could ever write about death. Sorry, Shakespeare."

"It's not that simple." Alex stretched his quads. "Historically, certain groups haven't been allowed to tell their own stories. Not only is it racist, but those writers are closer to those experiences, so wouldn't you rather hear from them?"

"Amen, hallelujah, and Shabbat shalom. Can we focus on the race now?" Marissa tightened her shoelace. "P.J., I hope you told Black Bear you're running. So they can publicize it to counter all the bad P.R. you're getting."

"That seems kind of—" P.J. said.

"Smart?" Marissa said.

"Narcissistic," P.J. said.

"Let me get this straight," Len said. "It's okay to want to be famous for writing a book but not for running a charity race?"

"People post potato chips shaped like penises," Marissa said. "They serve pictures of fresh afterbirth. Why shouldn't you publicize participating in a charity race? It might inspire someone to make a donation. Besides, if you don't serve it on Crave, it never happened. I'll take a picture and you can send it to Black Bear." The four friends squeezed together. "Smile!"

Marissa took the selfie and showed it to P.J.

"I look depressed," P.J. said.

"I told you to smile."

"Crop me out."

"I'm trying to rehabilitate your image. And you're in the middle. Let's take another. Come on, Alex, Len."

Len touched his toes. "I'm stretching."

Marissa snapped his photo from behind. "I'll send this to you, Len. Serve it on Crave, and I guarantee you'll grow your diners. You may even get a few new clients out of it."

P.J. couldn't help laughing, and while she did, Marissa took her picture.

When the gun went off for the start of the race, Len and Marissa joined runners at the front. Though he could have maintained a faster pace, Alex stayed toward the back with P.J. Cottonwoods and maples shaded the first part of the route. Runners fell into a rhythm, the *pat pat* of their soles filling the air.

P.J. thought her book shed light on an important issue, but instead of being hailed as a fresh, new voice, she was being portrayed as another clueless white lady. She didn't understand how it had happened or what steps she could take to fix it. She believed she had the right to tell the story of a sexual assault, but organizations she respected disagreed. Like the shriveled irises along the trail—fresh and exciting only weeks before—her book now seemed from another time and smacking of decay. Before anyone had even read it.

"Nothing from your agent?" she asked Alex.

"Not a word."

"Send your manuscript to Sloane. I've been telling her about you for years."

"I'm sure Jack will get to it soon," Alex said.

"You're not desperate enough. That's your problem."

Alex smiled, revealing teeth that overlapped like a poker hand. P.J. remembered how they'd felt against her tongue. "If you never sell it, at least no one will accuse you of stealing their story," P.J. said, trying hard in that moment not to think of George Dunn.

***

"This is not how I raised you girls!" Lawrence bellowed. He drained a glass of Scotch, ignoring his own rule about drinking in front of Mia. They were in her parents' living room at a family conference Lawrence had called. Mia sat cross-legged on the bamboo floor, P.J. and Dina at opposite ends of the sofa.

Lawrence unplugged a crystal decanter and refilled his glass. "It's like you're at war."

Dina examined the umbrella pattern on her skirt.

"She's trying to humiliate me in front of the whole world," Mia said. "What do you expect me to do, let her? She doesn't understand because she's always had it easy." She sipped her virgin mimosa, then set the glass down on the coffee table. "This stuff is gross."

"I haven't had it easy," P.J. said. "You try writing three books that don't sell and then having your sister undermine you when one of your books finally lands with a publisher that offers three hundred fifty thousand dollars for it."

A wave of orange liquid crashed over the lip of Dina's glass. "*How much?*"

"Who knows if I'll see a penny of it now," P.J. said.

Lawrence sat in an armchair. "Mia, is it true you had a friend claim P.J. stole your story?"

"What if I did? That's what happened." She clutched the lifeguard whistle.

Dina wiped the spill from the couch with a napkin.

"Tell them about the Better Day Fund," P.J. said, leaning toward her sister.

Mia was quiet.

"Her friend set up a Better Day Fund, so Mia could get paid for ruining my life. How much is in it now, Mia?"

"Fuck you," Mia said.

"Language!" Lawrence sipped his scotch. "How much is in it?"

"Sixteen thousand dollars as of this morning," Mia said.

"What exactly is the money for?" Lawrence asked. "How did you earn it?"

"That's not how a Better Day Fund works," Mia said. "People just give it to you. To help you."

"So it's begging," Lawrence said.

"It's not begging," Mia said. "It's people helping one another."

"How is that different from begging?"

"You don't understand because you're not on social media,"

Mia said. "Someone makes a joke on Crave and asks people to send money if they laughed."

"What joke did you make? I'd like to hear it," Lawrence said.

"I'm sure it was very funny," Dina said.

Mia tapped the whistle against her lip. "I didn't make a joke."

"Then why should people send you money?" Lawrence said.

"I give up," Mia said. "I don't know what you hope to accomplish by calling us all together. P.J. is going to do what she's going to do, and I'm going to do what I'm going to do. We're not children. You can't send us to our rooms."

"Surely, I can appeal to you for peace in this family," Lawrence said.

"Appeal to *her*," Mia said, looking at P.J. "She started this."

"You see what I'm dealing with?" P.J. said, but if she hoped for sympathy, she was disappointed.

Lawrence carried his glass back to the decanter. Dina stared at her children's wall-mounted school portraits, while folding and unfolding the mimosa-dampened napkin.

"She doesn't care who she hurts," P.J. said.

"Your sister cares," Dina said. "She's just afraid."

"That isn't an excuse," Lawrence said.

"She's not afraid, she's vindictive," P.J. said. "She's—"

Shreeeeeeeeeeeee!

Mia plucked the whistle from her lips. "I'm not afraid. I'm trying to live my life without being reminded every minute of what happened." She stood and swung her backpack over her shoulder. "You all think I'm fragile. A woman on the edge of some kind of breakdown or slip-up. You have for years. Well, I can take care of myself."

CHAPTER EIGHTEEN

Correspondence covered Janelle's desk, a testament to her abiding popularity among would-be authors who pictured their debut books selling for a million dollars. Although blessed with powerful imaginations, these writers envisioned themselves only at the beginning of George's journey, with all of his wins but none of his losses, Adam still frolicking in the garden. George couldn't blame them. Fantasies fueled motivation that failures and rejections sapped. He'd engaged in them himself, a masturbatory pleasure.

Though it was the third week in June, hot air blew through the vents in Janelle's office, finding George no matter where he positioned his chair. Janelle had cancelled a happy hour with another agent to meet with him. He'd promised her it would be worth it.

Next to her stapler, a ceramic dog pecked at a typewriter. George picked up the small paperweight and held it as he told her about the senator.

"That's some story," she said, when he finished.

His neck flushed. "It's not a story. It's the truth."

"You know what I mean."

Did he?

She took a pad from her drawer. "Who knows about this?"

"I told my parents when it happened."

"What did they do?"

"Nothing." He stood and examined her framed diplomas

for undergraduate and master's degrees in creative writing, the second dated two years before. Did she still want to be a writer? He considered warning her against it.

The pad remained blank. She didn't seem to know what to make of what he'd told her, what it would mean for him or for her, or how to advise him. "Will your parents back you up now?"

George's father was still active in Democratic politics. His mother still deferred to his father. He was ashamed to admit that after so many years, they still might not support him. "I don't know."

"Okay." Janelle's computer chimed with an email, but for once she didn't check it. She didn't seem to hear it at all. "Accusing a senator. That's something."

"A former senator." He wanted to tell her it was time to earn her giant commission, but he couldn't afford to alienate her.

"She'll probably come after you. You sure this is what you want?"

He returned to the impossibly hard chair. "I don't know what else to do." A red-and-white bird dropping marred the view through her window. That was life. Shit dropping from the sky, leaving a stain that was unreachable and impossible to clean.

"Let's meet with Saturn and see what they say." Having rediscovered her ability to write English, she jotted a few notes on the pad.

"I thought they wanted me to reveal the personal story behind the book," George said.

"They were hoping for a few fireworks, not a hydrogen bomb."

"It's the truth."

"I believe you. Let's see if Saturn does."

"Jesus," George said. "I thought the senator would be the

problem, not my publisher."

"They're not your publisher yet."

The paperweight had grown warm in his hands.

"It was a gift," Janelle said.

"What was?"

"The paperweight. It was a gift."

"I wasn't going to steal it." Light reflected off the dog's glazed muzzle as George set it back on the desk.

***

When George entered Mary's office the next day it was already crowded. Annette from public relations and Janelle were there. Mary introduced him to Renee Ambrose, one of Saturn's many lawyers. Hair in several shades of blonde fell around her narrow face, and she had the kind of large, elastic mouth found on sea creatures that vacuum ocean waste. He wondered if they'd been talking about him before he arrived, making up their minds about whether he was trustworthy. He sat on a black leather couch and in response to the lawyer's questions retold his story.

"Don't identify the senator." Reading glasses hung from a suede cord around the lawyer's neck. She took hold of them as she spoke but didn't put them on. "Don't even identify her gender. That way, if Sands wants to come after you, she'll be identifying herself as the perpetrator, which seems an unlikely course. You served numerous Democratic senators during your time as a page, right?"

"Yes," George said.

"Men and women?"

"Yes."

"Don't even say it was a senator." The lawyer nodded, approving her own advice. "Say it was someone who worked on

Capitol Hill. Say they're retired and no longer in a position to hurt anyone. The media will pressure you for a name. They'll say you have an obligation to reveal who it was. But it will be your choice."

"Won't refusing to give details make me less credible?" He was reconsidering going public and prolonging his time in an unforgiving spotlight.

"Maybe, but it will mean no one can deny your story. People are going to ask why you didn't go public sooner. They'll say you invented the story to rebut P.J.'s claim. But they'd say that even if you identified the senator."

George could see the wisdom in the strategy, though it let Sands—who he wished to humiliate—off the hook.

"I'll go through the manuscript and make sure you've done enough to disguise her identity," Renee said. "Is there anyone else who could back up your story?"

"Besides my parents?"

"Yes."

"Her chief of staff knew something happened," George said. "But the senator told him I came on to her."

"Not sure that would be helpful. Do you have any other evidence of what she did? That could support your story if the senator came after you?"

"You said she wouldn't come after me if I didn't name her."

"I said it was unlikely. Situations like these tend to be fluid."

Fluid? "What kind of evidence?"

The lawyer held up her glasses and looked through them. She took a cloth from the interior pocket of her black suit jacket and wiped the lenses, then let them dangle again. "Notes she might have written to you, or emails or texts that you saved."

"She didn't write me any notes."

"Did she give you anything personal or intimate?"

George told the lawyer about the volume of Montaigne essays, the engraved pad.

"Nothing really inappropriate there," she said. "More like gifts from a mentor. Anything else?"

"There were a few other things," George said. "I'd almost forgotten about them."

"Yes?" the lawyer said.

"She gave me a silk tie. She said she bought the same kind for her husband and told me not to tell anyone where I got it. That they might not understand." Sands had asked him to take off his jacket and the tie he'd put on that morning. It was perhaps the fifth time he'd met with her. She lifted his collar, her fingertips cold as iron on his neck. He knew how to knot a tie. She was so close, he could smell the lunch on her breath, something with onions. He didn't want her that close but was afraid to insult her. She wrapped the tie around his collar. She was being kind, wasn't she? It was an honor that she'd taken an interest in him. She could help him with a career in politics, introduce him to the right people. She tightened the knot, fixed his collar. When she handed him his jacket, he put it on. "That's better," she said. "Thank you," he'd managed to croak.

George touched the collar of his polo shirt and exhaled, returning to the present.

They were all staring at him, but he didn't explain.

"Silk tie. That's good," the lawyer said.

"And once she gave me cologne. She asked me to wear it. I thought it was bizarre and stuck it in my suitcase and forgot about it."

"Also good," the attorney said. "Do you have them, the tie and the cologne?"

"I might," George said. "They'd be in my parents' house in D.C."

"Go home and see if you can find them."

CHAPTER NINETEEN

For Immediate Release
Black Bear Press, New York, NY
Contact: Steve Blast

STATEMENT REGARDING *GIRL IS IN THE HOUSE*

The novel *Girl Is in the House* by P.J. Larkin is a work of fiction. The events and characters portrayed are products of the author's imagination. Assaults against women and sexual harassment in the workplace are all too common, so it is not surprising that some women may think they recognize themselves in the book. Larkin thought the subject was important enough to write about. To ensure the book would be as true to life as any work of fiction can be, Larkin researched her subject thoroughly. She hopes her novel will educate people regarding the issue and prevent these kinds of assaults from happening in the future. She has pledged to donate a portion of her royalties to an organization combatting domestic violence in her hometown of Denver, Colorado.

The Authors Union praised the statement. "Writers must be free to do what writers do: reflect on society's problems and write about them in the form of fiction, nonfiction, and anything in between. They must be allowed to follow their curiosity wherever it leads and to choose as subjects whatever inspires them, without facing a charge that they don't have firsthand knowledge of the material. That's what research is for. Historically, publishing has included too few voices, not too many. Censorship, no matter who it is aimed at, should be scrutinized and rarely accepted. While we don't think it is necessary for Larkin to contribute to a domestic violence shelter, and fear a precedent that would unnecessarily burden writers who already struggle to make a living at their craft, we commend Ms. Larkin for her generosity."

Scribblers for Justice wasn't buying it. "P.J.'s story isn't fiction at all," they wrote. "It was stolen from a person who was raped, further violating them. Moreover, a writer, no matter how talented or well-intentioned, should never tell the story of a victimized group of which they aren't a member. No amount of research can give them enough insight. No amount of charity can make right what Black Bear and P.J. Larkin are doing."

P.J. wanted to hide in her apartment but she would have scrolled Crave endlessly, and besides, she had a mortgage to pay. She'd been invited on the TV show *Rise and Shine America* and on NPR's *All Things Considered*. The *Guardian* wanted to interview her, as did *USA Today* and *Time*. The last thing she wanted to talk about was where she'd gotten the idea for *Girl Is in the House*. She didn't want reporters researching her background and discovering she had a sister who'd interned at the State Capitol. But Black Bear said if she avoided reporters entirely it made her look like she was hiding something. They arranged an exclusive with Rise and Shine, a friendly outlet. The ground rules provided for the interview to be short, ten minutes at the most.

Marissa took P.J. on an emergency shopping trip. Though

P.J. preferred a thrift store, her friend convinced her the interview called for something new, something pastel in a solid or a large print, which Marissa had read looked best on TV. In a department store, Marissa found a pale blue dress that hugged P.J.'s chest and thighs, and made her walk as if she were a gymnast on a balance beam.

"You look great!" Marissa said.

P.J. stood in front of the store's slenderizing mirror. She tugged at the synthetic, dry-clean-only fabric. "I can't breathe."

"You'll breathe after the interview," Marissa said, prying P.J.'s hands from the dress. "The important thing is that you look like a famous author."

"I'm not a famous author. I'm not even a published author. Not yet." P.J. turned to the side so she could see her ass in the dress. It looked pretty good. Round and tight. "How much is it?"

"I'm buying it for you. Don't forget me when you really become famous. You're going to be wonderful."

"Or not," P.J. said.

"It's a no-lose situation," Marissa said. "If you crash and burn, the video will go viral. Then, when your book comes out, people will be like, didn't I see something about that? And they'll buy a copy."

"*Crash and burn?*"

"Forget I said that. You're going to be eloquent! You're a writer! Words are your thing! Hey—it's your first major interview. Let's celebrate at Baxter's when you get back." Marissa took off the necklace she always wore: a pearl and diamond chip set at either end of a gold infinity symbol, hanging on a delicate chain. It had belonged to her mother. She fastened the clasp behind P.J.'s neck. "Wear this, too."

"That looks nice," P.J. said.

"*You* look nice."

Was there even a dry cleaner in her neighborhood?

The next morning, P.J. was on a flight to New York. Anna Gordon, her Black Bear publicist, had prepared a document as long as a Thomas Mann novel for her to review: questions to anticipate and ways to answer the tougher ones; things she wanted P.J. to be sure to mention, such as the statistics that showed how widespread sexual harassment and sexual assault were; and general advice for talking to the press, which included, don't answer a question if you don't want to, answer the question you wish they had asked instead. The publicist had sent links to interviews conducted by the host, Priscilla Logan, so P.J. could get a sense of her style. P.J. opened her laptop and stuck in earphones. On her drink napkin, she doodled an open manhole, a woman poised to step through.

***

Priscilla Logan was in her early forties and had been with *Rise and Shine* for five years. She had perfect posture and a face preserved by the same surgeon who'd worked on Hollywood's most famous leading woman. She greeted P.J. warmly, kissing her on the cheek and gesturing for her to sit in a leather armchair. P.J. had forgotten to check if she could sit in the new dress. When she tried, the "supportive" material wouldn't give, and she tipped like a plank against the back of the seat, barely managing to keep her legs together. That was all she needed, to flash the entire country. With great effort, she bent at the waist and sat. A bank of lights blinded her.

"I'm so glad you could stop by," Priscilla said. "As soon as I heard about your book, *Girl Is in the House*—great title, by the way—I knew I had to have you on. It covers such an important subject. And your publisher was kind enough to give me an early peek at the manuscript."

"I'm delighted to be here," P.J. said, a lie. The truth was that she was terrified and struggling to breathe in the vise-like dress. Her mouth was dry and she had to bite her tongue to get even the smallest drop of saliva to flow, a tip her publicist had hidden in the last paragraph of the endless document she'd sent, and that P.J. only noticed when she was checking to see if the epic ever ended.

"I love to read, so I have a lot of writers on," the host said. "But it's not always that I can say to our viewers, not only is this book engrossing, but it's important."

"Thank you," P.J. said, forcing her butt back in the chair, which had the unfortunate consequence or raising her feet off the ground and making her look like a child. "That's what I hoped when I was writing it. That it would be a compelling story and also have an impact. Because so many women find themselves in terrible situations at work, where they have to choose between keeping their jobs and being harassed or worse." She quoted statistics about sexual harassment on the job.

"That's awful. We've had our own share of problems in the television industry." Priscilla was holding a coffee mug with the R&S logo and she tightened her grip.

"Yes." P.J. knew all about the network scandal, which she'd researched while writing the book. Squelching her usual rant about it—her publicist had warned her to avoid the topic—made P.J.'s head hurt. In front of her was a mug just like the host's. Would she get to take it home? A selfie holding it would be good for several nibbles and proof of her growing fame, but maybe not the best look given the network's history.

"But let's talk about you!" Priscilla said. "This is your first book, right?"

"My first published book," P.J. said. "I wrote two before this one but they seem destined to live on my hard drive."

"That's not uncommon, is it?"

"I think most writers end up with a 'practice' novel or two."

"A 'practice' novel. I love that! Most of us have to practice whatever we hope to get good at, don't we? Now here you are, coming out with your debut novel. How does it feel?"

"It's what I've worked toward for such a long time. It feels great," P.J. said, and for a moment it did.

"That's wonderful. And a good lesson about patience and persistence for anyone chasing a dream." The host paused and the studio audience filled the gap with applause. "Now, there's been a bit of controversy surrounding your book. Didn't someone nibble that you stole a sexual assault victim's story?"

P.J. steadied her hands. "The sad thing is that sexual harassment and sexual assault are so widespread, a lot of women may recognize themselves in the book." It was a sentence she'd memorized and practiced in front of the hotel mirror.

Priscilla nodded, one finger curled under her chin. "If it wasn't another woman's story, what made you choose to write about this subject?"

P.J. could see the words the publicist had prepared. They were true even if they left something out. "It's a subject I've been keenly aware of for a long time. I wrote the novel hoping to educate people about it. Frankly, I wish fewer women recognized the situations I describe."

"Yes, we all wish that." Priscilla's finger migrated to her lips.

P.J.'s thighs were sweating. The clamp of a dress had cut off the circulation to her arms, not to mention her boobs. Could you develop gangrene in your boobs?

They went to commercial and when they returned, the host

expressed admiration for plot twists she hadn't seen coming, giving away more of the story than P.J. would have liked. At least she'd stopped talking about the trouble Avery Baron had stirred up.

"I understand you plan to donate part of your royalties to a women's shelter in Denver, and I think that's fantastic." Priscilla applauded, and the audience joined in. Their reaction felt as good as P.J. had imagined being famous would, though in her fantasies, they were clapping for her work. "We here on *R&S* were so inspired by your generosity, we decided to make a donation of our own to a New York City shelter," Priscilla said. "Their C.E.O. is here, and we were hoping you would help us present the check to her."

"I'd be delighted to," P.J. said.

"Let's welcome C.E.O. of Lavender House, Aaliyah Palma."

A small woman in a navy pantsuit and flats walked onstage as the audience cheered. P.J. stood, tottering on her heels. Could she have worn something comfortable, too? A producer handed Priscilla a giant check for twenty-five thousand dollars.

"Thank you for the work the shelter does. We hope this helps." The host handed the check to the C.E.O. The audience clapped again.

"We're so grateful," Aaliyah said. "To you and P.J. These funds will make an enormous difference to us and to the women who use our services."

"If any of you at home want to help as well, we put the information for Lavender House on our website," Priscilla said.

Music began to play, the cue for P.J. and Aaliyah to exit the stage.

In the green room, Aaliyah mentioned to P.J. that part of the money would be used to help women in the shelter with substance abuse issues. "Some women try to deal with their trauma by self-medicating," the C.E.O. said. "We've had some unfortunate situations."

P.J. wondered what she meant by unfortunate situations. She hoped Mia was doing okay.

Sloane joined P.J. in the green room and hugged her. "You were perfect," she said. "Better than perfect."

As a person who valued precise language, P.J. disapproved of the phrase "better than perfect." But she was so delighted with the compliment, she let it go. The experience hadn't been as scary as she feared. Three million viewers had heard her name and the title of her book. She had addressed the question of the book's genesis without seeming like she was hiding something.

"*Tell me, did the wind sleep you off your feet!*" Sloane sang.

P.J. was about to correct the lyric when her publicist called. "You were awesome!" Anna said.

A horribly overused word. Nevertheless, P.J. smiled.

***

As P.J. waited for her flight back to Colorado, she checked the Better Day Fund and saw it had reached fifteen thousand dollars. Among the items covered by the fund was tuition for the anonymous recipient to go back to school. P.J. hadn't known Mia wanted to finish her degree. She was glad the money would help her sister, even if Mia was raising it by slandering her.

P.J. had just landed when Sloane called and told her the interview had gone so well, Black Bear wanted her to do another. Though P.J. had enjoyed appearing on Rise and Shine, she knew not all interviewers would be as kind as Priscilla Logan. Sloane listened to P.J.'s concerns but told her she couldn't say no. Black Bear had already arranged for her to meet with Padma Kumar from the weekly newsmagazine *Pedestal*.

CHAPTER TWENTY

"If you tell me what you're looking for maybe I can help," George's mother said. They were standing in his parents' basement. After running a successful clothing boutique for twenty-five years, Faith had sold the business and retired, trading high-heeled boots and A-line dresses for yoga pants and sneakers. She'd shorn her gray hair, revealing a readout of worry lines that George imagined he was responsible for.

"You don't want to know." He hated to return home with this particular trouble. He wouldn't have if Saturn's lawyer hadn't insisted.

His mother fingered the fuzz at the back of her neck while seeming to weigh whether to pursue the subject. "Okay, well, everything's down here." She waved toward a hill of boxes in a corner of the room, cardboard sagging from years of humidity and gravity's press. "We packed your stuff when we remodeled. It wasn't anything you had looked at in years, but we didn't want to throw it away, just in case. Call me if you need anything." She climbed the stairs to the living room.

The basement smelled of mildew and concrete. Empty garment racks loitered against a wall. Jumbled on a shelf were the large gold letters that had once spelled out Faith's Closet and that had now lost their meaning. Furniture from his childhood bedroom—a Scandinavian desk papered with Bill Clinton bumper stickers, a corkboard sprouting Barbara Mikulski pins—mocked his old aspirations.

In the boxes, George found college textbooks and notebooks; papers on Hemingway, Plath, and Primo Levi; pennants he'd hung in his dorm. And from farther back in time: a tiny tuxedo, jeans, and Oshkosh overalls; soccer uniforms, cleats, and shin guards. Upstairs, his mother made fundraising calls for a local community center in the high-pitched voice she'd once used to peddle sweater dresses.

He was surprised she hadn't donated his childhood things, given her penchant for charity. Perhaps she was nostalgic for a time before his summer at the Capitol, when his promise was still uncomplicated, his accomplishments shared with colleagues and friends at backyard barbecues between bites of Caesar salad and grilled chicken. Even his father was proud of him before he brought messiness into their lives. Before he turned his back on politics and announced his intention to become a writer, and not a respectable one, a biographer or a journalist, but one who made up stories, a dreamer who wrote books for other dreamers.

He unearthed crayon drawings, corners missing where the tape had been; tests he'd aced; letters admitting him to colleges. Faith had saved his diplomas from kindergarten, middle school, and high school. His scout badges. His magic supplies: ropes, silk handkerchiefs, and boxes with false bottoms. Purchased to take to magic camp the summer after a woman named Madhim had performed at his ninth birthday party and George decided magic was his destiny. But when he'd learned how to do the tricks under a hot tent in D.C., he'd cried, because they weren't miraculous at all, just ways to fool people. "There is no magic," the instructor had said, "only hours of practice and blindness on the part of the audience." George hadn't wanted to go to camp after that, but his parents had paid for a three-week session, and his father insisted he finish what he started. He thought back to that summer sometimes and wondered if in writing he was still searching for real magic. The work of authors he admired seemed transcendent, but he worried his own writing was merely manipulative, full of the kind of cheap tricks that had made him cry.

Beneath the magic supplies, George saw the Montaigne, and next to it, the engraved stationery. He felt a wobble in his stomach like the snap of a rope. He pushed aside the stationery and found the tie and a bottle of Eau de Parfum Le Renard, then another item he'd forgotten. A journal his father had given him to record the names of the people he met at the Capitol and one or two details about each of them. Not just the senators, but their chiefs of staff and campaign managers and secretaries. "Practice remembering what they tell you," his father had said. "So the next time you see them, you can call them by their names and make reference to what you learned. Dale Carnegie says, 'There's nothing more pleasing to a person than the sound of his own name.'" Had he written anything about the senator? The cover of the journal was black. Each page was dated. He was about to look through it when his mother appeared at the top of the stairs. He shoved the journal into his briefcase.

"Did you find what you needed?" she asked.

"I did. Just putting things away."

He repacked the boxes, leaving them as quiet as he found them. When his mother invited him to stay for dinner, he couldn't say no.

***

Cyrus and George sat on the back patio in Adirondack chairs, his father with a glass of cabernet and George with a beer he'd found behind aging sauces in the refrigerator. The grass had been given a military cut, and along the borders of the property, tall hedges prevented interactions with neighbors.

"We got a dog," George said.

"Why?" Cyrus had hung up his suit jacket but still wore a pink dress shirt and navy tie. His skin had a synthetic quality to it, like an old rubber toy, its flexibility long gone.

"I've always wanted one." George hadn't visited in months. He'd forgotten how his supply of oxygen diminished in the presence of his father.

"Another thing you were deprived of." His father loosened his tie.

"That's not what I meant."

"What breed?" Cyrus said.

"We got him from the shelter." George rose and walked toward a line of plum trees. "His name is Mutt."

"Is that a joke?" Cyrus said.

"It's short for Mozzarella." On one of the trees, George found the spot where he'd carved his initials when he was eleven.

Upon discovering the letters, his father had said, "You've scarred it forever." He'd meant it as a rebuke, but George had liked the idea that he couldn't be erased.

As he sipped his beer, George wondered if that was why he'd become a writer. To leave a mark. Like the etchings on prison walls and the tags on Subway tunnels. A demand to be seen: *George Dunn was here*.

"You're the talk of the town," Cyrus said.

"I suppose so."

"Tricky business for a new writer, I'd think, getting accused of plagiarism."

"Inevitable when you're writing your own book and reading for a publisher at the same time," George said.

"Inevitable?"

George pulled on a branch, testing its strength.

"You're going to break that," Cyrus said.

He let go of the tree. "Maybe not inevitable. But not surprising."

"I didn't realize editors got accused of plagiarism so often." Cyrus's glass was empty. "Faith!" he shouted toward the kitchen. "Could you bring me the bottle of wine?"

"I'll get it," George said.

He filled a glass with water at the kitchen sink and drank it down before returning to the patio with a fresh beer and his father's wine.

"What are you going to do about it?" Cyrus said.

"Wait for it to quiet down. Then, once my novel comes out, people will see how different the books are." George wasn't ready to tell his father about the visit from the senator or his plans to go public about what happened when he was a page. His parents would have been impacted no matter where they lived, but in D.C., they would be at the center of the tumult.

"You should be more proactive. Sue the woman who accused you for defamation. Especially if you didn't borrow anything from her book."

"I didn't borrow anything."

"Good. I know an excellent personal injury lawyer. She's not cheap, but your mother and I discussed this, and we're willing to pay for it."

George was grateful for the offer and ashamed to need their help. Maybe a defamation suit was the way to go. The idea of making Larkin's life more difficult was attractive. "Thank you, but a lawsuit could take years, and my publisher might drop the book in the meantime. To be honest, I'm doing whatever Saturn wants at this point. There's so much money at stake."

"Money. Always the driver. You might consider your reputation. It's your decision, of course."

***

It was dark out when George returned to his car, but he couldn't wait any longer to examine the journal. He switched on the overhead light and pulled the book from his briefcase. Maybe something he'd written would save him by providing a record of what the senator had done. He rubbed his neck, the muscles aching. He couldn't remember the exact date the senator had touched him, so he flipped through the pages until he came to October. The first few days of the month contained ordinary entries. The names of Senate staff he'd met and what he'd learned about them in brief introductions. Notes about how the Senate operated. Not what they taught in the page school he attended every morning, but the way the institution really worked, the power dynamics. Lined sheets crammed with his immature handwriting, dispatches from a time before he was reduced to his vulnerability.

Then he came to a weekday entry in October that was blank. He turned to the next two days, and they were empty, too, and so were all the pages that came after though his time at the Capitol hadn't ended until January. George closed his eyes. He remembered wanting to banish everything that had happened from his memory, to erase the entire fall and winter.

Determined to find something to help his cause, he opened the journal to his first days as a page and looked through it again. He stopped when he came to Senator Sands' name. He must have written it the day he met her, then returned to the page later to add her husband's and children's names when he learned them. He'd listed gifts from her on the dates he received them so he would be sure to remember to send thank-you notes.

He'd filled every line on each business day, sometimes the margins, too, then abruptly stopped in early October.

***

It was past midnight when George got home. Kiara was in bed, streaming a crafting show, something she watched only when they weren't together. He thought briefly about what else he kept her from, the other parts of her that were eclipsed by their relationship.

"I didn't mention to my parents that I'm planning to go public," he said, after she muted the show. "I thought I'd hold off until I'm sure."

"I thought you were sure."

"I don't know. Saturn's attorney made me nervous. Maybe I should just wait two years until people forget about Larkin and let them publish it then." He removed the journal from his briefcase. "I did find the tie and the cologne, and something else interesting from when I was a page."

He handed the journal to her.

"I'd forgotten about it," he said. "I didn't write about what happened. But I completely stopped writing after it happened. That says a lot, don't you think?"

She looked through the book. "People will have different theories about why you stopped, depending on what they think happened."

In bed that night, George wondered how Saturn would react to the empty pages in his journal, whether they would publish his book, if he would be rich or poor. Would anyone believe his story? If another writer made the same accusation would he believe it? It moved him that his father, who questioned every decision George made, wanted to help. His parents were worried about him, not knowing they should be at least a little worried about themselves.

Sometime after three, he fell asleep and dreamed the senator had returned to his house, only it was his parents' house, and Ryan, his former boss, was preparing dinner for her.

As soon as he awoke, he hurried into the shower to wash off the nightmare.

"You had a tough night," Kiara said, when he joined her in the kitchen. It was Saturday, and she'd made pancakes and bacon.

"I had a lot of visitors."

"Want to talk about it?"

"No," he said.

"How were your parents?" she asked, handing him a full plate.

"The same. My dad said I should sue Larkin for defamation." He poured a river of syrup over the food, surprised he had an appetite.

"That doesn't seem like a bad idea."

"Lawyers think the solution to everything is a lawsuit. Just like surgeons think the solution to everything is surgery. If my dad were a nutritionist, he would have recommended that I eat more fiber. I don't have time for a lawsuit." He cut into a stack of pancakes.

"Maybe just the threat of a lawsuit would scare Larkin into apologizing."

"She doesn't seem like the apologetic type. But I'll think about it. I suppose I could mention it to Saturn." Though any lawsuit would be a civil matter, George envisioned P.J. in a prison jumpsuit and took an enormous bite.

CHAPTER TWENTY-ONE

"Terrific interview," Franklin said, as a server set down papadam and small pots of green and tamarind chutney. He'd asked P.J. to dinner after seeing her on *Rise and Shine*. Franklin's shirt pocket was empty. He must have used the bandage earlier that day or switched to comfortable shoes. P.J. glanced under the table. His sneakers didn't look particularly *un*comfortable, but could you ever really know the condition of another person's feet? "How'd you get here?" she asked.

"Light rail."

"Very eco-friendly. Still not driving?"

"I started the car the other day. I was worried the battery would die. I don't suppose that counts," Franklin said.

"It counts."

"That's what my therapist says. She's very encouraging. But I write her a check at the end of every session, so I'm never sure if I should believe her." He dipped papadam in green chutney. His bangs had grown out and were parted unattractively down the center.

"Well, you're not writing me a check. And I think you'll be driving any day now, cruising down Colfax, eating fries and trying to squeeze the last few drops of ketchup from a packet." P.J. picked up a laminated menu. "Why is there never enough ketchup?"

Franklin breathed an exaggerated sigh. "The proper ketchup-to-fry ratio is one of the modern era's great unsolved problems.

Like the Goldbach conjecture or the Riemann hypothesis. McDonald's once offered a million-dollar prize to anyone who could come up with a solution."

P.J. lowered the menu. "Needless to say, the prize went unclaimed."

"Needless to say."

In the arched window next to the table, she saw their reflections. They looked like a couple on a date, but were they? Or did Franklin just want to hang out with someone who'd appeared on national TV? The quiet street outside, the unhurried meal, and the woman at the next table getting an earful from the man opposite her about his ex, created a date-like atmosphere. But when they first saw each other outside, Franklin had merely waved in greeting. If he'd hugged her, she might have interpreted it in several ways, but a wave, what was there to say about a wave other than that it was decidedly platonic? Which was too bad because she wouldn't have minded getting a noseful of his soapy smell or tangling her smooth feet with his calloused ones. "How are your kids?"

"They're kids. They want to hear 'Baby Shark' on an endless loop and scream if I turn it off. The little one asks about her mother sometimes. When she's coming back. But then the older one reminds her Mama's in a box in the ground, and that seems to satisfy her." He gazed at a family with a full complement of parents two tables over. "Was it fun being interviewed?"

"Yes. Sort of."

"You don't sound sure." He sipped his water.

"It's complicated." P.J. leaned over the table and brushed his bangs to the side. Better.

"Things usually are. Complicated."

"When I dreamed of being published, it wasn't. I imagined

rave reviews and making *The New York Times* bestseller list."

"It could still work out that way, right?"

"Sure."

P.J. signaled the server, and they ordered.

Franklin refilled her water glass. "People who live in the buildings I engineer rarely know my name. But I still feel good about the plans."

"Okay."

"Couldn't publishing your book be a great accomplishment even if it's not a bestseller?" he said.

"Why isn't it a bestseller?"

"Not every book is, right?"

"Let's talk about something else," P.J. said.

"Okay. Sorry. Meet any interesting passengers lately? Besides me?"

P.J. sat back. "Do you want to hear about the washed-up actor who's doing the voice of a hemorrhoid in an animated commercial? Or the receptionist at a sperm bank who was fired after warning clients that the owner of the place had fathered their children? It's amazing what people share to fill the silence or boredom of a ride or because they think they're never going to see me again."

"Like I did," Franklin said.

"Like you did. To be honest, I like it. I'm interested in stories. That's why I became a writer."

"Do you ever write about what passengers tell you?"

P.J. wondered if Franklin had googled her. He must have. She had googled him: Masters in Architectural Engineering, B.S. in Civil Engineering, Associate at The Conrad Group, reached state finals in fencing as an undergraduate, listed as the surviving spouse in the obituary he must have written. She brought a piece of warm cauliflower to her mouth but didn't eat it. "I won't write about you if you don't want me to."

"I don't want you to."

Was he on Crave? She'd looked and hadn't found a menu under his name, but that didn't mean anything. He could be nibbling under a different handle. For all she knew, he was one of her diners. She didn't recognize most of them. Had he seen Avery Baron's nibble?

"I'd hate for my kids to read one day that their mother died because she was hurrying to pick them up."

"She was hurrying to pick them up," P.J. said.

"Yes, but I'd hate for them to know that." Franklin glanced at his phone.

P.J. wondered if he regretted coming. "How do you like being an engineer?"

"I like it. I solve problems. I enjoy seeing things from different angles. My wife used to tell me that sometimes I asked too many questions. That people felt like they were being interrogated. She felt that way sometimes."

"I can see that," P.J. said.

"Sorry. And I was trying to be on my best behavior," Franklin said.

"That wouldn't be a deal-breaker for me in a relationship." As soon as the R-word slipped out, she regretted it. "A relationship with someone else, I mean." There it was again. "With anyone else." Which wasn't what she meant, either. She drank some water to stop herself from talking.

He tore off a piece of garlic naan and wiped his hands on his napkin. "I'm not ready for anything like that."

"I didn't mean—"

"I hope I didn't mislead you." He combed his bangs with his

fingers, restoring the center part. "I just thought it would be nice to have dinner with someone over the age of five."

Looking down at her bowl of chana aloo curry, P.J. gave it a stir. She knew he wasn't ready for a new relationship. Was she even interested in him? She was when he was funny. Not when he suggested her book might fail.

"The thing is, I don't have very many friends," he said. "When Sharon was alive, I didn't feel like I needed any. I had her. Work and the kids kept me busy. But now I wish I had some adults to talk to other than my brothers. They care about me, but we've never been close. I get the sense they're waiting to make sure I'm okay so we can go back to seeing each other only on the holidays."

"My sister, Mia, and I were close growing up. But we haven't been lately. Even before she found out about the book."

"What happened?"

"She's a recovering alcoholic. She almost died a few years back. I didn't know what to do for her. How to help her."

Franklin lifted a red drumstick from his plate. "Maybe you couldn't. Maybe that was something only she could do."

It was true. In the end, Mia had been the one to rescue herself. "I took your advice and tried to talk to her," P.J. said.

"How'd it go?"

"She called me a vampire and then had a friend attack me on Crave."

"Glad that worked out."

Silence settled over the table as they ate.

"I bought a net-zero condo," P.J. said after a while.

"The ones Sunflower put up?"

"Yeah."

"I worked on those," Franklin said. "See, you didn't even know I was one of the engineers on the project. We got an award for it.

I was supposed to attend the ceremony, but it was after Sharon died. I think they mailed me the plaque."

"You think?"

"My mail's been piling up."

"For how long?" P.J. said.

Franklin reached for the Band-Aid that wasn't there. "Weeks? Months? One of my brothers came over and paid a bunch of bills out of my account a while ago. But he refused to do it again." He wiped his mouth with a napkin. "Sharon took care of the bills. I think of her every time I look at them."

"I could come over and help if you like," P.J. said. "Like a friend would do. Open the bills, put them in stacks: due tomorrow, due last month, pay or lose house. Stand over you while you set up autopay."

"I would appreciate that. I'll repay you by inviting you to dinner with my kids. I hope you like peanut butter."

"Sounds delightful."

***

With P.J.'s permission, Padma Kumar turned on a voice recorder, the reporter's wiry fingers resembling a snare. Though they were in P.J.'s new apartment, she hardly felt in control. The women faced each other across the coffee table, Padma on a desk chair and P.J. on the old couch. Padma asked where P.J. had grown up, what she did for a living, and what she'd studied in college. She inquired about P.J.'s favorite authors and how long it had taken her to write *Girl Is in the House*. Softball questions intended to relax P.J. and to get her to let down her guard.

The reporter leaned forward, her plum-colored sport jacket straining ever so slightly at the button. "Where did you get the idea for it?"

P.J. was prepared. She adjusted her seat, gripping the hem of the clamp-like blue dress so it wouldn't ride up. After the *Rise and Shine* interview, she'd decided it was her lucky dress. "Sexual harassment and #metoo have been in the news so much," P.J. said. "As a writer and as a woman it was natural for me to think about the victims and to imagine what it was like for them. I did a lot research on the subject, too."

"Is the book based on your own experience?" Padma asked.

"No. I've been lucky. But as I'm sure you know, it's common for fiction writers to choose as subjects things we haven't experienced personally." The reporter nodded, and P.J. wondered why she had worried about the interview. It would be fine. Another success like Rise and Shine. One that would reassure Black Bear they'd made a good bet on her and on *Girl Is in the House*. "I forgot to offer you a glass of water," P.J. said. "Would you like some? Or a beer?"

"I'm fine," the reporter said. "Thanks."

P.J. took in the five-star view of the Rockies. Perhaps the novel really would be reviewed in *The New York Times*. Wouldn't that be something? Her father opening the paper and seeing her name. His colleagues seeing it, too, and congratulating him. "Thanks for coming out here," P.J. said.

"I'm based in Denver. *Pedestal* calls me when they have a local story."

"That's great. Maybe we'll see each other around. At a professional meeting or an awards ceremony or something."

"Maybe," Padma said.

"I haven't been able to attend many of those," P.J. said. "Too busy working." Which was half true. P.J. had been reluctant to join organizations for professional writers. She'd been ashamed of her status as someone whose books had failed to sell, and she hadn't known if she'd be welcome. "Maybe after the novel comes out."

When Padma glanced at her phone, P.J. figured she was checking a list of questions. "Do you know anyone who's been sexually assaulted?" the reporter asked.

"Know anyone?" P.J. said. "Sure. I mean, yes. I think most women do."

"Probably so," the reporter said.

P.J. felt as if she'd narrowly avoided a rock slide.

"Was it someone close to you?" Padma said. "The person you know who was assaulted?"

P.J. itched for a pen and paper, but she'd tidied up before the reporter arrived. The coffee table was bare. "The book is an invention. I know someone has claimed it isn't. But that's not true."

"Yes. You've said that. The person you know who was sexually assaulted, was she a close friend? Someone in your family?"

"The book isn't about anyone I know."

Padma nodded. "Okay. But if you know someone who's been sexually assaulted, surely that must influence what you write about the subject and how you think about it."

P.J. picked up a throw pillow printed with the words *I'd Rather Be Reading* and pressed it to her chest. "Everything I experience has an impact on who I am as a writer, but that doesn't mean I'm writing about all those experiences."

"Yes, but that's different from learning about an experience from a friend and then writing about it. Just how close were you to this person? Were they someone you saw every couple of years? Once a month? Every week?"

"Even if someone close to me was sexually assaulted, I wouldn't necessarily be writing about them or what happened to them when I wrote about the subject. The book I wrote is based on what goes on in every quarter of society."

"So it was someone close to you," Padma said.

"I didn't say that."

"No, you didn't. You don't seem to want to answer that question." The reporter looked at her phone again. "Let me ask you something else. The book is a political book. Have you ever been involved in politics?"

"No." P.J.'s neck felt clammy. To save energy and because it wasn't that hot out, she'd kept the air conditioner off. The polyester dress trapped heat like insulation.

"Has anyone in your family been involved in politics?" Padma said.

P.J. wiped her neck against the throw pillow. "That depends on what you mean by 'involved in politics.'"

"Elected to a public office or worked for someone who was."

"I know several people who have been involved in politics in that way."

"Were any of them sexually assaulted?" Padma said.

"If they were, that would be a private matter for them."

"Too private for you to write about?"

The snare tightened around P.J. She stood up. "I just realized I'm late for an appointment.

CHAPTER TWENTY-TWO

George sat in Renee Ambrose's office, the items he'd brought from his parents' basement laid out on the attorney's black lacquer desk. On the wall was a picture of Ambrose, standing at a microphone, the president of Saturn to her right. He wondered if she'd been receiving an award, or more likely announcing a merger, Saturn gobbling up a small publisher like Peapod.

Janelle and Mary looked on as the lawyer examined the items.

Ambrose picked up the cologne. "The seal isn't broken."

"I never used it. It freaked me out," George said.

She nodded and leafed through the journal. "Odd for a sixteen-year-old to keep a paper journal. Even back then."

"My father gave it to me. He suggested I take notes about the people I was meeting."

She reached the blank pages. "Nothing obviously incriminating."

"I stopped keeping notes after it happened. Doesn't that show something?"

"Hard to prove anything from a negative. It would have been better if you'd written down what you claim she did."

"I don't *claim* she did it. It happened."

Ambrose rotated in her large ergonomic chair to face George. "Get used to words like 'claimed' and 'alleged.' You'll hear them a lot if you say someone at the Capitol assaulted you. Even if you don't specify who. And given the evidence you have, I would caution you again not to go after Wilma Sands personally. She'd come back hard. They always do." The lawyer took notes with a mechanical pencil, a writing instrument for people who lacked conviction. Ryan had used one at Peapod. She examined the tie without commenting.

"My father suggested suing Larkin for defamation," George said.

"Could take years. And are you sure you didn't accidentally borrow from her book? Not intentionally. But you read it and it was similar to your book and something, a paragraph, a few sentences, slipped into yours? Because if that happened, the media will have a field day running similar language from the books alongside one another."

"I didn't steal from her accidentally or on purpose. But I don't like that a lawsuit could drag out."

Ambrose stood. "Let us know what you decide to do. If you still want to go public with what happened to you, P.R. will help you craft a statement."

George stuffed the items he'd brought back into his briefcase, then followed Janelle and Mary out of the office. He wondered why he'd gone to the trouble of excavating his past in his parents' basement.

Outside the building, he turned to Janelle. "What do you think?"

"I'll support you whichever way you want to go," she said. "I never told you this, I haven't told very many people, but I had my own experience with sexual harassment. While I was getting my master's. With the professor who was supposed to be advising me on my thesis. It's one of the reasons I decided to work for myself and not join a large agency. One of the reasons I fell in love with your book, too."

"Sorry to hear that," George said. "Not about the book."

"Thanks. And about the book. It'll work out. You'll see."

"I hope so. I don't even know whether to go public."

"If you're not sure, why don't you sleep on it? Talk to Kiara. Call me tomorrow."

***

"Forget what Saturn wants. What do you want?" Mutt strained against the leash in Kiara's hand. The sidewalk was crowded with people returning from work, jostling one another as they stared at phones, groceries in reusable sacks hanging from their fists.

The humidity weighed on George. "I want the world to know what Wilma Sands did. But I don't want it to take over my life. I don't want it to define my reputation as a writer."

"It might."

"But if I don't say anything, there might not be any book or reputation to worry about."

Mutt sniffed the base of a sign that read *Don't Even Think About Parking Here* and pissed next to it.

"How was work?" George said. He was afraid their life was becoming entirely about his problems. "You used to tell me stories."

"Let me think—drop it!"

Mutt had caught the unused shoulder strap of a woman's leather briefcase in her mouth, and Kiara knelt and pried it out.

"Probably a relative of hers," George said to the briefcase owner. Ignoring him, the woman hurried away.

Passing a church, Kiara said, "Here's something. This woman Esther. I've told you about her. In her seventies and has been volunteering at the center for years. I always wonder if one day we won't see her again. It's a terrible way to think. Anyway, she has a new student she's tutoring in English. Lela, a young girl from France. Esther knows a fair amount of French. Apparently, Lela was asking her how to say condom in English. Well, this girl is only thirteen, and Esther didn't think she should need condoms. She asked the girl if a man was bothering her, and Lela said, 'no.' Esther wasn't sure what to do. One day, she followed the girl home in her car to make sure she was okay. That's not really allowed, but she didn't ask. When Lela arrived home, a very pregnant woman handed her a baby, while saying in French, 'Watch her for me.' Lela said, "Okay, *Maman*." Five other children, all smaller than Lela, surrounded her. Well, the next time Lela was leaving the center, Esther handed her a box of Trojans. Let's hope they find their way to *Maman* and get put to good use."

George reached for Kiara's free hand, catching her scent, a mix of buffalo dog treats, sweat, and lavender body cream, and a reminder that beneath their history, their occupations, their childhoods, and their vows were bodies that might give each other pleasure if he could find a way to let them. He bent and kissed a spot below her ear, lingering while Mutt whined, annoyed with the delay.

"What was that for?" Kiara said.

"Do I have to have a reason?"

"No, no you don't."

***

He returned to Saturn the next day and met with Annette in public relations. "Ambrose suggested disclosing that I was assaulted at the Capitol without revealing the perpetrator," he said.

"I talked to her," Annette said.

They sat together behind her desk, George feeding her his history at the Capitol and Annette crafting a statement designed to create sympathy for him and clear his name.

That night, he called his mother to warn her.

"Let me just get your father," she said.

Once both of his parents were on the call, George said, "I'm going to go public. About what happened when I was a page." He was sitting in his kitchen, and Mutt wandered in and leaned her head against his legs.

"I thought we were done with all that," Cyrus said.

"No." George stroked Mutt's ears, and she groaned with pleasure.

"Why dig it up again? It's been more than twenty years. You're fine," his father said.

"I need to show the world the book is based on my life and not stolen from anyone," George said.

"Your book. Your book. There are other things in life besides your book. Other people. This won't affect only you."

"I just wanted to let you know," George said.

"Thank you," Faith said. "Take care of yourself. I hope it works out the way you want it to."

***

For Immediate Release
Saturn Books, New York, NY
Contact: Annette Love

RELEASE REGARDING SEXUAL ASSAULT OF GEORGE DUNN WHILE SERVING AS A PAGE

George Dunn served as a page in the United States Senate when he was sixteen years old, an experience that provided the background for his forthcoming debut novel, *Up the Hill*. While he worked at the Capitol, George was sexually assaulted. The experience changed the trajectory of his life, which he had planned until then to dedicate to public service. It propelled him to write *Up the Hill*. He had hoped to keep his personal history and the events at the Capitol private because of the trauma they caused and continue to cause him. He was reluctant to relive that devastating period of his life on a book tour or while answering questions from the press and readers. However, because of an unfounded accusation that *Up the Hill* is based on another writer's book, George now finds it necessary to come forward with more of his background and the true genesis of his novel. George was a junior in high school when he was groomed and sexually assaulted by an individual he came in contact with at the U.S. Senate. He doesn't wish to name his assailant, except to say they no longer work at the Capitol. George hopes this statement will put to rest the baseless speculation that his book came from anywhere other than his own mind as he wrestled with the most painful experience of his life.

George's phone rang nonstop as reporters tried to reach him. They contacted him on every social media platform where he had a presence. On Crave, he received so many private meals, his app crashed when he loaded them. In his inbox, emails multiplied faster than he could delete them. Annette had instructed him to let her answer any questions, unless she set up an interview for him with strict parameters.

Not everyone believed his account. @editrix100 nibbled, "How convenient for @GeorgeDunn. Twenty years after the fact he conjures an assault that he claims is the basis for his book. Yet he refuses to name the predator."

@pencilgeek nibbled back to Saturn's statement: "How many more people has @GeorgeDunn allowed a predator to victimize by refusing to name and shame them? All while George peacefully wrote a novel. I'm not buying it."

Yet many other diners re-served Saturn's statement with the hashtag #believesurvivors.

A conservative radio show gave most of its drive time to the story, the host gleefully speculating that if it were true, the person who'd assaulted George had to be someone "affiliated with the Democrats, since Dunn was a Democrat page." The announcer reveled in the idea that, "the Party of PC has been protecting one of its own at the expense of a child." He invited listeners to call in and rename the "Democrat Party" in light of the scandal. A good portion of the calls had to be bleeped.

The next day, Randall Buck, an ethics professor at Columbia, published an Op-Ed in *The Wall Street Journal* arguing that George, who was now an adult and out of harm's way, had a moral obligation to name the predator. Journalists scoured George's time in the senate. They interviewed other pages who had served with him, asking if they were aware of George being sexually assaulted and whether anything similar had happened to them at the Capitol. Few remembered George and none remembered a sexual assault. As far as anything inappropriate happening to them, they stated categorically—from their lower Manhattan law offices, their state senate seats, and their judicial chambers—that they would have said something if it had.

As Cyrus attempted to go to work, a reporter blocked his car: "Who assaulted your son?" she shouted. "Did George tell you about it when it happened?" She stuck a voice recorder outside his window. "Did your son seem different after his time at the Capitol?" she yelled. "Did you believe him?" When the reporter didn't get anything from Cyrus, she knocked on the front door. Faith drew the curtains, transforming her bright home into a claustrophobic cave.

After the woman left, Faith stepped outside. The reporter's card, which had been shoved between the door and the jamb, fluttered to the ground. Faith recognized her name, Tovah Sparrow, from all of the exposés she'd written about sexual predators.

On the Fourth of July weekend, George and Kiara ate boiled hot dogs and store-bought potato salad in their apartment, then joined the hordes alongside the East River watching fireworks. They'd planned to spend the time with friends who had a place in Montauk, but George cancelled, afraid he'd be asked too many questions, or not asked them, the questions hanging over every conversation.

"Of all the asinine strategies," Cyrus said to George over the phone. "Teasing the media while refusing to give details. Do you realize the position you've put me and your mother in?"

George pedaled his exercise bike. "Why didn't you tell the reporter I came to you when it happened?"

"Did you?"

He pedaled faster. "*Did I?*" Could his father have forgotten a conversation that had carved such a deep and painful groove in George's memory? A conversation George had returned to over and over at every stage of his life, even now, at forty, though he'd thought he surely would've gotten over it by then.

"It was a long time ago," Cyrus said.

"Not that long."

"Why does everything have to be public? Can't anything remain private anymore?" his father said. George couldn't help sympathizing with Cyrus's desire for privacy, which he shared.

"The senator might have done this to other boys. She might have done it to other people working under her. And we let her," George said, breathing hard.

"What did she really do?"

George stopped pedaling. He wiped his face with a towel. Is this what it would be like from now on? Constantly explaining what had happened to people who didn't want to understand or to believe him? Having to remind himself that it really did happen despite his father and the senator trying to convince him otherwise?

"Are you there?" Cyrus said.

George clutched the handlebars. "She sexually assaulted me."

"I thought teenage boys liked older women coming on to them."

"No, Dad."

You're making a big deal out of it, but it doesn't seem like such a big deal. I'm sorry if I don't get it. You didn't like what she did, so you stayed away from her. Problem solved," Cyrus said.

"I was so frightened, I pissed myself. If I hadn't, I don't know what she would have done after she kissed me, or what I would have felt I had to do, or whether I could have protected myself from her. Lucky for me, she was disgusted."

"You pissed yourself?"

"I told you."

"I don't remember," he said, his voice lacking its usual

authority. "Maybe your mother remembers." Cyrus called to Faith, "I have George on the phone. Come in here." The two men were quiet as they waited for her. Then Cyrus said, "Do you remember George telling us about the senator kissing him?"

George heard Faith in the background. "Yes, I remember. He was traumatized."

"Why didn't we do anything?" Cyrus said.

"You were afraid the senator would come after you and your firm. She was very powerful back then," Faith said.

"I said that?"

"No. You said maybe George imagined it," his mother said.

"Is that what you thought?" Cyrus asked Faith.

"I didn't want to believe we let something bad happen to him."

"I'm still here," George said.

"I'm sorry," his mother said. She'd taken the phone. "I'm sorry we let the senator get away with it. I'm sorry we didn't do more. I'm sorry we didn't believe you."

The knot in George's chest loosened. He'd been waiting for decades to hear his mother say that. He let go of the handlebars, his arms dangling at his sides. "Say it again."

"I'm sorry," Faith said.

It helped to be believed. It reinforced what his body knew. What his mind knew when he wasn't repeating to himself the lies he'd been told in the aftermath. Even after so many years, it meant a lot for his mother to take his side. But not what it would have meant earlier. George tried to imagine what the trajectory of his life would have been if his parents had supported him when he first came to them. Would he have gone into public service? Something else? He might not have needed therapy to have sex with his wife. But then, he might not have met Kiara at all and he wouldn't have written his book. He didn't know how to erase the harm without wiping out all the rest, everything he loved and that gave his life meaning. "It's not too late to help me," George said.

"What do you want us to do?" his mother said. "I'm putting you on speaker so your father can hear, too."

"Contact that reporter who tried to interview you," George said. "Tell her I told you what happened. As soon as I saw you. Thanksgiving."

"What about Wilma Sands?" Cyrus said.

"Don't mention her."

"It will look like we're hiding something," Cyrus said. "That's not a good look for a lawyer."

"At least you won't have to worry about the senator coming after you," George said.

"She's not as powerful now that she's retired," Cyrus said.

"Don't mention her," George said. "For me."

CHAPTER TWENTY-THREE

"How was I supposed to know?" P.J. wailed after she read Saturn's statement about George. She was in her car, waiting for Ride With Me to send her a job. Was it true? How bad a person was she? Some people on Crave were skeptical because Dunn hadn't gone public when it happened, but P.J. knew victims often chose to remain silent out of shame or because they were afraid no one would believe them. It had taken Mia years to tell their parents. She called Marissa. "Did you see it?"

"Yeah."

P.J. pulled on the prosperity cat. "Am I screwed?"

"People aren't really talking about you. They seem more interested in figuring out what really happened to Dunn," Marissa said. "If they believe him, they want to know who the predator is and why he waited so long to say something. Plenty of people don't believe him. Guy can't win."

"He was only sixteen," P.J. said.

"Do I detect a note of sympathy? What happened to 'he stole my book'?"

"I can't believe someone would make up a story like that knowing what would follow."

"Maybe he didn't know," Marissa said.

"What should I do?"

"Nothing. If you say anything, you'll become a target. The trolls will destroy you. Your book might get cancelled. This is a no-win situation for you."

"Okay," P.J. said. "But I feel bad."

"Too late for that. But if it helps, I feel bad, too."

As P.J. whispered an apology to George in the car (where it did no good) and gave the prosperity cat a final tug, the cheap chain from which the kitty hung snapped and metal beads scattered everywhere, some finding their way to car purgatory where they joined a large collection of ballpoint pens, sandwich crumbs, and a pair of sunglasses P.J. had been looking for and would likely never find.

***

"It's a hatchet job," Marissa said, after reading the *Pedestal* article. "That reporter just fed you gotcha questions." She sat on P.J.'s bed on Saturday morning, drumming her phone against her chin. "She probably knew all along that Mia worked in politics. She could have interviewed people who worked with your father back then, professors in his department who remembered when Mia was an intern. Or people who went to school with Mia. They might remember. She could have talked to the woman who set up the Better Day Fund."

"It makes me look like an uncaring bitch," P.J. said. "But I'm not, am I? I care about you. I care about Mia, even if I'm not willing to give up my book for her."

The article didn't identify Mia specifically or say the book was about P.J.'s sister, but it quoted an unnamed source who said a relative of P.J.'s had been sexually assaulted while working for a politician. It said P.J. had been the victim's confidante and that the victim had learned about the book on Crave and felt violated.

"The existence of the book raises ethical questions the author refuses to address, as if she can pretend the entire world isn't asking," Padma Kumar had written.

The entire world? It was, at the very least, a terrible exaggeration.

Marissa was scrolling. "Like she's never used someone for a story."

"She never mentions that I changed all the details. No one would know the book was inspired by a real person if it weren't for her writing the piece. Maybe someone should write an article about that. About all the lives journalists destroy in the name of a free press, but really just to get more clicks. Where's the outrage about that? It's not novelists who are the problem. At least we disguise our subjects."

"They want people to get angry. That's how journalism works these days," Marissa said.

"That's how everything works. Journalism. Social media. I guess I should know." P.J. thought about the nibble she'd served that started it all. She closed her eyes and lay back on the bed. Mia's Better Day Fund was up to twenty-four thousand dollars. Where was the Better Day Fund for her? For the trauma she'd suffered as a struggling writer and was suffering now?

"What did Black Bear say about the article?" Marissa said, her thumbs moving furiously. P.J. hoped she was attacking the story.

"They said it would get people more interested in the book. But I know if too many people come out against me, they'll cancel the deal." If Black Bear refused to pay her advance, P.J. would have to drive eighty hours a week for the next twenty years to pay Marissa back for the down payment on her condo.

"It's not like *you* sexually assaulted someone."

"No, but from that reporter's article you would think I had." P.J. sat up. "Fuck it. Are you ready for your interview on

Monday?" The opening was for a high school assistant principal.

"I found a substitute for my summer school classes, but I have nothing to wear."

"How is that possible? You've been interviewing for a year."

"Everything I own is cursed. Besides, it's too hot for a wool suit. I'm almost afraid to say it, but I might have a chance. It's pretty late in the hiring cycle. They must have lost someone at the last minute."

"I have something you could borrow." P.J. searched in her closet for a black dress with a floral pattern and a cotton jacket. She laid it on the bed, then set some black pumps on the floor. "I wore it when I interviewed for that job with Earth Protectors."

Standing in front of the mirror, Marissa held the dress up against herself. "I like it, but—"

"You think it's too funereal?" P.J. said.

"No. It's pretty. It's just—"

"Too short?"

"No, no. It's the perfect length. Very professional," Marissa said.

"Then what's the problem?"

"You didn't get the job."

P.J. sighed. "Try it on. I bet it will fit perfectly. Just don't mention at the interview that you think environmentalists who eat meat are hypocrites because the head of the hiring committee might be planning to go to a hamburger joint for lunch."

"Sorry," Marissa said.

"Too much information, I guess."

Marissa slipped on the outfit and examined herself in the mirror. She handed P.J. her phone. "Take a picture of the back so I can see it." As P.J. photographed her, Marissa said, "With or without stockings?"

"It's too hot for stockings."

P.J. showed Marissa the picture.

"I look *good*." When she finished admiring herself, Marissa put the dress back on the hanger. P.J. stashed the shoes in a gift bag.

Marissa hugged her. "The interview is at nine."

P.J. crossed her fingers and held them up. "No one is more qualified than you."

After Marissa left, P.J. checked Crave to see what was happening with the *Pedestal* article. To her surprise, it didn't seem to be going viral. Was the public growing tired of her story? A Hollywood divorce was a popular menu item, and so was the engagement of a royal. People were mocking a family-values politician who'd been photographed canoodling with his mistress in Cabo—a more satisfying target than an unknown writer whose book hadn't come out yet—the scandal temporarily exhausting the platform's store of outrage. P.J. was relieved and a little disappointed. It unnerved her how easily she could be forgotten.

The weekend stretched out before her. Although she hated to admit it, P.J. had enjoyed knowing she had somewhere to be every Sunday, before her father revoked her invitation to brunch and then, annoyed with Mia, too, cancelled the tradition altogether. She'd liked the idea of a gathering that was incomplete without her and of having people who were responsible for her happiness, or at the very least her Sunday morning plans. She texted Franklin, offering to come over on Sunday afternoon to help him with his mail.

As if Dina had sensed P.J. thinking about her, she called. "Have you heard from Mia?"

"I'm fine, Mom, thanks for asking." P.J. opened Crave

and munched some other writers' good news: university appointments, residencies in exotic locations, prizes. She nibbled back, "Fantastic!" "Congrats!" and "Wonderful!" adding strings of fire emojis, though what she mostly felt was envy. Despite having her own book contract. Despite not having applied for a university appointment and not being qualified for one. Though she couldn't afford to take time off to travel. What was wrong with her? Would she ever be satisfied? How many books would it take?

"P.J.?" Dina said. "Are you there?"

"I'm here." She'd missed part of the conversation, a thing that seemed to happen more and more often, notwithstanding her vow—taken after listening to a Brené Brown podcast—to be more present.

"I asked how you are," her mother said.

"I'm fine. But I'm the last person Mia wants to talk to."

"It isn't like her not to return my calls," Dina said.

"There are a couple of conventions in town. Ride With Me instituted surge pricing and we've been super busy. The hotel is probably full and she's working a lot. Or maybe she's trying to create more drama. As if she hasn't created enough already." P.J. drafted a nibble, attaching an image of her mountain view. She'd served a similar picture right after she moved in. "Still can't believe I get to look at this every day!!!" she typed. She deleted two exclamation points, added one back, then hit *serve*.

"Do you want to try texting her?" Dina said.

When P.J. looked up her sister's menu, she saw that Mia hadn't nibbled anything for weeks. It was the same on Mia's other social media sites. Recently, P.J. had nibbled an image of the two of them in their Little League uniforms. She'd captioned the picture, "sisters," and tagged Mia, hoping it would remind her of what they'd once meant to each other. It was P.J.'s second-most popular nibble, but Mia ignored it. P.J. scrolled back to it now and felt her own longing for the friendship made unique by shared history and DNA. "She's not answering my texts," P.J. said, staring at the photo. "I suppose I could go over to the hotel. Make sure she's okay."

***

P.J. parked in front of the Avalanche Hotel. "I'll just be a minute," she said to the attendant, taking advantage of the large Ride With Me sticker on her door.

A wave of cold, sanitized air hit her when she entered the lobby, and her sneakers sank into the royal purple carpet. In a large black and white photo hanging behind the front desk, snow muscled down a mountain. P.J. imagined some reckless skier who'd strayed into the back country trapped beneath the avalanche's dense blanket. "I'm looking for Mia Larkin," she said to the clerk.

The woman turned to her computer. "What room?"

From a bowl, P.J. grabbed a firm green apple and shoved it into her backpack. "She's not a guest. She's a housekeeper."

"Let me check with the manager. She'll know if your friend is working today."

When the clerk disappeared into an office, P.J. helped herself to two more apples. She wondered how much a night in the hotel cost. Black Bear had paid for her room in New York, and the cashews, Swedish fish, and numerous small bottles of wine she'd plucked from the minibar. Not to mention the movie she'd watched and a veggie burger that cost more than her flight.

The clerk returned with a woman whose suit matched the carpet and whose nametag read *Manager*. "Mia Larkin no longer works here," she said.

It wasn't unusual for her sister to change jobs. Still, P.J. felt a spark of concern, a specter of trouble floating in her peripheral vision that disappeared when she tried to examine it. "Are you sure?"

"Am I sure? I'm the manager of this hotel. Who are you?"

"What happened? Did she quit?"

The manager rearranged the apples, making the bowl appear full again. "I can't discuss personnel matters."

"When did she leave?" P.J. said.

"It's been about two weeks."

"Is she working at another hotel?"

"I haven't the faintest idea," the manager said, turning back toward her office.

When the woman was gone, P.J. said to the clerk, "I'd like to use your bathroom."

The clerk pointed. "End of the hallway to your right."

"Thanks." P.J. walked until she was out of the clerk's line of sight, then ducked onto an open elevator and pressed the button for the second floor. When the door opened, she peered out but didn't see a housekeeper or a cart. She stopped at the next floor and the next, until she spotted a cart and got off.

The housekeeper was stripping a bed.

"Do you know Mia Larkin?" P.J. said. "She used to work here."

"Not here anymore."

"I know. I'm wondering what happened. Did she quit? Get fired?"

The woman yanked a fresh sheet onto the bed. "Who did you say you were?"

"I'm her sister."

"The asshole!"

"My name is P.J."

"Like I said." She fluffed a pillow.

"We haven't heard from her and my mother's concerned."

"What about you? Are you concerned?"

"I guess I am," P.J. said.

The housekeeper bent to pick up a dirty towel. Lowering her voice, she said, "She was pretty out of it for a couple days. Forgot to do the bathrooms in some of the rooms. Guests complained."

"Shit." Had Mia relapsed because of her book? P.J. wanted to ask the woman more questions, but the manager appeared in the doorway.

"I hope you're able to get the rooms done on time with all this chatting," the manager said to the housekeeper. She turned to P.J. "Are you trying to keep everyone in the hotel from working?"

After she returned to her car, P.J. texted Mia: "Looked for u at the Avalanche. Everything ok?" Her sister didn't reply.

Dina called back that night.

"I didn't have a chance to go to the hotel," P.J. said.

***

A tower built from empty cereal boxes rose from the floor in Franklin's kitchen. Plastic horses and cows grazed on a Cinnamon Toast Crunch rooftop. P.J. was impressed that someone—Franklin? Sharon?—had reused what others might have thrown away. At the table, she opened bills and sorted them, careful to avoid the strawberry jam drying on the checked tablecloth. The room smelled faintly of sour milk. She unwrapped the plaque honoring Franklin's work on the Sunflower condominium project. "For meritorious conduct in designing a net-zero building," she announced, and tipped her head while handing it to him.

A smiley-face magnet secured a photo to the refrigerator. In the picture, a woman who could only be Sharon held the girls' hands, Franklin behind her, resting his chin on her head, his smile more lighthearted than any P.J. had seen. The woman was short with a utilitarian buzzcut. Maybe P.J. reminded Franklin of her. Maybe that was why he wanted her around.

"She was always happy writing the checks," Franklin said. "Like it was her birthday or something. I'm afraid if I pay them, it'll mean she's really gone." Franklin set the plaque on the table next to a necklace of plastic beads. "I guess that's dumb."

"I don't think so," P.J. said. No one close to her had died. Her mother's parents had lived on the East Coast. She'd seen them only on holidays and they died within a few months of each other when she was six. Her father's parents had died before she was born. In her alumni magazine, she'd read about a classmate who'd suffered a fatal pulmonary embolism, but P.J. hadn't known the woman. She tried to imagine what it would be like to lose Mia.

Franklin picked up the plastic necklace and gazed at it as if he didn't know what it was, pale brown circles beneath his eyes.

"You want some water?" P.J. said. He should have been the one offering, but he didn't seem up to it.

He shook his head.

"Tea? Or maybe we should continue another day. What's the worst that could happen? They shut off your lights? You could make a fort in the living room with your kids. Curl up underneath with a flashlight." P.J. had done that with Mia, and they'd told each other ghost stories. Once, when they were too old for forts, they'd made one anyway, and Mia shined the light in her face and described going to the library and discovering all the shelves were empty and their favorite librarian had morphed into the one they hated who let them borrow books only from the children's section. They screamed, but softly so their father wouldn't hear, and laughed so hard they spit out the s'mores Dina had made on the kitchen stove.

Franklin stuck the necklace into his pocket. "It's all right. Let's pay them."

P.J. returned to opening envelopes. "My sister won't talk to me," she said.

"Give her some time."

"I don't know if she hates me or if she's in some kind of trouble. She was fired from her job. I keep picturing terrible scenarios."

"It's the terrible scenario you forget to picture that you have to worry about," Franklin said.

An envelope sliced through the joint on P.J.'s right index finger. "*Ow!*" She sucked a thin ribbon of blood. Until it healed, every time she typed a *U* or a *Y* it would sting. She waited for Franklin to offer her the Band-Aid sticking out of his shirt pocket, but instead he pushed a used paper napkin in her direction.

"Why didn't Sharon sign up for autopay? You could have saved a lot of paper and stamps," P.J. said.

"She grew up poor. She liked the feeling of paying everything and seeing there was still a healthy balance in our account. It wasn't something she took for granted. She'd been hungry as a kid. Her mother had made pasta so often, Sharon wouldn't let us have it in the house."

"Paper bills and envelopes are so wasteful," P.J. said, blotting the cut. "Paper napkins, too." She waved the crumpled napkin like a flag. "With two kids, I'm surprised she didn't care more about the planet."

"She cared about the planet."

"People say they do, but then they continue to live the way they've always lived, driving gas cars, heating big houses." Franklin's house had to be more than two thousand square feet. Not huge, but not sustainable.

Franklin pushed his chair back and stood up. Next to the horses and cows on the cereal box tower, plastic pigs rooted in a pen. He picked one up. "What about you?" he said. "Ride With Me is pretty wasteful if you do the math. People could take light rail or buses or carpool and it would be better for the environment."

"At least with me they get an electric car."

"That makes it a little better," he said, examining the pig.

"A little?"

"Someone has to manufacture your car and the batteries, and that comes at a cost to the environment. The batteries will have to be disposed of eventually, also at a cost to the environment. And you drive all those miles between passengers, going to pick them up, which they wouldn't be driving if they took themselves directly to where they were going. It's better, but not great."

That was the thanks she got for helping him. P.J. shoved a pile of bills that included the mortgage and car payment toward Franklin, knocking two envelopes off the table. "These are very overdue. Call the companies today and give them a credit card. Then put them on autopay."

"Okay."

She pushed over a second stack that included life insurance and hospital bills. "Also very overdue. Same instructions, except don't put the hospital bill on autopay."

"I wouldn't have." He replaced the pig in its pen, then reached down to pick up the envelopes. "We're all human, P.J. That's all I was trying to say. I think it's great that you drive an electric car and live in a net-zero building. Really, it's great. I loved working on that building. But we're all human. I have flaws. I make mistakes, including being too busy to take my wife shopping. I'm sure you have a few flaws yourself."

"Whatever."

"I have to pick up the kids from my mother's. Why don't you come?"

"I should go home. I haven't gotten much writing done today."

"I was just kidding about peanut butter. I could stop for middle eastern food on the way back. My kids love falafel."

The skin around the papercut was pink and her finger throbbed. "Maybe another time." She pushed back her chair and swung her backpack over her shoulder, accidentally taking three stories off the cereal box tower and sending farm animals flying. "Shit. Sorry."

"Don't worry about it. Demolitions are common around here. Though I'll probably have to enter into an ice-cream settlement with the builders. You're sure about dinner?"

He seemed like a good dad. P.J. regretted the argument, but she wanted to return to her condo where no one criticized choices she was proud of. Stepping around the scattered boxes, she made her way out of the kitchen. "I don't have much of an appetite."

"Okay. I appreciate the help."

"Autopay is your friend," P.J. said, as she stepped out the front door.

"I thought that was you," Franklin said.

Before she could answer, the door swung shut.

CHAPTER TWENTY-FOUR

"How did it go?" George asked his mother over the phone. She and Cyrus had met with Tovah Sparrow earlier that day.

"Fine," Faith said. "She's very nice."

"And?" George said. His mother was running water somewhere.

"We didn't mention the senator's name. And we said you told us about the assault on Thanksgiving.

"Good. Where's Dad?"

"He's lying down."

"Is he okay?" George said.

"He's not used to, you know, not being in charge."

"I know." The microwave beeped, and George took out his reheated coffee, burning his lips when he sipped it.

"We said we made a mistake not coming forward."

"Thanks."

That wasn't all his parents had told the reporter. Sparrow's article appeared online the next day and in it Faith described how George had changed after his time at the Capitol. "Before he was a page, he was so full of energy. He volunteered for political campaigns. He couldn't wait to go off to college. But after he came home, he wasn't interested in politics anymore. He dropped out of scouts, though his father promised him a car if he made Eagle scout. All he wanted to do was hide in his room and read *The Bell Jar*. I don't know where he got that book. It definitely wasn't in our library.

"I had to beg him to eat, to change his clothes after going to school in the same khaki pants and polo shirt four days in a row. He couldn't bear to be touched."

Asked why they hadn't come forward at the time, Cyrus had said, "We weren't sure what happened. We weren't there. We hadn't witnessed it. We just didn't know what to believe."

George called his father. "Jesus Christ. I told you what happened. You should have believed me."

"I meant we didn't understand," Cyrus said. "Now we do. But then we didn't."

Flashing his middle finger at the phone, George hung up. His father was still denying what had happened. His mother had seen how the senator's actions had hurt him. She'd known something was wrong and did nothing. The senator had paid no price for launching a wrecking ball against his life.

At the end of the article, Sparrow noted that sex scandals involving pages were nothing new in Washington. In the 1980's two congressmen had been censured for having sex with pages, and in 2006, a third congressman had resigned after sending sexually explicit instant messages to a page.

George wondered how many politicians were missing from that list because they'd gotten away with their offenses. He stared at the names of the congressmen, their reputations destroyed and rightfully so. Why shouldn't Sands' name be added to that ignominious club? Why should she escape the consequences for what she'd done? He certainly hadn't.

Sitting next to him on the couch that night, Kiara completed the last few rows of a sand-colored rug. Though it was two weeks past Independence Day, neighborhood kids continued to set off illegal fireworks. Mutt lay under the coffee table whimpering, her tail tucked. George hoped one of the little felons blew off a finger. "I'm going to talk to Tovah Sparrow," he said.

"You sure that's a good idea?" Kiara said.

"No." He wasn't sure, but he was tired of wondering if the assault was somehow his fault. Tired of feeling like less of a man for allowing it to happen. Tired of being afraid of the senator. "I'm going to do it anyway."

Sparrow had left him a phone message after she'd spoken to his parents. George redialed the number, his hands shaking. When he got her voicemail, he blurted, "Wilma Sands." His heart tumbled in his chest. "That's who assaulted me at the Capitol. Senator Sands."

Three minutes later, she returned his call, and they spoke for an hour. George told his story again, his face warming as it always did. He wondered if he'd ever be able to speak of it without feeling ashamed, damaged somehow.

The piece ran the next day. George felt an enormous satisfaction picturing the senator blanch as she read it, her pulse firing unevenly, her phone buzzing like a disturbed hive. Yet, he knew the turmoil he'd unleashed would catch up with him, too. He couldn't eat his Cheerios, setting the bowl in the refrigerator where the little life preservers would soften and bloat.

He'd found part-time work as a copyeditor for an electrical engineering journal, but all he could do that morning was go through the motions: greet the distracted receptionist, turn on the shuddering fluorescent light in his office, fill a stained coffee mug, read technical articles he failed to absorb.

He kept a tab open to Crave. Pressure built in his head as his accusation against Wilma Sands was re-served over and over. He was afraid to open the private meals that were sent to him; they piled up as high as the garbage that floated around the city on scows.

A COMPLETE FICTION

When he returned home that afternoon, reporters congregated outside his apartment. They shoved microphones in his face, shouting, "Who else did you tell?" "What do you want to happen to the senator?" "Why did you wait to come forward?"

While George fumbled for his keys, Mutt barked behind the door. Finally. "She's a trained guard dog. I suggest you all back up." The reporters shuffled back. George opened the door a crack and slipped inside. "Good girl."

An hour later, he found himself on a conference call.

Saturn's lawyer said, "This isn't what we agreed on. You weren't going to mention her name."

"It's important to coordinate your responses with us," his editor said.

"Are you okay?" Janelle said.

CHAPTER TWENTY-FIVE

The seventy-five page publishing contract was too dense for P.J. to read, so she skimmed it, cringing when she came to the title—*Girl Is in the House*—and whooping when she saw the advance. "Don't they care about the *Pedestal* article?" she asked Sloane. "Or Avery Baron? They're not going to cancel the book because of George Dunn's statement, are they?"

"The Dunn thing is complicated," Sloane said. "And people seem to have forgotten about Avery Baron. Those kinds of stories can disappear as fast as they catch on. The *Pedestal* article didn't get many eyeballs. Black Bear's lawyer vetted your book and thought it was clear that even if you'd been inspired by real life events, the novel was a work of your imagination. Let's hope by the time the book comes out the fact that anyone thought you shouldn't write it will have been forgotten. Sign the contract and send it back, and you'll receive a large check. And don't forget." Sloane cleared her throat, then sang: "*Celebrate good times. Come on!*"

"Oh my god! Those are the words!" P.J. said.

"What else would they be?"

"Thank you," P.J. said. "For everything you've done for me."

"Of course."

"No really, thank you. For believing in me all these years even though my books didn't sell."

"You're welcome."

After returning the contract, P.J. ordered a new sofa and

matching arm chair on a payment plan. She knew it would be better for the environment to buy used, but just once, she wanted her ass to be the first on the furniture. For the cushions to be free of stale farts and other bodily excretions she preferred not to imagine. Free of fur and feathers. To take delivery without imagining the bed bug colonies that were moving in, too. The frames were made from recycled water bottles, the fabric from recycled polyester. The set cost twenty-five hundred dollars, more than P.J. had ever spent on something that didn't come with wheels or its own address.

The next day, she received an email from Babette Aller with suggested revisions to the novel. P.J. was surprised to find that she agreed with most of them, and though she wasn't looking forward to working on the book again, she could see they how the changes would make the novel better.

***

P.J. pulled up in front of the house Mia shared with an ever-changing group of roommates. She'd forgotten how grim the exterior of the property was: remnants of a chain link fence, the gate missing and half of the posts knocked to the ground; house paint worn to the color of muddy water; a looming dead cottonwood. The tree would fall one day, crushing the roof and anyone standing below.

She should have been revising her novel and resented her sister for interfering with her work. But no one was forcing P.J. to check on Mia. A week and a half had gone by since P.J. had visited the hotel, and she hadn't heard from Mia and neither had her mother. The night before, P.J. had dreamed that Mia drove off a mountain pass and crashed into a rocky creek below.

She climbed the stairs to the front door. The bell hadn't

worked for as long as Mia had lived there, so she knocked. When no one answered, she tried again.

A bearded man shoved aside a window curtain, then opened the door. "Yes?"

"Is Mia here?"

"I haven't seen her, but I've been working in my room."

She briefly wondered what kind of work he was doing. "Can I come in?"

"Only with a housemate. I don't know you. Stuff gets stolen. The wrong kind of people try to get in. Ex-boyfriends. Ex-husbands. It's a rule we agreed on."

P.J. wondered if she was the wrong kind of person in Mia's eyes. "I'm her sister," she said. She held out her hand. "P.J."

"Wendell," he said, shaking her hand. As worried as she was about Mia, P.J. couldn't help but notice how strong his hand was, how warm, just hairy enough to be manly without being simian. But he didn't step aside.

"Would you at least see if she's here?" P.J. said.

The man shouted Mia's name.

"I meant go upstairs and check."

"I will if you'll promise not to come in," Wendell said.

"Fine."

"Fine what?"

"I promise."

Wendell climbed the stairs and knocked hard on a bedroom door.

P.J. craned her neck, but couldn't see much other than the staircase. She itched to cross the threshold. In the past, she would have. It would have been easy to justify. Instead, she forced herself to respect Mia's privacy.

Wendell came back down, skipping every second step.

"Sorry. She's not here."

"Thanks for checking."

"Thanks for not coming in. I'll tell her you stopped by."

After he closed the door, a suspicion arose in P.J.'s mind, but when she called Mia's phone it didn't ring in the house.

CHAPTER TWENTY-SIX

Wilma Sands stood before a bank of microphones wearing an off-white suit and a large wedding ring, her husband at her side. The press conference, which she had called, was being held on the long driveway outside her gothic D.C. mansion, the day after she was publicly identified as George Dunn's alleged assailant.

George closed his office door and watched the proceedings on his phone.

The senator cleared her throat. "It's been a while," she said, and waited for the respectful laughter to die down. "Not exactly how I thought I'd make my comeback." She paused, hoping for more laughter, but the reporters were silent. Sands' expression turned dour. "The would-be author George Dunn has made the most preposterous charge against me, and I find myself forced to come before you to set the record straight.

"Nearly twenty-five years ago, when I was a senator representing the great state of Tennessee, a sixteen-year-old page named George Dunn tried to kiss me in my office. It was so ridiculous, I almost laughed. In fact, I may have laughed. You had to see him, this skinny, awkward boy, thinking I could possibly welcome his flirtations. He said, 'You're so beautiful.' Can you imagine? I think I told him to find someone his own age. And that was all there was to it.

"As a woman in a predominantly male institution, I later wondered if there was some sexist dynamic there, something larger at work that would lead a young page to sexualize me in that manner. Some ultimate conquest he was after. But as I say, that came later. At the time, I just thought it was silly and went about my incredibly hectic schedule. And for him to now claim that I came on to him, because he got into trouble plagiarizing a woman's novel and hopes this will result in sympathy for him—I don't even know what to say."

A reporter from *CBS News* shouted, "Did you tell anyone about it?"

"I told my chief of staff, more as a humorous anecdote than anything else. I knew he would get a laugh out of it."

The reporter asked a follow-up, "Did you consider terminating Dunn's page appointment?"

"No. Nothing like that. We—my chief of staff and I—discussed having someone from the page program give him a talk," Sands said. "And we probably should have. But I could tell Dunn was embarrassed. I thought it was just a case of him admiring me and getting confused about his feelings, a case of puppy love or a crush, if you will, and I decided I wouldn't give him any more page assignments, since there were other pages that I could call on. So I didn't. I would occasionally catch him glancing at me from the other end of a hall or on the stairs, and he would turn and go the other way, which led me to believe he was ashamed and had learned his lesson."

A reporter from *The New York Times* asked, "Weren't you afraid he would behave inappropriately with someone else?"

"In retrospect, you may be right. But it wasn't the easiest time to be a woman in the Senate. Whenever I could, I preferred not to call attention to my gender."

Sands pointed to an *NBC News* reporter.

"Are you the senator in George Dunn's book?" the reporter asked.

The senator's mask fell briefly and she glowered at the reporter, before recovering herself. "I haven't read Dunn's book. From what I understand, it's fiction."

"Did he base the character on you?" a *Washington Times* reporter asked.

"As I said, I haven't read it, nor do I intend to. I can only tell you what actually happened while he was a page and my reasons for responding the way I did. These kinds of things happen in offices. Young men develop attractions. I didn't want to give it a whole lot of my attention. I wanted to focus on my legislative agenda, work for the good of the country and for the people of Tennessee, and not get sidetracked by what would almost certainly have turned out to be a tabloid story." Sands stepped back from the microphone, took out a handkerchief, and blew her nose. Her husband huddled with her a moment, squeezing her shoulder. She put the handkerchief away and returned to the microphone.

"Dunn's book isn't out yet. Do you intend to try to stop Saturn from publishing it?" asked another member of the press.

"You'll have to talk to my lawyers about that."

Lawyers. Plural. George had trouble breathing for a moment.

Reporters continued to shout questions, but Sands ignored them as she and her husband walked back to the house.

George wondered if he could hire someone to kill her. He would order something slow and painful. It was no good if she didn't suffer. Maybe he could arrange for her to be poisoned. He'd read that was a terrible death. Or perhaps a stoning, like in the story, "The Lottery." His phone rang. It was Kiara, likely calling after seeing the press conference, but George hated to be interrupted. He had Sands in the electric chair and was fastening the straps.

A COMPLETE FICTION

The story led the evening news. Clips appeared on social media.

The next day, Saturn's attorney informed George he would have to hire his own lawyer. George called Cyrus, who agreed to find an attorney and pay all the fees. George and Kiara couldn't afford the bills lawyers sent.

***

Maxine Leland had been practicing law for twenty years. She specialized in high-profile sexual assault cases, and the walls of her lower Manhattan office were covered with framed newspaper articles about victories she'd secured for her clients. She'd sued a former U.S. President and an NFL star. Housekeepers and Hollywood stars, alike, turned to her for justice, and she was the first attorney Cyrus had called.

Alone with the lawyer, George repeated his story.

"You'll have to appear before the press," Leland said. She wore a white suit with a black-and-white collar and sparkling teardrop earrings, as if to remind everyone she'd turned her clients sorrows into diamonds. "Bring the gifts the senator gave you. All of them. You'll have to tell the reporters exactly what happened."

"I can't." Though George had by now told Kiara and Sparrow, and Saturn had released a statement, confessing his shame in a room filled with national reporters and cameras poised to transmit his image across the globe would be something else entirely. It would be humiliating.

"You have to. Wear a suit. Kiara will appear with you. We'll work up something for you to read." The senator would sue him for defamation, the lawyer cautioned. "The case will be difficult." She paused to make sure George appreciated the warning before reassuring him she would see him through it.

***

Leland had arranged to use her firm's largest conference room, but it still wasn't big enough to accommodate all the press. Filled with bodies and lighting equipment, the space quickly overheated. By the time George and Kiara arrived, it was tropical. George took his place behind the lectern, Kiara on his right, the lawyer on his left. On a table at the side of the room were the journal he had kept that summer and the gifts from Sands. A copy of the statement Leland had drafted and selected pages from the journal were handed out to reporters.

George kept his eyes down as he read what the lawyer had prepared about the long-ago time when the senator had started out seemingly kind; how her behavior had made him more and more uncomfortable until the day she brushed his hair from his forehead and pressed her lips to his neck. Haltingly, and with blood saturating his ears, he described pissing himself, and Sands pulling away. Then he was silent. The reporters were momentarily speechless.

Behind the lectern, Kiara squeezed his hand.

Through a door propped open to let in some air, George heard the *cachunk, cachunk* of a copy machine as it spit out a large job. He heard a receptionist transfer a call. Then the shouting began. Leland pointed to a *CNN* reporter.

"Did you tell anyone at the time?"

"I told my parents," George said.

And a follow-up: "What did they do?"

"Nothing." Which was precisely what George felt like now. How else to explain his parents' neglect other than that he was a person unworthy of care? The reporters leaned forward because he had spoken softly, his mouth pointed away. Leland whispered to him to speak into the mic, then pointed to a *CBS* reporter.

"Did you tell anyone other than your parents?"

"I wrote a whole—" *screeeeeee*. The feedback made him jump. He pulled his head back from the mic. "A whole book about it. That's what got me here."

A reporter from the online site *Breaking* shouted: "Why did you wait to come forward?"

"I was sixteen," George said.

"The senator has said that you had a crush on her and that you tried to kiss her," said a *Washington Post* reporter.

"I know what she said."

"Do you deny it?"

"I was a junior in high school. I was terrified of her. Even before she assaulted me." He tried to sip from a glass and spilled water on his hand, his shirt, and the lectern. Pulling a napkin from her purse, Kiara wiped the lectern. George brushed his hand against his pants.

"So you deny trying to kiss her?" the *Washington Post* reporter said.

"Yes."

From *PBS*: "You described the senator grooming you. Did you ever see her engage in that kind of behavior with any other page?"

"No."

Asher Stone from *CNBC* shouted, "Some people might think it's convenient, you coming forward with this after P.J. Larkin accused you of stealing her #metoo story."

"I can't control what people think," George said.

"How do we know you didn't buy the tie and the cologne yourself?" Stone said.

"I didn't."

"What do you think should happen to the senator?" A *Guardian* reporter asked.

"I don't know." George couldn't inflict any of the terrible punishments he had imagined. She wouldn't go to jail. It was too late for the Senate to censure her or for her to resign.

An *Al Jazeera* correspondent asked: "What do you want us to make of the blank pages in your journal?"

"When I started as a page, I was trying to remember everything that happened and everyone I met. But after what the senator did, all I wanted to do was forget."

***

The press conference was covered by every major news outlet, and of the many people it reached, at least three were kept awake by it.

Neal Sands, the senator's husband, understood who his wife was. He drank four highballs that night, two more than usual, and said a silent prayer for George and all of the other people Wilma had taken advantage of or destroyed during her long career. He had stayed married to her by reminding himself that the legislation she had sponsored helped the poor and middle classes and, more importantly, that their wealth came from her side of the family.

P.J. Larkin sketched a tie and a bottle of cologne on the cover of a *New Yorker* magazine she'd been saving to read. She had listened to the press conference on the radio and had no doubt George was telling the truth. She remembered Mia's anguish when she described being raped, and while what happened to George was perhaps less awful, there was a similar quality to his suffering, an aspect of shame, as if he believed, as Mia had,

A COMPLETE FICTION

that he had somehow brought the assault on himself. It was her fault that George had to relive his trauma in front of the entire country.

Alice Barsham watched the press conference sitting next to her husband. She'd been a custodian at the Capitol when George was a page. One afternoon, she'd gotten a call on her radio from her manager, telling her Senator Sands had put in a request, which was unusual. If the senator needed something, a member of her staff would generally ask for it. The manager told her the senator sounded upset. Said a dog had pissed on her carpet and to send someone to clean it up right away.

You didn't see many dogs at the Capitol other than service dogs. Alice didn't even know if they were allowed. She stopped what she was doing and headed to the senator's office with cleaning supplies. The room was empty when she arrived, but a little while later, a tall young man came out of the senator's bathroom with his suit jacket wrapped around his waist. It didn't take a detective to figure out he was the one who'd had the accident. She couldn't imagine what had caused him to lose control. Not at the time, anyway. She was on the floor, scrubbing the stain, and didn't think he saw her as he hurried out.

She remembered how young he'd looked, how frightened. He didn't seem capable of attacking a senator. Everyone at the Capitol knew about Sands. You would sometimes see young male staffers coming out of her office in the evening. The custodial workers had been told never to knock if the door was closed. To come back another time, instead.

Alice wanted to say something, to call one of the networks or get in touch with George. But her husband was afraid the senator would come after them. "I don't need any more drama than I get watching my soaps," he said.

***

The Capitol Scoop ran a small item on the scandal. The French cologne George said the senator gave him sold for three hundred dollars a bottle and was available in only one shop in D.C. The ancient shopkeeper had many nice things to say about the senator, who'd bought countless bottles over the years. "Such a lovely woman. It's her husband's favorite, you know." When shown a picture of George in a denim shirt, the owner couldn't recall ever meeting him or selling him anything. "Not a fellow who looks like he has three hundred dollars to spend, is he?"

***

A week after his press conference, George opened the door to a man claiming to be from UPS and was served with a lawsuit brought against him by the senator, naming his parents and Saturn as additional defendants. The senator was seeking ten million dollars in damages, public apologies from all the Dunns, and an injunction to prevent Saturn from publishing his book.

CHAPTER TWENTY-SEVEN

"A lot happening with your old friend George Dunn," Alex said.

"Don't remind me," P.J. said.

They were standing behind the registration table at a charity run for multiple sclerosis. Len's father had been diagnosed three years before, and since then they'd always volunteered on race day, checking people in and handing out numbered bibs and swag.

"What's that old saying? 'Don't call someone a plagiarist in a nibble because they may turn out to be a survivor in real life,'" Len said.

P.J. fastened a pin to a bib, but not before she thought about sticking Len with it

"I don't see your name," Len said to a runner who came up to the table.

"I registered," the man said.

"I'm not doubting you. I just don't see it."

"What am I supposed to do?" the runner said. "I'm not paying again."

Len handed him a bib. "Thanks for coming out." When the runner walked away, Len put twenty-five dollars in the cash box. "I was going to donate anyway."

Hoping to feel better about herself, P.J. dropped a twenty in the box.

Len raised his eyebrows at Alex and Marissa.

"Don't look at me," Marissa said. "I have to buy a whole new wardrobe for my—drumroll please—new job."

They gathered around Marissa to congratulate her, though P.J. already knew.

Alex high-fived her.

A runner waited at the table. "Would you mind?"

"Yes, sir." Len checked off the runner's name and handed him a bib. "Thanks for coming out today."

"Sure," the guy said. "What are you celebrating, anyway?"

"Our friend got a job as an assistant principal," Len said.

Marissa curtsied.

"Well, congratulations. I hope you're as excited a year from now." He walked away, pinning his bib to his shirt.

"Thanks. I think," Marissa said. "Will I be unhappy with the job in a year?"

From listening to passengers, P.J. knew a lot of people were unhappy at work. But not everyone. "If you feel like you're making a difference, you'll be happy."

"Okay, then!" Marissa said. "This is why we're friends. Free therapy."

"Not free." P.J. held out the box and Marissa dropped in a five.

"I'm already sponsoring a runner," Alex said, but his friends glared at him until he added a ten.

They separated during the race, taking up stations along the course and handing out water to passing runners who drank and threw what was left on their faces, tossing the cups aside. P.J. had tried to get the organizers to use compostable cups, but they were unwilling to spend the extra money that would otherwise go to medical research. She cringed at the waste. Watching as they sped by, she wondered who in each of their families was sick.

She was grateful her parents were healthy. They didn't depend on her, and she didn't worry about them. That wouldn't be true for Len as his father got worse. He didn't seem to dwell on it. Though she'd never tell him, she admired the way he moved through life with equanimity.

Reaching for a cup, a runner lost his balance and fell hard on the road. P.J. rushed to see if he needed the medic. The man was tall with light-colored hair and she helped him stand as other runners skirted around them. He winced as he put weight on the injured leg. Using her as a crutch, he hobbled to the side of the course and sat on the grass. She got him another cup of water.

"My wife is waiting for me at the end," he said.

"What's her name and what's she wearing? I can call down there and have someone find her." She unclipped a walkie-talkie from her belt.

The runner gave his wife's first name. "She's wearing green shorts and a black T-shirt that says, 'Give Back.'"

"Okay." P.J. pressed the button on the walkie-talkie. "This is Patricia from station 3. We need a medic." She described the runner's wife. "Can you bring her here, too?"

"Copy that," she heard.

"You want some more water?" she asked the runner.

"That's all right," he said.

"Medic and your wife should be here soon."

"I heard."

"How bad is it?" she said.

"My knee hurts. But, mostly, I'm embarrassed."

"Everyone falls. It's you today. It'll be me tomorrow."

"Are you a runner?" He planted his arms behind him and leaned against them.

"A slow one."

"Nice of you to volunteer."

"My friend's father has M.S.," P.J. said. "What about you? Do you know someone with the disease?"

"My mother-in-law."

"Is this your first time running it?"

"Yeah. I've been pretty stressed out, so my wife suggested it would be a good way to blow off steam," the man said. "We're not from Colorado. We just flew in for the race and to relax a bit. She's always wanted to see the Rocky Mountains. Hike. So much for that."

"Where are you from?"

"New York."

"Oh yeah? What do you do there?"

"I was an editor, but I lost my job. Hence the stress."

"Sorry to hear that." P.J. was afraid to ask his name. It was a longshot, anyway, considering how many editors lived in New York. But what if it was him? She'd seen his thumbnail image on Crave. The man didn't look *unlike* George Dunn. Was she responsible for this, too? As if he wished to bury himself, the runner pulled out a fistful of grass and dumped it on his thigh. She noted the number on his bib.

The medic drove up in a golf cart, and the man's wife jumped out. "Oh Sweetie," she said, sitting next to him and wiping the sweat from his forehead with the race T-shirt he'd received when he registered. P.J. looked away, the scene oddly intimate.

Later that morning, as they packed up the race paperwork, P.J. looked up the runner's number. When she saw the name associated with it, she called Marissa over and told her what had happened.

"So, it wasn't him," Marissa said.

"No," P.J. said.

"Just another unemployed editor from New York."

"Seemed like a nice guy," P.J. said.

"But it wasn't him." Marissa grabbed a leftover race T-shit and stuck it in her bag.

"No. But it could have been him."

"What are you two whispering about?" Len said.

"Which restaurant you're taking us to, to thank us for volunteering." Marissa patted her stomach. "One with a brunch buffet. I'm starving."

"Nice fantasy. How about hurrying up with those lists so we can get out of here sometime today?" Len said.

"So bossy," Marissa said.

"Take notes. You're about to be a boss."

"I'm going to be a boss, but I'm not going to be bossy."

"We'll see," Len said.

P.J. was staring at the list again.

"What are you looking for?" Marissa said.

"Could Dunn have been running under an alias?"

"Dunn is in New York. You just feel guilty."

"Contribute another ten. That will help," Len said.

P.J. set a ten in the box.

"Feel better?" Marissa said.

"No," P.J. said.

Len locked up the cash. "It takes a while to work."

***

Mia had had an on-again, off-again relationship with a guy named Aram, who'd been in P.J.'s high school class. P.J. didn't know if they were on-again, but it was worth a try. Anything was. She'd gone to Mia's house twice since that first time and hadn't managed to find her sister home.

Once, Wendell had opened the door again. P.J. tried to imagine his life when he wasn't standing in her way. Maybe he was a handyman or a security guard who worked a night shift. He held a new hose.

"You're still not going to let me in?" P.J. said.

"Not unless your sister tells me it's okay."

P.J. nodded toward the hose. "I hope you're not planning to waste water on a lawn."

"It's for a rain harvesting system I set up out back. Are you familiar with rain barrels? We collect the water to fill the toilets. Conserves water and cuts our bill."

"Oh."

He went upstairs and came down shaking his head. "Last time you were here, I told her you stopped by. That you seemed concerned."

"And? What did she say?"

"Are you sure you want to know?" He held the hose with two hands, as if he might decide to lasso her, an image she couldn't help but linger on.

"I'm not sure I want to know, but tell me anyway."

"She said you were a spy and to be careful not to answer any personal questions."

"I'm not a spy," P.J. said.

He slung the hose over his shoulder. "Isn't that what a spy would say, though?"

During P.J.'s third visit, a different housemate had answered the door. P.J. thought she glimpsed Mia through a bedroom window, but the woman said Mia wasn't home.

P.J. could've called Mia's sometime-boyfriend Aram before driving out to Westminster, the Denver suburb where he had a townhome, but she didn't trust him not to cover for her sister.

She wanted to surprise Mia and see if she was drinking.

Aram opened the door, wearing a pair of cut-off sweats. He yawned and stretched. "To what do I owe the pleasure?"

"Can I come in?"

He made way for her but didn't ask her to sit. A Gillian Flynn paperback was spreadeagled on a red leather couch.

"I haven't been able to find Mia," she said.

He picked up the book, lay on the couch, and closed his eyes. "And you thought she might be here."

P.J. nodded, then realized he couldn't see her. "I hoped she would be here." She looked around the apartment. Down the hall, she saw two closed doors. She figured one had to lead to his bedroom.

Aram opened his eyes. "No tours today. No tours for people who stop by without an invitation."

"I'm worried about her."

"And you didn't call her because…"

"I've called. I've texted. I've paid unannounced visits to her home and job, though the truth is, I don't know where she works, anymore. She was fired from the Avalanche. You don't know if she got another job, do you?"

"I do not. I haven't seen your sister in three months," he said. "I have, however, been following your saga on Crave, and I can understand why she might not want to see you. Maybe you should give her some space."

P.J. wondered if he was lying about not seeing Mia. "I'm worried."

"So you said, and I can understand that. But here's the thing." He stood up and walked to the front door. "She has friends. Real ones who don't share the private details of her life in novels. If she's in trouble, they'll know and try to help."

"I didn't—" P.J. started to say, but then thought better of it. He was right that she and Mia weren't exactly friends anymore. Maybe she should leave her sister alone.

***

Dina paced P.J.'s apartment in her Garfield scrubs and white sneakers, having come straight from work. "I called the hotel. Mia hasn't worked there for weeks."

"I know," P.J. said.

"Why didn't you tell me?"

"I didn't want you to worry. She probably just has a new job." It was her mother's first time in the apartment, and she had yet to comment on the view.

"Don't you think she would have told me if she got a new job?" Dina said.

P.J. planted herself in front of the windows, her back to her mother. "She's mad at us because our lives don't revolve exclusively around her."

"That's not why she's mad at us." Dina ran a hand along the top of the wood card catalog. "I always liked these. I guess the computer is more convenient."

"Aren't you going to say anything about the apartment?"

"It's beautiful," Dina said. "Good for you for buying in a next-to-zero building."

"Net zero."

"Net zero. We're happy for you."

P.J. turned around. "Why do you always say 'we'? Dad doesn't give a shit." She thought about how defensive her father got every time she discussed environmental issues with him. She'd urged him to make small changes, put solar panels on the roof, drive a hybrid, but he'd insisted all of that was just a way of signaling you cared without actually doing much, which she couldn't help but take as an insult.

"Your father cares about you." Dina pulled open one of the card catalog's narrow wood drawers, the friction causing a shushing sound not unlike the one librarians sometimes made. For a moment, P.J. was back in her childhood library with her mother and Mia, P.J. on tip-toes trying to see what was in the drawer.

"If he cares so much, why didn't he come with you?" Stepping into the kitchen, P.J. grabbed a bottle of pomegranate-flavored seltzer from the refrigerator. She poured two glasses.

Dina followed her and set her white purse on the island. "He has to teach tomorrow, and he was hoping to get some work done tonight, and I could see he was tired." She sipped the sparkling water.

"He's mad at me for publishing the book," P.J. said.

"He's troubled by it," Dina said. "I should try this seltzer at brunch."

"That would be a good idea if we were having brunch."

Dina peered into her glass as if she could discover her family's future in the bubbles. "We will again."

"Maybe if he ever manages to finish his own book, he'll be happy for me," P.J. said.

"Your father's not that petty."

"He's not that self-aware either."

Touching the glass to her cheek, her mother said, "When did you get so angry at everyone?"

P.J. thought about the argument she'd had with Franklin. "I don't know."

"Well, I wish you would figure it out. Everyone has struggles. Your father, as you mentioned. Mia, certainly."

"What about you?" P.J. said.

"What do you think?" Dina picked up the seltzer bottle and examined the label. "It doesn't have sugar."

"It can't always be easy being married to Lawrence," P.J. said.

"It isn't."

P.J. went into the bedroom and returned with a cardboard box she sometimes thought of as her motivation box, other times as her perseverance box, but most often as her fuck-you box. Large enough to fit a dozen reams of paper—not that P.J. printed anymore—it was filled with emails containing bad news of one kind or another related to her writing. She held it out toward her mother. "Pick one from the bottom of the box."

Dina pulled out an email from an agent who'd declined to represent P.J.'s first book.

"Now pick another. From the middle," P.J. said.

The email Dina chose was from Sloane, forwarding a publisher's rejection of P.J.'s second book.

"Now from the top," P.J. said.

"I think I get it," her mother said.

"Do you? I've spent years writing books only to have them rejected. When I finally manage to sell one, my family tries to keep me from publishing it. Wouldn't that make you angry?"

"Maybe it would." Dina sipped from her glass. "What other flavors does it come in?"

"A lot, Mom." P.J. took a pineapple and a blueberry seltzer from the refrigerator.

"Can I take one home? I want your father to try it."

"Sure."

Dina pulled the bottle of blueberry seltzer toward her. "I read your book. I know it's not Mia's story."

"Thank you." She returned the box to her bedroom closet,

Dina following her.

"What a beautiful view."

"Thanks for noticing," P.J. said. *Finally*.

"The thing is," Dina said, "people might figure out your sister was in politics. They might think it's her story, even if it isn't. And maybe certain parts are her story? I'm not saying you shouldn't publish it. Just that it's complicated."

"I wasn't trying to make Mia's life harder."

"I know that," Dina said. "But it's not like her to disappear. It reminds me of when she was drinking."

"It reminds me of that, too," P.J. said.

"Call her."

"I will, but she won't answer."

"Try."

"I said I would."

"Thank you," Dina said.

"You don't have to thank me. She's my sister."

After her mother left, P.J. checked Mia's Better Day Fund. The website said it had been paid out and the account was closed.

***

P.J. sat at her desk, *Girl Is in the House* open on her computer. She was thinking about George Dunn, as she had regularly since his press conference and the news about the senator's lawsuit. She felt oddly like she was in his camp now, though he didn't know it and it did him no good. He had a new, more powerful adversary. Even if P.J. were to state publicly that she believed him and that he hadn't plagiarized her, she had no evidence to support his account of sexual assault. She had turned his life upside-down and couldn't fix it.

Yet perhaps some good had come from it. Dunn's #metoo

statement was a single wave in the enormous tide of truth sweeping society about how people in power sometimes abused subordinates. She had written her book to bring attention to that very issue, and what could possibly bring more attention than the exposure of a former senator as a sexual predator? If, as her mother worried, people connected her novel to her sister and assumed what P.J. described was real, that, too, would enlighten people about the kinds of things that went on in the world and create awareness that change was necessary. She considered calling Dunn and apologizing or serving a statement on Crave but decided not to. Her nibble accusing Dunn had gone viral for reasons that had little to do with her and everything to do with an environment ripe for upheaval and change.

She turned her attention back to her manuscript but soon was distracted again, this time by fantasies of what her life would be like once she was a best-selling author. Maybe she would move to one of the larger units in the building. Travel to Prague and write her next book at a café, gathering with other successful writers at night to drink and fuck.

As the sun began to set, she lifted her head. She tried to watch it every day if she wasn't driving, the mountains becoming silhouettes as night fell, everything alive disappearing, leaving only gray and black forms beneath a bleeding sky. Evening brought a kind of claustrophobia, but not before the sun's dramatic display.

She texted Mia. "Thinking about you. Hope you're okay. Saw the Better Day Fund closed. Text me." She didn't expect a reply and didn't receive one.

CHAPTER TWENTY-EIGHT

Cyrus insisted they countersue. Although George didn't want to complicate matters further, he felt obliged to go along since he was responsible for their legal troubles.

He and his parents joined Leland around the table in her office, and the lawyer had George go over his story again. Repeating it in front of his father was nearly as hard as sharing it with the press. He couldn't look at Cyrus who'd asked on the way over why George didn't just stand up to the senator and refuse to come around the desk when she beckoned. Cyrus, who blamed George for shattering his carefully arranged life.

"No one saw you come out of the office?" Leland said.

"No," George said.

"And you didn't tell anyone besides your parents? No friends?"

"I was too embarrassed."

"Understandable," Leland said, and George wanted to hug her.

The lawyer asked Faith about George's time as a page. As she answered, Leland took a metal box of mints from her suit pocket and tapped it on the table before putting one in her mouth. "Trying to quit smoking," she said. She held out the box. "Anyone?" They shook their heads, though George was salivating. The lawyer set the mints down and picked up her gold Montblanc pen. She flipped to a fresh page on her yellow pad.

"We should have done something, but we were afraid," his

mother said. She rubbed the sleeve of her crepe dress, testing the fabric, a habit from her time in the store.

"That's good," Leland said and wrote it down.

Better late than never, George thought. The next time Leland offered a mint, he took it, ignoring his father's disapproving glance.

Leland had Cyrus recount what happened when George came home for Thanksgiving. "We couldn't believe a senator would do that," his father said, his hands resting on the arms of his chair, an open posture he recommended for clients when they took the stand.

The lawyer stopped writing. "That's precisely the kind of thing we're not going to say."

"Right," Cyrus said, turning pink.

"Here's what we'll do." The lawyer tapped the box of mints on the table. "We'll depose the senator. She'll hate that. She'll talk too much. They all do. Can't follow their lawyer's advice to just answer the questions. Always think they're the smartest ones in the room. She'll contradict herself. Lie. It will be a beautiful thing." *Tap, tap.* "But first we'll depose her chief of staff. They know everything." *Tap, tap.* "It doesn't matter if they didn't witness what happened. They find out to protect their boss." Leland chewed what was left of the mint in her mouth. "They'll depose all of you, too. It will be tougher than the journalists' questions. We'll prepare you. The key is to say as little as possible. You'll be surprised how hard that is." She opened the box. "You'll want to explain. Don't. You'll want to convince them. Don't try. They're not the jury. We'll practice. In the meantime, I'll be the one handling the press. If they call, refer them to me. We'll assign a public relations team to the case. Questions?" When none of them spoke up, she popped a mint in her mouth. "My paralegal has some paperwork for you."

Faith clutched the buckle on her purse, and George wondered how much it would end up costing his parents, his embarrassment at not contributing outweighed by the feeling that they deserved to pay.

***

When the senator made the rounds of the talk show circuit, it wasn't as the formidable figure who'd come to his apartment or the political powerhouse who'd called the press conference. Instead, she wore makeup that did little to hide her wrinkles and may have accentuated them. Her hair was puffed like cotton candy and tinted a brassy gold. She hobbled across sound stages in a vintage nineteen seventies suit. To the public, she must have cut a sympathetic figure, an elder stateswoman attacked by an unknown writer. No other accusers having come forward, she could claim George was using her to dig himself out of a hole. During one interview, she speculated he would have accused her of assault even without P.J.'s claim of plagiarism to cause a scandal that would gin up sales.

George occasionally caught himself wondering if the senator's version was true. His therapist told him that was normal, that having been offered a version of reality different from his own by his parents, it was natural for him to question his memory. Nevertheless, when it happened, he couldn't help but feel a traitor to himself.

In every interview, Sands said about George, "Perhaps he's having some kind of psychotic break, in which case, he deserves our sympathy." The hashtag #DeservesOurSympathy took off on Crave, becoming a popular menu item that people posted with images of everything from bent fenders to spoiled crops.

"Do you consider this a form of elder abuse?" the editor of *Second Chapter*, a magazine for seniors, asked the senator.

"You know, I hadn't considered that. But I think you're right," Sands said. "Who knows how many years this is taking off my life? I don't have the energy. And I'd much rather be playing with my grandchildren." On YouTube, a satirist's song, "Don't Have the Energy," got two million hits.

Some Democratic politicians called for an investigation into Dunn's charges. But others nibbled in support of Sands. One Republican congressman pointed out their hypocrisy, but most members of the Party of Lincoln weren't interested in defending a man who claimed he'd been sexually assaulted. It wasn't in keeping with their brand.

The P.R. firm Leland hired was quiet. George emailed the lawyer, asking when they would respond to the senator's media blitz. "Patience," the attorney counseled, but it was easy for her to say. She wasn't the one whose notoriety was growing.

The lawsuit against Saturn was dismissed as premature on the grounds that the publisher had never signed a contract with George. His parents hadn't identified the senator in their interview with Tovah Sparrow, so the suit against them was thrown out, too. There was little comfort for George in those victories.

He waited to be fired from the engineering journal and wasn't surprised when the editor came into his office one day looking as troubled as if he'd just learned "ain't" was in the dictionary. Rafi was a large man who wore his double-breasted suit jackets unbuttoned, his ties loosened, and had a Stanford ring jammed onto his finger. He'd treated George with only kindness. A reader or advertiser must have noticed George's name on the masthead and registered a protest.

George steeled himself. When he looked for his next job, he would use an alias. He hated to tell Kiara—who would stock up on canvas and bleak wool—that he'd been fired.

The editor took a seat opposite George. "How's it going?"

"Fine," George said, wishing he'd get on with it.

"People are so quick to judge," Rafi said. "They see something on the news, on Crave, and it makes them angry." The editor ran his hand through his thick black hair, then rested it on his stomach, as if the assignment were giving him indigestion.

George took a deep breath. If the man wanted to justify his decision, he would let him.

"Your work is excellent," Rafi said.

"Thank you."

"Everyone says so."

"I understand," George said. "I appreciate the opportunity you gave me."

"Okay, then."

George had known not to bring many personal items this time. Everything would fit in his briefcase. Lifting it to his lap, he said, "I'll clean out my desk."

The editor's eyes widened. "Oh, no! No, no, no! Is that what you think? No. No." He waved his hand. "I'm not here for that. I wanted to make sure you were okay. When I saw the news, I felt terrible. We don't want to fire you. You're much better than our last copyeditor. He kept hyphenating magnetic field even when it was used as a noun. No. No. I was just checking on you. I know what it's like to be unfairly judged."

"Thank you." George sank into his chair. He was so exhausted he felt he might slip to the floor, pooling there, his bones turned to ink.

"You have a job here as long as you want it. You will probably sell your book and leave, and that's fine, too."

George smiled. "I hope I do sell it. It took a long time to write it."

"I hope you sell it, too," Rafi said.

CHAPTER TWENTY-NINE

It was almost P.J.'s birthday. She was turning thirty-six, which was perilously close to forty, which was by anyone's standards old. Might as well throw herself a party while she still remembered how to enjoy one, she thought, and sent out electronic invitations:

When—Sunday, August 18, 3 p.m.
What—P.J.'s Birthday Party and Housewarming!
Feel free to bring two presents—JK!!!

At Eco Emporium, she registered for gifts, selecting a cork briefcase for her book tour, a toaster oven that doubled as an air fryer, running clothes, and online subscriptions to the magazines *Invisible Living* and *Unpaved*. A few days later, packages began to land in her lobby. She set the bounty on a card table she borrowed from Marissa.

The morning of the party, P.J. cleaned the apartment and hung pictures that had been leaning against the walls since she'd moved in. Several were from a trip to Peru she'd taken while she was married, images of Machu Picchu and the Plaza de Armas, but none of her or Vlad, who'd made a habit of trailing the fit, teenaged guide and sitting too close to her on the bus, before tipping her twice what was recommended.

At two-thirty, P.J. arranged platters of vegetables and white bean dip, cashew cheese and crackers, baba ghanoush and pita bread. While loading a cooler with beer, she jammed in three bottles of Bulldog non-alcoholic ale on the off-chance Mia would show up.

Her parents were first to arrive. Giving himself a tour of the condo, Lawrence inspected closets and turned on faucets, as if he might decide to purchase the unit next door if the water pressure were adequate. "Very nice. Very functional. Good for you, you're living your values," he said to P.J.

She savored the rare compliment while Lawrence examined the kitchen cabinets. When he came across a bottle of locally sourced, peach-infused vodka, he poured some over ice.

A woman P.J. hadn't seen since high school arrived with three small children. Glancing at the table full of sloppy foods, P.J. wondered if she could throw a sheet over her new sofa without insulting the woman before remembering she didn't have a clean one.

The doorbell rang, and P.J. let Franklin in.

"Happy housewarming birthday," he said.

"Thanks for the running shorts."

"Maybe we'll run together some time."

"Would you like to introduce us to your friend?" Dina said, appearing behind P.J. with Lawrence.

"Mom and Dad, this is Franklin. He was one of my passengers."

"I hope you gave her five stars," Dina said.

"She more than earned them," Franklin said. "Provided much more personalized service than I usually receive."

Lawrence's eyebrows—those neglected hedges—rose.

"Advice," Franklin quickly added. "She gave me some great advice."

"Ah," Lawrence said, his brow relaxing.

P.J. brought Franklin a glass of wine, then circulated among the guests.

Marissa let herself into the apartment, trailed by Len. After grabbing two bottles from the cooler, she greeted P.J. "We carpooled."

"You did?"

"Len was helping me select a retirement plan." Creases spiderwebbed across her white cotton shirt. "It was getting late, so we decided to head over together."

Bending to tie his shoe, Len said, "The plans are very involved. I wanted to make sure we went over them very, very thoroughly before Reese made her decision."

"Reese?" P.J. said.

"That's what my mother called me when I was a kid," Marissa said.

"Why didn't I know that?" P.J. said.

"I never used to like it." Marissa handed P.J. a gift bag. "From both of us."

"Which one of you forgot to buy me a gift?"

Len stared at a photo of the Amazon.

As P.J. pushed aside crepe paper, she said, "You have excellent taste in sports bras, Len."

"And thongs," he said.

P.J. dug beneath the bras. "And thongs. Thank you." She hugged her friends and sent them off to mingle.

People streamed in, ate, and paused in front of the window. They congratulated P.J. on her book and on the apartment. But no Mia, and, surprisingly, no Alex. She texted him, in case he'd forgotten.

P.J. refilled a bowl of corn chips, added crackers to a platter, and considered wiping the baba ghanoush from a small boy's fingers. She checked to see if Alex had responded. He hadn't. When she looked up, Franklin was standing in front of her.

"Everything okay?" he said.

"Fine. Just thought a friend of mine would be here."

"I've seen you looking at your phone."

"He's just a friend," P.J. said.

"Okay."

She stuck the phone in her pocket. "Are you having a good time?"

"I am. I had a talk with your father about teaching at the university."

"Why?"

"I think about it sometimes." Franklin swirled the wine in his still-full glass.

"Did he talk you out of it?" P.J. said.

"He loves the teaching part. He did say trying to publish something has been hard. He can't seem to sustain an idea for three hundred pages. He doesn't know how you do it."

"He said that?"

"That was the gist. He used bigger words."

"He does that."

Across the room, Dina handed Lawrence a slice of birthday cake. Len whispered something into Marissa's ear. When her friend laughed, P.J. briefly wished she'd been the one to make the joke. "I shouldn't have gotten upset at your house," P.J. said to Franklin. She glanced toward the door. "Or criticized Sharon. Thanks for coming."

"We're friends, remember?"

"Do you want something else to drink?" she said. "You don't seem to like the wine."

"I'm afraid to drink it. I drove here."

"You did? I mean, of course you did!"

"My therapist said to try short trips on the weekend when the roads are less crowded. I thought I could have one glass of wine but every time I'm about to take a sip, I picture myself running someone over on my way home."

P.J. took the wine from his hand and brought it into the kitchen. She returned with a glass of peach seltzer.

The crowd had begun to thin when Alex arrived empty-handed. He headed for what was left of the food. P.J. hadn't seen him since the charity race. The last few times she and Marissa had gone to Baxter's, Len had been there with colleagues from work or alone at the bar.

"Nice of you to show," she said.

He bit into a pita triangle topped with a lump of cashew cheese and covered his mouth with his hand. "I was in the middle of revising a scene and hated to stop."

"It's just my birthday."

"And your housewarming." He shoveled watery three bean salad into his mouth. "Nice couch."

"It came three weeks ago."

"I've been busy."

"Too busy to see your friends?"

"I'm trying to get the book done," Alex said. "Miracle of miracles, my agent finally got back to me. He had a few good suggestions, so I'm revising it again."

"A call would have been nice," P.J. said. "You know, with George Dunn being in the news so much."

"No offense, but it's always something lately. I have to focus. We don't all have huge book deals."

"Offense taken. I expected other writers to be jealous, but I didn't expect it from you. And I didn't think you would disappear."

"I'm here, aren't I?"

"Barely."

"Look, P.J. We're all getting older. I don't know how much longer I can keep going without having success. I'm not like you. I can't cause a scandal to draw attention to my novel."

Had he really just said that? While stuffing his face with her food?

Alex pinched corn chip crumbs, opened his mouth like a baby bird, and dropped them in. "Don't you feel even a little bad for Dunn?"

"I do feel bad for him. But I'm not sorry to have exposed the senator as a sexual predator."

"Whatever." He looked around for something else to eat.

"I don't understand why you're so angry at me," P.J. said.

"I'm not angry."

P.J. collected soiled plates. "You sound angry."

"We hooked up once and then you ignored my texts," Alex said. "I thought we had a good time, but I guess I was wrong."

"It's not that," P.J. said. "If we could have sex without all the other stuff it would be fine."

"What are you talking about?"

"What if your book doesn't sell?" P.J. said.

"Thanks for the vote of confidence," Alex said.

"Forget I said that. What if your book is wildly successful and mine flops?"

"It isn't going to flop."

"But what if it does?" she said. "And you're on *NPR* and *Good Morning America* and *Late Night*, a constant reminder to me that I failed."

As he considered the possibility of himself on national shows, Alex grinned.

"This is what I'm talking about," P.J. said.

***

"What are you in town for?" P.J. asked Darlene, a twenty-something in daisy leggings who slid into her car at the airport. A silver serpent corkscrewed through the girl's eyebrow, piercing it twice.

"The big writer's conference," Darlene said. "My first time. I'm ready to be deflowered."

"You'll like it. I went a couple times."

"Are you going this year? We could hang out."

"Too busy." P.J. had hoped to be invited to the conference to give a reading from *Girl Is in the House* or to sit on a panel of debut authors. When the conference organizers rejected all of her proposals, she cancelled her plans to attend.

She remembered what it had been like to be a young writer attending conferences. The thrill of being part of a crowd whose members all shared the same dream. How it had cemented her identity in a way that writing a book alone in her apartment couldn't. Her belief as she sat in hot, oversubscribed seminars that one day she would make her mark. The conversations with jaded authors whose novels had disappeared three months after they were released, people she'd learned to avoid while repeating the mantra: *not me*. Now, here she was, about to be a famous author.

Darlene was staying at a downtown Airbnb. P.J. hoped she wouldn't talk for the entire ride, but as it turned out, she needn't have worried. Once her passenger looked down at her phone, she didn't seem inclined to look up again.

For a while they drove in silence. Then P.J. said, "I've got a book coming out next year."

Darlene continued to scroll. "That's cool." Her phone clattered as she served a nibble, the sound inordinately loud. Had it always been that loud?

"Maybe you heard of the book. The title is *Girl Is in the House*."

"No."

"Are you sure? It's about a woman who's sexually assaulted by the chief of staff in a congressional office."

"Nope. Haven't heard of it," Darlene said.

"You probably will. Black Bear is publishing it."

"Okay."

P.J. bit into a cinnamon donut and offered one to Darlene.

"Sugar is poison," Darlene said. "Causes inflammation. You want a lemon slice? I always travel with them."

P.J. returned the half-eaten donut to a reusable container. "Um, no thanks. Maybe you saw my interview on *Rise and Shine America*. You know, the morning show? The host, Priscilla Logan, loved the book."

"Yeah. I don't watch that."

What was wrong with young people? Didn't they follow the news? P.J. drummed her hands on the steering wheel. "P.J. Larkin. Look it up."

Darlene sighed and typed something on her phone. "Says you accused an editor of stealing your book."

Was that the first thing people saw when they googled her? P.J. was tired of being known for the scandal rather than her work.

"I remember something about this," Darlene said. "But it was a while ago."

"A few months."

"Anyway, that's great that you sold your book. Things have

a way of working out, right? What happened to the editor? Did he lose his job?"

"It's complicated," P.J. said. Oil refineries pushed up from the ground, their smokestacks marring the view, their stench permeating the car through sealed windows. P.J. felt for the people who lived downwind, not coincidentally some of the city's poorest residents. Maybe she would write a book about them.

"Let's have a drink while I'm in town," Darlene said. "I'd love to hear the whole grisly story of how you took that editor down. Maybe my friends could come, too. That's what you should write a book about. I mean, I would read that. Your other book sounds fine. Kind of depressing, though. It's bad enough sexual assault happens. Does anyone really want to read a novel about it? Not me. I like a mystery or something funny. Have you read Sophie Kinsella? *Confessions of a Shopaholic*? I love that book.

"There's a bar down the street from where I'm staying. My friends and I are meeting there tonight. Why don't you come?"

P.J. would rather swim in an oil spill. At least the fish would be quiet. "I'm busy tonight," she said.

CHAPTER THIRTY

The Times ran a feature on the Wilma Sands controversy and in two concise paragraphs buried at the end debunked P.J.'s plagiarism claim. The reporter had read the two manuscripts. She wrote that although both dealt with sexual assault and included the points of view of the victimizer—which she noted had been done in *Lolita*, too—the plots couldn't have been more different and Dunn's novel contained not a hint of borrowed language. "There is paltry evidence that he was influenced by reading Larkin's manuscript," she concluded, "let alone that he plagiarized it."

The reporter had found a second male page who claimed he'd been sexually assaulted by the senator. The man agreed to be interviewed but insisted on remaining anonymous. Like Dunn, he described the senator grooming him with chocolates and cologne. Unlike Dunn, he hadn't managed to stop Sands when the relationship turned sexual. He'd been too shocked, too afraid to alienate her and forfeit his political career. A month after he returned from the Capitol, his mother found him in the garage with the car running and rushed him to the hospital.

Presented with the man's accusation, the senator was quoted as saying: "It's complete fiction. Work in politics as long as I did, and you make enemies. Perhaps I refused to give the young man a reference or gave him a bad one. I have often suffered because of my insistence on honesty and truthfulness when it came to people with whom I worked. Why don't you people talk to my chief of staff, who was by my side for my entire career and who could attest to the exemplary way I treated everyone from the least important Capitol staffers, the janitors and secretaries, to presidents who often sought my counsel? It's not lost on me that these complaints come from men who might resent a powerful woman, who might prefer power remain in male hands. With regard to anonymous sources, we live in the United States of America, a country that last time I checked believed people should be allowed to confront and cross examine their accusers. The Times has robbed me of that opportunity and sullied my good name. Shame on you, shame on the paper."

Waiting in bed for his turn to shower, George opened the story on his phone and read it in a kind of trance, forgetting periodically that the second page to whom it referred wasn't him. When he reached the end, he read it again. He hadn't invented what happened to him. He hadn't blown it out of proportion. He hadn't misinterpreted the senator's intentions. Her intentions were worse than he'd imagined.

The water went off in the bathroom, but George didn't move. He wondered if the other page had confided in anyone at the time of the assault and if his account had been dismissed like George's was. Could he have protected the other boy by going public sooner? George had extricated himself before the senator's behavior worsened though it had meant humiliating himself. His body had sensed how dangerous she was before his mind understood.

George set his phone on the nightstand and pulled the sheet over his head.

***

Alice Barsham, the Capitol custodian who'd cleaned up George's mess, read the paper online over coffee and cheese Danish. When she came to the senator's assertion that she'd treated custodial staff well, Alice said, "Everything that comes out of that woman's mouth is a lie."

Because he was used to Alice talking back to the newspaper, Bernard, her husband, didn't respond.

For decades, Alice had spent her nights at the Capitol, dusting, vacuuming, polishing furniture. Scrubbing stalls and urinals. She'd run across Sands when the senator worked late or when Alice picked up a day shift, but Sands rarely acknowledged her, and when she did, it was always as "you." "You, do that later." "You, the trash wasn't emptied yesterday." "You, everything on this desk is private. Do you understand the word 'private'? Who in God's name does the hiring around here?"

It infuriated Alice that the senator might get away with abusing children or that George might be penalized for telling the truth. She was ashamed to have remained silent for so many years, but she'd needed the job and she'd never had proof. All she'd had were the rumors that spread like a virus among the staff. It wasn't until she heard George at his news conference that she realized she might be the only person who could corroborate his story. If she came forward would Sands sue her, too?

Alice and her husband lived on small pensions, hers from the Capitol and his from a career as a D.C. Metrobus operator. They couldn't afford lawyers. Maybe she could talk to the reporter anonymously, like the second page had done. People would know it was a custodian but not which one. She ran the idea by Bernard.

He turned to the editorial section of the paper. "If George Dunn had become a politician like he wanted, he would have treated you as badly as the senator did. You don't owe him anything."

"You didn't see him. He was just a child."

"No, I didn't see him. But I know people like him and the senator. Let them destroy each other. We earned a quiet retirement."

"He didn't deserve what she did." Alice swept crumbs from the table onto her hand. "And that other page didn't, either. Poor man. I think I have to say something."

Bernard rattled the paper. "You don't have to. But I know you. It doesn't matter what I say."

"It matters."

From behind a theater review, he said, "Go ahead and call that reporter. Make sure she agrees not to use your name."

***

George called Janelle later that morning. "What does Saturn think of the *Times* piece?"

"Mary talked to legal," Janelle said. "The article helps with public opinion that's for sure. But without knowing who the other page is, it doesn't help you in court. They won't sign the contract while you're still being sued."

George couldn't seem to win. He knew writers produced stillborn books all the time, fat novels and memoirs buried forever in hard drives after they failed to sell, but he wasn't ready to accept that fate for *Up the Hill*.

"How's the job?" Janelle said.

George looked around the sparsely furnished office. Tacked to a battered corkboard were the style guide he'd been handed his first day and a photo of Mutt with her tongue out, poised to lick icing off a cellophane wrapper. At least it was an actual office. One with a door he'd been able to shut before calling his agent. "The job is fine. I'm learning a lot about capacitors and resistors."

"Maybe you'll write a book about an engineer."

"Maybe," George said. "I'm working on something else right now."

"Do you want to tell me about it?"

George swiveled his chair to the left. He didn't like talking about new projects, was afraid to dissipate the creative impetus that way instead of channeling it into the writing. He swiveled his chair to the right. But he was curious to hear his agent's feedback. He swiveled left. Yet what if she thought the idea for the book was crazy? Would he really abandon it? Right. Left. Right.

"No pressure," Janelle said. "No need to share it with me until you're ready."

He took a deep breath and in three sentences described the new book.

"Wow," Janelle said. "I love it. Send me what you've got."

Thank god.

***

P.J. laid a thick coat of peanut butter on a slice of toast before reading the *Times* article on her phone. How many people had the senator victimized? When she arrived at the paragraphs dismissing her plagiarism claim, she carved a tombstone with the epitaph *RIP PJ* in the peanut butter and took a bite. Still chewing, she called Sloane. "How badly will this hurt me?"

"P.J.?"

P.J. swallowed and sipped her coffee. "It's me. Did you read the article? Is Black Bear going to cancel my book?"

"I haven't heard from Black Bear and if they were concerned, they would have called. Hard to say if this will hurt you. If you're in the all-publicity-is-good-publicity camp, then it won't hurt you. Personally, I would have preferred you weren't in the piece."

"I shouldn't have accused Dunn."

Sloane didn't say anything.

"I think I need to apologize," P.J. said.

"Please don't. At least not publicly. Maybe just leave things alone?"

For once, P.J. could hear her agent thinking. "Okay."

After she hung up, P.J. looked at the article again. Without meaning to she'd attacked a survivor. An apology would reinforce the idea that survivors should be believed, a point she'd tried to make in her book. She called Marissa to see what she thought.

"I'm kind of busy," Marissa said. "Can we talk about this once I get home?"

"Sorry to bug you at your new job," P.J. said.

P.J. checked Crave. No one was nibbling about her. Though she should have been relieved, it irked her. She wondered what would happen if she nibbled an apology and tagged Dunn. Some people would condemn her for having accused him in the first place. But others might congratulate her for owning up to her mistake.

If Dunn forgave her, they could do a reading together when their books came out, their personal history guaranteed to draw a crowd. P.J. pictured the event at The Strand bookstore in New York.

When she was a child, her family had taken a Christmas trip to New York. Staring up at a Rockefeller Center tree far taller than her house, she'd tried to imagine the freakish ladder someone had climbed to place the star at the top. She ice skated with Mia in the famous rink, holding her sister's hand to steady her, while their parents watched from the sidelines. This time, she would invite Marissa to come along. They would visit museums, take in a show, and eat at fancy vegan restaurants, but the highlight would be the event with Dunn, two literary newcomers appearing in front of a packed audience anxious to have their hardcover copies signed. Any ill will the authors once felt for each other behind them.

More likely, Dunn wouldn't want to have anything to do with her. Why should he? But she would still apologize, so that when *Girl Is in the House* came out, guilt wouldn't mar her accomplishment.

P.J. typed: "I made a terrible mistake when I accused @GeorgeDunn of plagiarism. I didn't know he was a survivor. I jumped to a hasty conclusion because he wrote about sexual assault after reading my book on the same topic. I hope you'll forgive me, George. We must all #BelieveSurvivors." She served it before she could change her mind.

She stared at the nibble. Thirty seconds passed. (Had time always moved so slowly?) Then a minute. No one munched it. She closed the app because watching a nibble had never proved to be an effective way of drawing attention to it. Her toast had hardened, but she bit into it anyway, mashing her epitaph. On an old, unpopular social media site, she watched an animal-rescue video that she'd seen a month before on a different app. She checked her nibble again, sure that someone would have munched it. No one had. No one had re-served it, either. No one had joined the meal to praise or to condemn her. Not a single diner. Rather than feeling proud of her contrition, P.J. felt embarrassed to be ignored. She munched the nibble herself though she'd always thought people who did that seemed a bit desperate.

That night P.J. dreamed she was at The Strand. The bookstore was under water and every time she tried to read from *Girl Is in the House* entire schools of yellow and gray fish swam into her mouth.

CHAPTER THIRTY-ONE

George didn't see P.J.'s nibble right away because he'd shut her menu. A friend, one of the few who'd caught it, emailed it to him with the message: "Arsonist regrets fire."

George contemplated the performative nature of a public apology. The shallowness of it. The cowardice of hiding behind a nibble, rather than reaching out directly to the person you've injured to ask for forgiveness and how you might make amends. He deleted the email.

Recently he'd noted with satisfaction that *Girl Is in the House* hadn't made any lists of books to watch for and that P.J. hadn't been invited to speak on any literary or #metoo panels at the large publishing conferences. An on-line novel-writing class she was supposed to teach for a literary magazine had been cancelled for lack of interest. Her book was still scheduled for publication, but no one was talking about it or P.J.

***

On a Saturday, George took Seth, his Little Brother, to see a matinee of the latest Marvel movie. He cringed when Seth ordered a jumbo popcorn, soda, and candy, but the teenager had no way of knowing George and Kiara were still trying to make up financially for the time George had been out of work.

"Aren't you getting anything?" Seth said.

"I had a big lunch." They walked to the middle of the half-empty theater, and George relaxed into a springy velvet seat, glad to disappear into a fictional universe for a few hours. Kiara rarely complained about the chaos and uncertainty he'd introduced into their lives, but the other day he'd noticed a giant callus on her finger, the result of jabbing a latch hook into canvas over and over.

"I saw your news conference," Seth said.

"Do you want to ask me anything about it?" George said, hoping he wouldn't.

"I talked to my mother."

"That's good." George wondered if Seth's mother believed him, but it wasn't fair to press his young friend.

"I'm sorry about what happened to you."

"Thanks."

Seth placed the bucket of popcorn between them as they waited for previews to start. "When does your book come out?"

"They postponed it until a lawsuit with the senator is settled."

"Are you angry?"

George considered the question and was surprised to find that his feelings were complicated. "I'm angry the book might never be published and that the woman who falsely accused me of plagiarism will probably get away with it. But I got a lot out of writing the book." He'd needed to deal with what happened with the senator. A part of him had to have known that writing about it could lead to going public. Even if P.J. hadn't accused him, interviewers would have asked why he chose the subject of sexual assault, and the honest answer would have been because it happened to him. "I really hope it gets published. No one should be able to shut down a book without having read it. It's a very ugly kind of censorship."

Seth sipped his drink. "What if a mass murderer wrote a book?"

"I'm not saying no one should ever be cancelled. I don't think mass murderers should be given platforms. But to cancel a book by a person no one's ever heard of based on speculation about what's in it? That's fucked up."

"I read they were going to give you a million dollars for the book. Will you still get the money?"

George helped himself to popcorn. "I don't know."

"If I had that kind of money, I'd buy two Ferraris."

"Why two?"

"One for my mother. She could drive it to her tiling jobs. It would mess with her clients' heads. That's all they'd talk about once she left. They'd be nicer to her. They wouldn't even realize they were doing it. If she was delayed because another job went long, instead of complaining, they'd say 'no worries.'"

"Maybe they'd want to pay her less because they'd think she didn't need the money," George said.

That's not how it works," Seth said, angling his head as if he were surprised he had to explain something so obvious to his mentor. "If you're poor, people think you don't need money. They think you're used to being poor. They think it's okay for you to earn minimum wage at a department store where they randomly cut your hours. But if you're rich, they think you have a lifestyle that's expensive and you need to be paid well. They might not even know that's what they think, but they do. They identify with you without realizing it."

George looked at Seth. When had the kid transitioned from The Hardy Boys to Bernie Sanders? "It might be hard for her to get all of her equipment into a Ferrari."

"Details."

The lights dimmed. Seth offered George the box of candy and he took it and shook some into his hand, appreciating the thoughtful person Seth had become. George didn't know if he'd played any role in that but at least he hadn't ruined him.

***

As the final credits rolled, George got up and stretched. They waited for the crowd to thin before making their way to the exit. Outside, rain threatened. Car headlights had come on. George drove them to a comic book store where they browsed, the owner recognizing them as past customers and leaving them alone.

"Dinner?" George asked, because it was their habit.

"How about if I pay this time?" Seth earned money programming video games during the summer, but George wanted him to save it for college, or for his own needs or his mother's.

"Nope," George said. "But let's go someplace cheap. Like Monster Burgers." Rain pelted his Subaru as they drove to the restaurant. When they hit a pothole, the car rattled like the collection of old parts that it was. "A Ferrari, huh?"

"Not really. My mother would make me put the money in the bank. I'd be lucky if she let me buy a pair of Jordans."

George made a mental note to try to get Seth the sneakers for his high school graduation.

***

On his way home, after dropping Seth off, George stopped at a craft store. He picked out two skeins of the darkest yarn he could find, a color called wine, but if there was any red in them, he couldn't see it. He tossed them in a basket, added a canvas, and asked the clerk to wrap them.

During a recent exercise suggested by his therapist, he and Kiara had sat naked opposite each other on the bed for twenty minutes without touching, describing what they saw, all the qualities they loved, physical and otherwise. It helped that George was a man of words, and that their ordeal had deepened his appreciation of her. Neither ran out of things to say before Kiara's phone timer went off, playing the song she had set for the occasion, Prince's "Do Me, Baby."

***

The New York Times ran a follow-up piece in which they interviewed Alice Barsham. As she requested, they didn't use her name. "His jacket was wrapped around his waist, but I could see he'd wet himself. Poor boy. He was so young and so distressed. I could tell something terrible had happened," she said. And: "They used to come out of her office at all hours, young male pages and staff." The senator had responded, "More anonymous sources. My goodness. A regular witch hunt. Some custodian claims they saw a bizarre thing decades ago but just remembered it now. Makes one wonder. I don't recall George Dunn pissing in my office, but I wouldn't be surprised if he had. He was unstable. If I told someone a dog did it, I was just trying to spare Dunn embarrassment. Treating someone with kindness wasn't a crime last time I checked. And it's true, I worked late. The people's business required it. Pages and staff sometimes helped."

The article was widely quoted by other news media, and public opinion swung farther from the senator. Unfortunately, like the account of the second page, it couldn't help George in court because Leland didn't know who the custodian was. Rather than encouraging the senator to drop the case, the developments made her dig in. "She's determined to use a trial to clear her name," her lawyers told Leland, who in turn told George and his parents during a video conference.

"I still don't remember seeing a custodian," George said.

"Not surprising," Leland said. "You were in shock."

The light in George's apartment, usually inadequate, glowed with the warmth of a Mediterranean sun. Was that what it felt like to be believed?

***

At 2 a.m., an Ivy League student served a nibble demanding her university cancel an invitation to Sands to give a prestigious lecture. After he munched it, a state college professor drafted a nibble of his own, calling on his administration to revoke an honorary doctorate it had bestowed on Sands. By mid-morning both nibbles had been re-served more than ten thousand times and Wilma Sands was a popular menu item. Later that day, the CEO of a corporation that employed Sands as a consultant had discreet conversations with its lawyer and a headhunter. The publisher who had bought the rights to the senator's memoir sent her an email and quietly removed the book from its list. Politicians from both parties drafted statements condemning her behavior. Neal Sands purchased as much digital currency as he could with money from the couple's joint account. After confirming the purchase, he bought a one-way ticket to the Seychelles, packed a suitcase, and ordered a rideshare.

When he looked up the senator on Wikipedia, George was gratified to see a new section. Yet despite the near-complete destruction of the senator's reputation and professional life, she still refused to drop the lawsuit.

CHAPTER THIRTY-TWO

The proposed cover of P.J.'s book featured a building with fluted columns and the shadow of a woman who'd just passed through. P.J. didn't love the pastel colors, or the outline of the woman in a dress, but at least the columns suggested the Capitol and the sun wasn't setting like in some cheap romance novel. Babette Aller approved P.J.'s manuscript revisions, added a few of her own, and sent the book off to copy editing. Famous authors who owed Babette favors wrote effusive blurbs, and the editor forwarded them to P.J. "No one captures the devastating effects of sexual assault quite like P.J. Larkin. Read this and weep." "Riveting…a great American novel for our times." After reading them, P.J. shook her fists at the ceiling like a victorious prize fighter, then fell into her armchair, relieved. Within minutes she'd nibbled them, bragged about them in an email sent to her entire contact list, and pasted them into an electronic scrapbook she'd begun keeping.

A few days later, her publicist contacted her about scheduling book store events in several Colorado cities, but when P.J. asked if she'd be reading in New York, Boston, or Los Angeles, or perhaps Seattle or Portland, the woman apologized and said there wasn't enough interest.

P.J. supposed she'd need something to wear to those book store readings, even if they were only in Colorado. Not wanting to distract Marissa from her new responsibilities, she invited her mother to shop with her.

***

"This is almost as much fun as when we looked for your wedding dress," Dina said, a stack of blouses draped over her arm as she and P.J. browsed in the vintage clothing store Madonna's Closet.

The "almost" nettled P.J. Was there a ruder word in the English language? In the dressing room, she tried on a structured sky-blue shirt.

"Your father has some good news," Dina called over the dressing room door.

"Did he finish his book?"

"No. I'm not sure he ever...." Her mother's voice trailed off.

"Then what's his good news?"

"A university press approached him about publishing a collection of his lectures. One of his former students is an editor there."

P.J. stepped out of the dressing room. "Which color do you like better, the blue or the red?" She held up the red so her mother could compare them. "Do you think he'll be able to do it?"

"The blue. I hope so. He's written the lectures. He just has to put them together, write an introduction, and maybe edit them a little?"

"The red makes a bolder statement." P.J. stepped back into the dressing room and took off the blouse.

"That won't be too much for him, will it?" Dina said. "The editor will help him, right?"

"He'll at least give him a deadline," P.J. said. "That could be just what he needs."

Dina opened the dressing room door a crack and handed P.J. a pair of off-white slacks. "Don't tell him I said anything. He wants tell you himself. Act surprised. And happy."

P.J. stepped into the slacks. "I don't have to act happy. I am happy."

"I can't always tell. And, P.J., when he talks to you about it, don't bring up your own book."

"Okay… I guess."

"Just let the conversation be about him," Dina said.

"I said, okay." P.J. looked in the mirror and saw an image of herself she would have preferred not to see.

***

While P.J. waited for George Dunn to acknowledge her apology, Labor Day came and went. In the mountains, backyard gardens froze, aspens began to turn, and bears broke into homes to forage in well-stocked pantries. When P.J. drove after dark, passengers insisted she turn on the heat—wasting precious charge—instead of making do with the blanket she'd thoughtfully left on the back seat. Following Aram's advice, P.J. had tried to give Mia space. But her sister still wasn't returning Dina's calls, and P.J. thought of one more spot where she might find her.

The Monday night AA meeting met in a church basement. P.J. had attended it with Mia when her sister first got out of rehab, and Dina had gone there to give Mia a cake on the fifth anniversary of her sobriety. P.J. looked around but didn't recognize anyone.

"Do you know if Mia Larkin's been coming lately?" she asked a man loosening his paisley tie.

"We don't talk about who comes here," the man said gently.

P.J. blushed. "Sorry. I forgot." She sat on a folding chair, not far from the door. The meeting started, and people got up and shared their stories. P.J. doubted she'd have the courage to speak so honestly about her screwups. Being a fiction writer allowed her to hide the darkest parts of herself behind invented narratives. It was a privilege she'd stolen from George Dunn.

When the door opened, P.J. turned. A woman Mia's age and demeanor entered, and P.J.'s heart lurched toward her, but it wasn't her sister.

***

It was perhaps odd to follow an AA meeting with a visit to Baxter's, but earlier in the day, Marissa had said she would try to stop by the bar for a drink. P.J. spotted Alex and Len in a booth. "I know you guys!" She flagged down a server and ordered a Cosmo.

"My agent loved the revisions," Alex said, before P.J. had even sat down.

"That's great!" She'd decided to forget their conversation at the party. He'd been stressed trying to finish his book. If anyone could understand that, she could. She slid onto the bench next to Len.

"Maybe you won't be the only success," Alex said.

"I'm a success," Len said.

Alex sipped his beer. "You know what I mean. Literary success."

Plucking the olive from his vodka martini, Len said, "Pretty narrow definition." He popped the fruit into his mouth.

Alex looked buoyant. His cheeks were flushed, as if he'd sprinted to the bar to share his good news. Maybe they would both have successful literary careers. If that were the case, why shouldn't they get together? Hadn't their relationship always been headed in that direction? They could be one of those literary power couples, like Nicole Krauss and Jonathan Safran Foer.

P.J.'s and Len's phones buzzed. It was a text from Marissa. "Can't make it sry. ☹."

"I thought she'd come, knowing she'd get to see you," Len said.

"That's funny. I thought you'd be the attraction," P.J. said.

Len slipped off his sport jacket, folded it, and set it next to him. "We rarely go out on weeknights. If I want to see her, I have to go to her place and watch her work. It isn't as bad as it sounds. She finishes eventually."

"What are your fantasies for when you make it?" P.J. said to Alex. "You, too," she added, not wanting to exclude Len.

"I already made it." Len loosened his tie. "Jesus, you're such snobs."

"If my book sells, I'm moving to New York," Alex said.

In the condensation on her cocktail glass, P.J. drew an airplane, nose up, though the first image that had come to mind was an empty bar stool. She took a long sip.

"Nice knowing you," Len said.

Alex looked at his phone as if he might find more good news from his agent on it. Or maybe he was seeing what rents were in Brooklyn or checking his company's remote work policy. "No offense, but this town is dead."

"Maybe it's just sleeping off a bad hangover." P.J. rotated her cocktail glass and scribbled a line of Z's in the condensation on the other side.

"Or in a coma after getting hit hard by a defensive end," Len said.

"Or maybe it consumed too many edibles," said the server. He removed their empty glasses and took orders for fresh drinks.

"Don't you guys ever dream of a different life?" Alex said.

P.J. thought about it, while absentmindedly scrolling

through Crave.

"I like my life," Len said. "I like my girlfriend, though I wish she wasn't so busy. I like my friends. I like helping people invest their money. I wish my father wasn't sick and that taking care of him wasn't going to make my mother's life hard. But other than that, no, I don't dream of a different life."

"I used to think I wanted a different life," P.J. said, putting down her phone, "a life where I was famous. But if it means losing my family, or Marissa, or you guys, I don't think so. I'm glad I have a book coming out, but no, I don't want a new life. I went to an AA meeting tonight."

"Is there something you want to tell us?" Alex said.

"It wasn't for me. I was looking for Mia. I'm worried that she relapsed and that it's my fault." P.J. went to work on the fresh Cosmo the server had set down.

Len turned to face her. "Because of the book?"

She lowered her glass. "Yeah."

"I know I've given you shit," he said, "but you tried pretty hard to conceal her identity, didn't you?"

"I did," P.J. said.

"And Mia could tell that when she read it, right?"

"Yeah."

"And she's a grown up, who's responsible for her own choices when it comes to alcohol, right?"

P.J. grunted and picked up the Cosmo.

"So maybe if anything happened—and I'm not saying anything did—but maybe you don't get to take the blame." Len turned back toward the table.

P.J. rested her head against the back of the booth, worn out from driving and writing and imagining all the awful things that could have happened to her sister. Tipping back her glass, she felt a drop on her tongue, and wondered where her drink had gone. Though she was starving, the idea of eating the bar's greasy food turned her stomach. When she tried to lift her water glass, it slipped through her fingers, crashing onto the table.

Len tossed a thin drink napkin onto the spill and slid toward the wall. P.J. leapt up. An alert server grabbed a pile of dinner napkins and sopped up the water. He dried P.J.'s seat. Raising his eyebrows, he took P.J.'s order for another Cosmo.

In the bathroom, P.J. had little success drying her shirt and pants with the hand dryer. Giving up, she peed while rereading Marissa's text, experiencing fresh disappointment. She wondered how much of her life she spent reliving bad news on her phone. Too much.

A flamingo pink cocktail awaited her at the table. Len was saying something about the markets, and ordinarily she would have paid attention because he knew his stuff, but just then she didn't believe she could follow it. She sipped the sweet drink. She'd have to ask one of the men to drive her home. Or order a Ride With Me, but the goddamn company didn't offer drivers a discount. She was on Len's way home, but she'd rather ask Alex and see where things went when they reached her apartment. She didn't care that she'd left her place a mess, the bed unmade, the sheets as crumpled as discarded paper. She laughed thinking about it.

"What's so funny?" Alex said.

P.J.'s head rocked against the back of the booth. "How's your sex life?" Alex's face fell, and through a muddle of alcohol, P.J. realized he thought she was mocking him. She tried to think of a way to explain without giving away her hopes for the evening.

"I'm actually seeing someone," he said. "Her name is Cheryl. We work together. Well, not together, but she works at the same company. She's in IT. And she doesn't ignore my texts."

P.J. sipped her drink. Her timing, as usual, was shit. Why had it taken her so long to realize that it could work with Alex? That she wanted it to work. "What is she, a geek?"

"She's smart, if that's what you mean."

"What do you talk about, semiconductors? Or maybe you don't talk at all. Is that it? Waiter!" P.J. lifted her empty glass. "Waiter!" she shouted, and a couple at the bar turned to look.

"You're drunk." Alex shook his head at the server who appeared.

"Are you going to show her your writing? Or will the two of you go to lectures about systems administration? That should be fascinating. Have you told her you're planning to move? Or are you keeping that a secret, so she'll keep fucking you?"

"You should stop talking now," Len said to P.J.

"At least she doesn't have to worry about me betraying her secrets in my work," Alex said.

P.J.'s head flopped to the side. "You're an asshole. You know that?"

Alex got up and threw two twenties on the table. "I'm calling it a night. Will you get her home?" he asked Len.

"I can get myself home," P.J. said.

"I'll take care of her." Len paid and helped P.J. to his car. As they drove toward her apartment, P.J. remembered that Nicole Krauss and Jonathan Safran Foer were divorced.

**

Later that night, too late, P.J. called Marissa. "What's wrong with me?"

Marissa sighed. "There's nothing wrong with you. But you should probably try to sleep. Don't you have to drive tomorrow?"

P.J. was sitting in bed in a nightshirt. She couldn't lie down without the room spinning. "Did I wake you?"

"You know what they say, 'I had to get up, anyway, to answer the phone.'"

"Is Len there?"

"No, but he told me what happened," Marissa said.

"I should have dated Alex when I had the chance," P.J. said.

"What about your rule?"

"It's a stupid rule."

"You'll meet someone else."

"I don't want someone else."

"What about Franklin?" Marissa said.

"He's getting over his wife. And he said he wants to be friends. And you know what that means. It means he's not attracted to me." P.J. got up and walked toward the kitchen, steadying herself on the back of the couch.

"Maybe you should focus on your book."

"That's easy for you to say. You have Len." P.J. filled a glass with water from the tap and drank it. "Maybe it was Alex who talked to the *Pedestal* reporter. You know, the anonymous source? He knew the book was inspired by what happened to Mia."

"He wouldn't do that. You guys are friends."

P.J. set the glass in the sink. "It sucked that you weren't there tonight."

"I shouldn't have said I would come. There's so much to learn, and I want to do a good job."

"I know," P.J. said. "I want you to do a good job, too. I should let you sleep."

"Think about the positive stuff," Marissa said. "Your apartment. Your book."

"I'd like to meet someone."

"You will. And then you'll get annoyed that he still calls you a teacher when he introduces you to his friends and forgets to wipe the sink after he shaves. And he'll get annoyed when you buy a new car with the money he suggested putting into tech stocks."

P.J. made her way to the window. "Things aren't perfect with Len?"

"Things are never perfect."

"Are you saying that just to make me feel better?"

"I'm saying it because it's true and also to make you feel better," Marissa said.

"You're a good friend. Go to sleep."

Marissa hung up. P.J. opened the window and breathed in the dry, cold air. Above the moonlit Rocky Mountains hung a distant sky. Galaxies in which her relationship problems, her forthcoming book, and the pain she'd caused George Dunn meant nothing. A universe of stars indifferent to the blue-green earth she was trying in her small ways to save.

She would call home tomorrow, congratulate her father again, and ask him to lunch, just the two of them, somewhere near campus. It had been years since they'd done that. She used to talk the whole time about the stories and essays she was publishing, never thinking about how it might make him feel. This time, she would ask about his collection of lectures and get his advice about being a homeowner. She would listen for a change. At least she would try.

CHAPTER THIRTY-THREE

Leland arranged to depose the senator's former chief of staff in a hotel conference room in Maryland. She called George and asked him to attend. "It may be harder for him to lie with you in the room."

"You're not sure?" George said.

"You have to remember the guy worked in D.C. for decades. He may not even know what a lie is anymore. But he may. If he still has a conscience, it'll be harder for him to lie with you there."

George heard mints rattling in a box. "I'll switch the days I'm working."

"Good." The lawyer hung up without saying good-bye.

On the day of the deposition, George left his apartment at four in the morning and arrived at the hotel at nine, wired from the three energy drinks he'd had on the way. His mother had invited him to drive down the night before and stay with them, but it would have meant listening to his father complain about Leland's bills. Instead, he and Kiara had curled up on the couch after dinner, eating pretzels and drinking wine from gas station tumblers. They'd binge-watched a show about a family with eighteen children. When Mutt barked at the doorbell on the show, George rewarded her with a handful of pretzels.

"When she barfs, you're cleaning it up," Kiara had said.

He'd moved his hand to the inside of her thigh. "I'll wear a butler outfit. You can give me all kinds of orders."

Handing his car key to the hotel valet, he wished Kiara was with him. He wished he'd listened to her and washed the car and thrown away the dozens of home brochures he'd plucked from yard boxes when he'd thought they were going to be rich.

The front desk clerk pointed him toward a large conference room with windows that looked out onto the street. George tried to read a good omen in the sunshine, but the weather was as bright for the senator's legal team. Approaching the roomful of lawyers in custom suits, he felt underdressed in his sport jacket and khakis. To his great relief, Sands wasn't there. He'd wanted to ask Leland whether the senator would attend but couldn't without betraying an anxiety of which he was ashamed.

The senator's attorneys introduced themselves. The older of the two was his father's age. On a legal pad in front of him lay a fountain pen with an extra-long nib that could serve as a weapon if things went badly. The junior attorney wiped a doughy hand on his suit pants before extending it to George. The lawyers flanked a man whose bristly white hair horse-shoed around his bald spot. His navy suit jacket strained at the button, and an American flag pin pierced his lapel. George had met Marshall Davis, the senator's chief of staff, several times at the Capitol. Davis nodded to George, and George, ever polite, nodded back, as if the man weren't there to destroy his reputation. Leland motioned for George to sit opposite Davis.

As they were about to start, the senator appeared in the doorway. George's leg began to bounce and he tried unsuccessfully to still it with his hand. The senator's hair hadn't been styled. Since George had seen her on TV, her white roots had grown out as thick as a skunk's stripe. She'd lost weight, and her black suit swallowed her. There was something newly feral about her. Having nothing more to lose, she seemed to have abandoned even the pretense of propriety. She stood over the junior attorney until he rose from his chair, opening up a seat for her next to Davis. "Water," she said to the young man, as he was pulling out a chair for himself. He filled her glass from the pitcher on the table.

The senator stared at George, and he felt a corset tighten around his chest. She patted Davis on the shoulder. "Just another chapter in our long history together," she said. "We'll get through this like we did all the rest. We're not the flavor of the month. So what?"

After Davis was sworn in, Leland asked a number of preliminary questions to put him at ease. Then she came to the heart of the deposition. "What did the senator tell you happened with George Dunn?"

"She said he came on to her," the chief of staff said. He clasped his hands loosely on the table, the tips of his thumbs touching.

"Can you be more specific?"

"She said Dunn tried to kiss her." Davis spoke with no more emotion than if he were commenting on traffic.

"Anything else?"

"Told her she was beautiful." The senator rewarded Davis with a smile. George's leg bounced faster. He doubted he would make it through all the questions.

"Now, Mr. Davis," Leland said, "does that sound to you like something a sixteen-year-old would say to a woman his mother's age, a woman who was one of the most powerful people in the country? You do know George was sixteen at the time, right?"

"Objection. Compound question," the senior attorney said.

"I'll withdraw it," Leland said. "How did the senator seem after the incident?"

"What do you mean, how did she seem?" Davis said.

"Did she seem upset?" Leland reached into her pocket and pulled out the box of mints. She tapped it gently on the table.

Davis looked at the candy.

"Mr. Davis?" Leland said.

"What was the question?"

Leland had the court reporter read it back.

"She wasn't upset," Davis said. "She was laughing. She said Dunn had a crush on her."

"And did you believe her?" Leland said.

"Naturally."

"Why, 'naturally'?"

"She was always honest with me," Davis said.

The senator nodded. She rested her hand briefly on Davis's arm, giving it a friendly squeeze.

Leland popped a mint into her mouth. "How do you know she was always honest?"

"I never caught her in a lie." Davis's eyes roamed the room and he tapped his thumbs together impatiently, as if the proceeding was an annoying chore.

"I see," Leland said. "But you investigated the incident, correct?"

"What do you mean?" Davis said.

"You talked to Mr. Dunn and asked him what happened."

The senator looked up from her phone.

"No," Davis said.

It had never occurred to George that he was owed this. That it wasn't only the senator and his parents who had injured him, but every other person who'd enabled the senator's behavior or covered it up or looked the other way. He felt more tired than he'd imagined possible.

"Let me get this straight," Leland said. "The senator said Mr.

Dunn tried to kiss her, and you didn't talk to Mr. Dunn about it? Not even to tell him how inappropriate his behavior was?"

"No."

"Why not?"

"That wasn't, it wasn't my job," Davis said.

"It wasn't because you thought George might tell a different story than the senator?"

"No."

"If George had told you something different, if he had said that it was the senator who kissed him, you would've had a problem on your hands, wouldn't you?" Leland said.

"Objection. Calls for speculation," the senior attorney said.

"I'll withdraw it. What exactly was your job as chief of staff?" Leland asked.

"To make sure the senator's office ran smoothly." Davis clasped his hands a bit more tightly now and his eyes had ceased to wander.

"If it got out that the senator sexually assaulted George Dunn, that would interfere with the smooth running of the office, wouldn't it?"

"That isn't—"

"Wouldn't it, Mr. Davis?"

"I suppose."

"Don't agree with her," the senator muttered.

Davis blushed.

"Let me ask you something else," Leland said. She tapped the box of mints on the table. "Did you talk to other Capitol staff to see if George had behaved inappropriately at other times?"

"No."

"Or to tell them he had behaved inappropriately with the senator?"

"No."

"What about the head of the page program? Did you tell him that George acted inappropriately?" Leland said.

"No." Davis looked at his watch.

"We have lots of time," Leland said. "Don't you think the head of the page program would have wanted to know if George acted inappropriately?"

"I don't know."

"You don't know?"

"I don't know."

"That's better," the senator said softly.

"You didn't talk to other Capitol staff or the head of the page program because what really happened was that the senator assaulted George Dunn. Isn't that right?" Leland said.

"That's not what the senator told me." He glanced at his old boss but she was looking at her phone again.

"You didn't tell the head of the page program because you didn't want him to talk to George, did you?"

"I didn't think about it."

"He would have asked George what happened, wouldn't he?"

Davis looked toward the senior attorney.

"Calls for speculation," the attorney said.

"I'll withdraw it," Leland said.

"You'll never know what the head of the page program would have said or done because you didn't bother telling him, isn't that right?"

"Stupid question," the senator muttered.

"Let's take a five minute break," the senior attorney said. "If that's okay with you, Counsel."

"Sure," Leland said.

"Senator, can we have a word outside?" the senior attorney said.

George stepped out to use the restroom. On his return, he passed the senator and her attorneys huddled and arguing.

They reconvened and Leland reminded Davis he was still under oath. "You didn't really believe the senator, did you?"

"I believed her."

"You're telling me you believed a highly ambitious sixteen-year-old boy who hoped to have a political career would jeopardize the incredible opportunities that went along with being a page in order to kiss the senator?" Leland tapped the mints on the table.

George wondered whether Leland was really trying to quit smoking.

The chief of staff rubbed his chin. "I don't know."

The senator put her hand back on Davis's arm, but it didn't seem friendly this time.

"Let me ask you something else," Leland said. "Without disclosing anyone's identity, while you were chief of staff did anyone else make complaints against the senator that you're aware of?"

Davis unbuttoned his jacket. "What kind of complaints?"

"Complaints that the senator assaulted them. Like George's."

"No, there were never any complaints like that that I was aware of during that time."

"And what about before or after you were chief of staff?" Leland said. "Did you become aware of any complaints against the senator then?"

"Other than the one by George Dunn?"

"Yes, other than that one."

Davis wrote something on the senior attorney's legal pad

and the attorney nodded. "I saw something in the paper about that the other day," Davis said, "but I don't know anything about it other than what the story said."

"No one gives a rat's ass what you read in the paper," Sands said.

"Senator, please," the senior attorney said.

Leland stared at the box of mints. "And, again, without disclosing anyone's identity, did the senator ever tell you that someone else acted inappropriately with her?"

The senator slid her empty glass in front of the junior attorney and he refilled it.

"Behaved inappropriately?" Davis said.

"Came on to her sexually. Like she says George Dunn did. Please take a moment to think about it." Leland mashed a mint between her teeth.

The chief of staff looked toward the senior attorney.

"Counsel, please instruct your client to answer," Leland said.

The senator stood. "No. Don't answer."

George trembled. He couldn't seem to get enough air. He wondered why Leland didn't intervene to have the senator excluded from the deposition.

Sands turned toward her senior attorney. "What does this have to do with George Dunn defaming me?"

"Senator," the attorney said, "please let me handle this."

"Handle it then." She sat down.

Marshall Davis drained the glass of water before him. He closed his eyes and then opened them. "What was the question?"

Leland had the court reporter read it back.

"Yes," he said.

"Just so I'm clear," Leland said, putting another mint in her mouth. "The senator came to you regarding a staff member or a page other than George Dunn and said they came on to her."

The chief of staff looked down at his hands which were clasped on his lap. "Yes."

"Please speak up so the court reporter can hear you," Leland said.

"Yes," the chief of staff barked.

"Was she upset when she told you?"

"She was laughing," Davis said. "She said a certain page was in love with her. She said they were always falling in love with her."

"And by 'they,' she meant pages?"

"Yes."

"How many times did the senator tell you a page or a staff member acted inappropriately with her?" Leland said.

"Don't you dare answer," the senator said.

"Senator, please," the senior attorney said.

"I couldn't say," Davis said.

"That's better," Sands muttered.

Leland ignored the senator. "Was it more than three?"

The senator laughed. She softly mimicked Leland: "'*Was it more than three?*'" Then she added, perhaps to reassure herself or perhaps because she'd forgotten there were others in the room, "You don't remember. Isn't that right, Marshall? You don't remember anything unless I say you remember it."

Davis unclasped his hands.

Leland tapped the mints. "Was it more than three?"

The senator turned toward her former chief of staff. She thrust her face into his. "Don't you dare. You may think I'm powerless. But I promise you, I'm not."

Out of the corner of his eye, George saw a smile flutter across Leland's face.

Davis turned from the senator. For the first time since the questioning began, he looked at George. Goose pimples covering his scalp, George ignored the scowl the senator was directing at him and nodded at Davis. "Please," he mouthed, though it drew the ire of both of the senator's attorneys. "Yes, it was more than three," Davis said.

The senator slammed her palm on the table. Water jumped in the junior attorney's glass. George flinched.

"Was it more than five?" Leland said.

George couldn't imagine so many victims. Trying to swallow a sip of water, he coughed, and Leland threw a stern look at him.

"Could I have some more water?" Davis said.

The senior attorney stabbed his pad with the fountain pen. "Why don't we take a short break?"

"I won't be too much longer," Leland said.

"I'm okay," said Davis.

"You sure you don't need a break?" the senior attorney said. It didn't sound like a suggestion.

Davis's chin slumped toward the flag pin. His tie was askew. He looked like he needed a break. "Let's continue," he said. The junior attorney refilled his glass and Davis drank. "What was the question?"

"I'll rephrase it." Leland tapped the box as she thought. "Would you say the senator came to you at least five times regarding staff members or pages other than George Dunn and said they had come on to her?"

The senator stood up. She hovered over her former chief of staff, and George thought she might strike him.

In the distance, George heard a pile driver and cars banging over a metal plate in the road.

Softly, the chief of staff said, "Yes."

With that, something broke in Sands. Shaking her head and mumbling, she walked toward the brightly lit windows and ignored the rest of the proceeding.

"Could it have been more than five times?" Leland said.

"Around that. She served for a long time. I can't say exactly."

George gripped his glass but didn't sip from it. How many pages had there been? Or had some of the others been staff members who were afraid to come forward because they valued their jobs and their places in the party?

"You can't say exactly?" Leland said.

"No."

"Because she served for a long time."

"Yes."

"Did you think it was odd that so many young people were acting inappropriately with the senator?"

Davis didn't answer.

"Counsel—" Leland began.

"I'm going to object for the record because what he thought was irrelevant," the senior attorney said. "But you can answer."

"Yes," Davis said.

"Yes, you thought it was odd?"

"Yes."

"But you didn't investigate what was really happening?"

"No."

"Because you didn't really believe the senator, did you?" Leland said.

"At the time, I trusted her."

"But you don't believe her now."

"No."

"You've had a long relationship with the senator, isn't that right?"

"Yes."

"Would you consider yourself loyal to her?"

"I was, yes."

"That's all. Thank you." Leland dropped the box of mints into her pocket.

**

Behind the wheel of his Subaru, George was trembling so hard he could barely see the cars darting around him. He found a nearby motel and checked in. After talking to his therapist, he called Kiara.

"You never have to see her again," Kiara said.

"I'm afraid I'll never stop seeing her."

**

The next day, the senator dropped the suit. George and Kiara were celebrating over sushi when Janelle called. "Saturn wants to sign the contract. They think *Up the Hill* is going to be huge because of the scandal involving the senator. And I sent them the pages from your new book and they love it and want to acquire it, too." When he paid the check, George left a tip so large the restaurant called him later to make sure it wasn't a mistake.

CHAPTER THIRTY-FOUR

"I had my last therapy session," Franklin said, as he and P.J. strolled past a display of motorized rollerblades at the alternative energy show, one of the many products P.J. figured were sponsored by orthopedic surgeons whose practices were slow. Franklin plucked two promotional toy cars from a table and pocketed them. "I mentioned you to the doctor."

"I told you I was sorry."

"Not about what happened at the house."

A solar golf cart beeped while backing up. Conference attendees gripping stiff tote bags jabbered about sessions they planned to attend.

"That first day in your car, I was distraught," Franklin said.

"I noticed."

"I was a stranger. You could have turned up the radio. Written me off as just another wacked out pot tourist. But instead you tried to help. When I thought about it later, I realized that even though I missed my chance to be kind to Sharon ever again, there will be other people I can help. It doesn't make up for what happened, it never will, but it's something."

"Yes. And for the record, I'm nice to pot tourists, too. A couple once left me an in-kind tip," P.J. said.

Franklin examined an electric bicycle. "How fast does it go?" he asked the manufacturer's rep.

The guy's suit was made for a larger man. His pants pooled at the floor. "Speed is overrated," he said, looking past Franklin.

"But if that's what you really care about, instead of saving the planet, twenty-eight miles per hour."

As they walked away, Franklin smiled.

"What?" P.J. said.

"He reminds me of someone."

P.J. gave Franklin the side-eye as she hurried to check out a luxury electric car.

A little after noon, they picked up lunch at a kiosk and sat at a table at the far end of the exhibit hall. P.J. tucked a stray piece of lettuce under the bun and bit into her veggie burger. "I want to run something by you."

"Yes?" Franklin ripped open a packet of ketchup.

"I'm thinking of apologizing to George Dunn."

"I thought you already did."

"Yes, on Crave. I wonder if he even saw it. I think I owe him a personal apology or at least a call. I'll feel better when I launch my book. I mean, I nearly destroyed his life."

"True."

"You don't have to agree," P.J. said.

Franklin dipped a fry in ketchup.

"You think he'd want to hear from me?" P.J. said.

"I don't know. But I guess he could hang up. Or ream you out. He might enjoy that."

P.J. set down her burger. Her appetite had fled.

"Here's the thing," Franklin said. "Don't do it for yourself, so you can enjoy your book launch. If that's what you're thinking, don't do it at all. Do it for him. To help him feel better."

P.J. wondered whether she'd want to hear from George if their situations were reversed. If he had nearly destroyed her life. She'd probably be too angry, too busy looking for a way to get even. She hoped George was a better person than that.

***

"I heard you were looking for me," Mia said, as she entered P.J.'s condo.

P.J. hadn't been expecting her and was in the middle of boxing up the research she'd done for *Girl Is in the House*. Spread out on the dining table were articles by therapists about the treatment of sexual assault victims; notes from interviews with survivors and mental health professionals; journal articles on PTSD; newspaper stories and academic papers about perpetrators. "Someone at the hotel said you'd been fired. Are you okay?"

"I'm fine. They thought I was stoned. I was, kind of. My doctor had prescribed a new anxiety medication, and the dose was too high. I didn't feel like sharing that with my manager. Not that it would have mattered. Anyway, the dose is correct now."

"I'm glad." The tightness in P.J.'s shoulders eased.

"What's all this?" Mia said, approaching the table.

"Background material. For the book."

Mia glanced through several piles. "Must have been hard to read all of it."

Placing a textbook into a nearly full box, P.J. said, "It was. I had to take a lot of breaks. Work on something else for a while. Sometimes I didn't think I'd be able to write the book. It was too awful."

"Why bother then? Or did you get pleasure from turning my life upside-down?"

P.J. said softly, "I thought it was an important subject."

Mia walked to the window. A gray front was moving in from the west and she stared at it or perhaps at the reflection of the two sisters in the glass or perhaps both. "I didn't realize you talked to so many people. I thought you just turned everything I confided to you into a book."

P.J. fit a cover onto the box. "I wrote the book because I couldn't stop thinking about what happened to you. I felt I hadn't been there for you. When we were kids, I always took care of you. But while you were working for the senator, I was in Michigan, and we didn't talk much. Mom and Dad knew Blackwell. They knew his family. I thought that guaranteed he'd treat you well. I couldn't imagine he'd do what he did. And after, I didn't know how to help you. I felt it was up to me to do something since you didn't want to tell anyone else, at least at first. But I didn't know what to do. Then your drinking escalated, and I really couldn't help you. But I thought I could write a book that would be a warning to other people."

Mia touched the window, and P.J. felt the chill of the glass on her own fingers.

"You're not responsible for what happened to me," Mia said. She turned back toward P.J. "Blackwell is responsible. He should be in jail. Not working in high tech. There was nothing you could have done. For a long time, I thought it was my fault for not preventing it. For not screaming or hitting him. But I wasn't responsible, either." Mia blinked rapidly, the way she always had when she was angry, ever since they were children. She unbuttoned her coat.

"I'm sorry," P.J. said.

"Okay."

"You want me to hang up your coat?"

"I'd rather keep it on."

P.J. cut a piece of packing tape. "Mom can't forgive herself for saying all those nice things about Blackwell when you got the internship."

Mia shook her head. "Everyone said those things. He was a rising star. Someone who was changing the world for the better. Wasn't I lucky? Didn't I know how many people applied for that internship? I'll never forget my political science professor telling me Blackwell was a moderate Republican who was always supporting pro-woman legislation. Who gave women opportunities in his office. It makes me want to vomit." She sat on the couch. "I never talked to any reporters. A few called me. They figured out I'd worked for a politician and wanted to know if the book was about me, but I never called them back."

"I appreciate that." P.J.'s mouth was dry. She thought about making tea, but she didn't want to interrupt the conversation. It had been years since they'd really talked. She hadn't realized how much she missed Mia, the only other subject of their father's dinnertime interrogations, their mother's overweening love. The only other person who'd experienced the pressure of Lawrence's and Dina's middle-class expectations, their need to see their children rise and rise.

"I wish you'd told me about the book while you were writing it," Mia said. "I might have helped. I could have been ready for it when it came out."

"I should have done that," P.J. said. "But we weren't close anymore. You had your friends from group therapy. I meant to show it to you before it was published. I didn't mean for you to find out about it on Crave. I'm sorry you learned about it that way." P.J. taped one side of the box. "At least now you'll be able to go back to school and get your degree. I saw the Better Day Fund was closed, but it must have been pretty big."

Mia shrugged off her coat. "The woman who set it up disappeared with the money."

"Avery Baron? How?" P.J. set down the roll of tape.

"I gave her all of my account information, password, security questions, everything. She said she needed it to create the fund. The Better Day Fund transferred the money to my account, but then she used the information to withdraw it."

"Can't you get it back? If you tell the company what happened?"

"They won't help because they paid it out to me. They said what happened next wasn't their fault. That it was my negligence. I should have known better than to trust her after she talked to the *Pedestal* reporter. I specifically asked her not to, and she shared enough information that someone could figure out who the book was about if they really wanted to. She did it to get more people to contribute to the fund. I wonder if she was planning to steal it all along. I was lucky the magazine has a policy of not naming victims."

"I wondered if she was the one who talked to them. But then I thought it might have been my friend Alex. What are you going to do about the money?" P.J. said.

"There's nothing I can do. Avery's gone. Her apartment's empty. She hasn't shown up to work or to any AA meetings where I used to see her. Her phone is disconnected. But I'll still finish my degree. I'll have to go more slowly, but I'll finish it. I'll take two courses next semester."

"Are you working at another hotel?" P.J. said.

"I got a job at the rehab where I was treated. They offer tuition reimbursement. And on weekends, I work at a library. It's just shelving books right now. But I don't mind. Handling them makes me happy, especially knowing they have nothing to do with me." PJ. cringed. Mia continued: "Sometimes, when no one's looking, I smell them. It's the only high I'm allowed anymore. I'm thinking maybe I'll get a library degree. It'll take a long time, but I have that now."

P.J. taped the other side of the box. "That's a good plan."

"Don't seem so surprised."

"I'm not surprised," P.J. said, though she was. While she was writing about the woman Mia had been, her sister had changed. The Mia sitting in her apartment was grounded and hopeful. She wore the lifeguard whistle under her sweater, but didn't touch it. P.J. had forgotten how her sister's progress could feel nearly as good as her own. Like Marissa's pride in her new responsibilities, and her father's excitement about the promotion he would receive once his book was out. He'd described the lectures he'd chosen for the book over lunch, waving his fork like a baton, a piece of asparagus coming loose and dropping into his soda. She'd managed not to talk about her novel. At least until he asked.

P.J. sat next to her sister. "I could help you with tuition. I'd like to."

"I'd rather help myself."

"Okay."

"My housemate Wendell said you seemed pretty worried when you stopped by," Mia said.

"I was."

"You made quite an impression on him. He asked for your number. Should I give it to him?"

"Sure." P.J. hadn't forgotten him. "He seemed nice."

"He's a good guy. Protective," Mia said.

"I noticed."

"Not bad looking, either."

"I noticed that, too," P.J. said.

"And you two have a lot in common."

"Because he's concerned about the environment?"

"There's that," Mia said. "But I meant because he's a writer."

P.J. sighed. Of course he was.

Mia looked at the stack of background material waiting to be put away. "There's something I've needed to say to you for a long time. I know it was hard for you when I was living with you and drinking. I'm sorry about the way you found me that day."

"It's okay." P.J. stood. "I'm glad it wasn't the last way I ever found you."

The sisters were quiet for a moment.

"You want some tea?" P.J. asked.

Mia nodded. "I told Mom I was coming over here. They'll probably start having brunch again."

"Should I bring flavored seltzer for them to serve?"

"I don't know," Mia said. "I kind of miss seeing dad choke on his fake mimosa."

P.J. laughed.

CHAPTER THIRTY-FIVE

George had just set a raw shoulder steak on a cutting board when his phone rang, displaying a number he didn't recognize. The phone lay on the counter. Wiping his hands on his apron, he accepted the call and put it on speaker. "Hello?"

"It's P.J. Larkin. Is this a good time?"

He was tempted to hang up. "Not really. Why? Do you want to accuse me of something else?" He moved a knife steadily through the beef, slicing it into strips.

"I want to apologize," P.J. said.

"I thought you already did," he said.

"I didn't know if you saw it. Why didn't you say anything?"

On P.J.'s end of the line, a Harley roared. George waited for it to pass. "It's not my job to make you feel better. And if I've learned anything, it's that someone will always find a way to twist whatever you say on social media. Anyway, I'm rarely on Crave anymore." He rotated the cutting board, slicing the strips into cubes.

"How will you let people know about your book?" P.J. asked.

"The book you tried to destroy? Thanks to you, that doesn't seem to be a problem. I doubt there's anyone who hasn't heard about it."

With all the buzz George's book was getting, P.J. thought he was probably right.

("Are you surprised the man ended up on top?" Marissa had said recently as they hiked.

"I guess not," P.J. said, huffing.)

"It was my fault you had to go public about what happened with the senator," P.J. said.

"It was."

"I'm sorry."

George didn't mention that he might have decided to tell his story even if P.J. hadn't accused him of plagiarism. He didn't say that the ordeal had gotten him into therapy and possibly saved his marriage. "What you did was wrong," he said, "horribly wrong, but I suppose it must have seemed weird, my book coming out not long after I read yours." He tossed the beef with a flour mixture.

"Yeah. And I'd just gotten word that my agent couldn't sell my book," P.J. said. "It was the third one that didn't sell. I felt like I'd wasted years of my life. Then I remembered how you'd sent a long email praising my novel, listing all the things you liked about it. It seemed like you really wanted to buy it. But in the last sentence, you turned it down. I couldn't understand why you wouldn't publish a book you liked so much. When you came out with a similar novel, I thought, *that's why*, because you planned to steal it. It was a bit of a leap, I know, but that's what I thought, and I'm sorry."

George remembered rewriting the last sentence of the email. He and P.J. weren't so different. They'd both been desperate to publish. "I accept your apology. It was no fun to be targeted by a mob, but I guess you discovered that, too."

"They don't warn you about Crave in writing workshops," P.J. said. "We should compare notes over a beer if we're ever in the same city."

"Sure," George said, though he didn't mean it. "*Up the Hill* and my new novel are keeping me pretty busy right now." He tested the temperature of the oil in the pot on the stove and added the beef and onions. He wasn't supposed to talk about the new book yet. Saturn wanted to make a big announcement. But if there were a writer who could resist sharing that kind of news, George hadn't met them.

"I'm so glad to hear that." P.J. walked toward the restaurant where she was meeting Marissa. She relished being outside, her body opening after being stuck in the car all day and passing strangers who didn't expect her to carry their bags. She hadn't destroyed George's life. He didn't even seem that angry. Well, maybe angry, but not furious. He was writing. Moving on. She was so pleased she'd called. She couldn't wait to tell Marissa. "What's the new book about, if you don't mind my asking? I know some writers don't like to talk about their work too early."

The smell of seared meat filled the room. Since P.J. had identified herself, he'd hoped she would ask about his newest novel so he could tell her he'd written about them: an editor who's falsely accused of plagiarism and the writer who accuses him. He'd made sure to alter the plot and disguise the characters. He knew enough to do that. If he never said anything, she could pretend it was about some other writer. But was that what he wanted? When he was first working on it, he'd fantasized about telling her, inflicting a wound. Yet now that they'd talked, he wasn't sure. What was the point? He wasn't in the business of writing for revenge, but rather to understand himself.

Entering the kitchen, Kiara mouthed, "Who is it?"

A week earlier, they'd found out she was pregnant. George had said to Mutt, "You're going to be a big sister!" and the dog had whapped her tail against the wall so hard, George had worried she would injure it.

"She's happy because we're happy," Kiara had said, though

George swore Mutt understood.

Now he muted the phone. "It's P.J. Larkin."

"Everything okay?"

"Yup."

"Are you there?" P.J. said.

He held a finger to his lips and pressed unmute. "Still here."

P.J. spotted the restaurant and slowed so she could finish their conversation. The wind picked up, and she pulled her wool cap over her ears. "I asked about your new book."

"You were right. I'm one of those writers who would rather not talk about it this early."

"I totally get it."

She didn't, but George didn't correct her. Mutt was nosing his knees. Kiara was pulling water crackers from a box. He was rich even without the giant advance he would soon receive. He didn't need to steal another writer's peace of mind to feel it.

"I better go," P.J. said. "I'm meeting a friend."

"I really did like your novel," George said.

After P.J. hung up, she found herself wondering again if he'd borrowed something. Not everything, as she'd initially thought, but something small that he'd admired. She supposed she'd never know.

When she entered the restaurant, she saw Marissa already at a table. The vision of her friend who was so busy but had still found time to have dinner filled P.J. with such happiness she forgot all about George Dunn and his new and old novels, and what he might or might not have gleaned from hers, forgot all about her own novel and its limited success. She lifted her camera, intending to capture and nibble the image with a pithy caption, something about friendship, but then stopped and lowered the lens. What good had ever come from serving something on Crave? Just then, Marissa looked up and the friends greeted each other with their eyes, the exchange one of joy masquerading as light and recognition of the corners of their souls reserved for each other. P.J.'s full heart tripped when she realized she had very nearly missed it.

ACKNOWLEDGMENTS

Rosie, my South Dakota mutt, and Arie, my little white stray, you sat beside me while I wrote. There's no better company.

My deepest thanks to:

Robert Lasner and Elizabeth Clementson, publishing mavens, who plucked this book from the slush, polished it, and reminded me that I have something to say and a funny way of saying it. One day they may even tell me what the Ig in Ig Publishing stands for.

The writers, a.k.a. angels, who read and commented on drafts of this book though it took time away from their own work: Elissa Cahn, Elizabeth Edelglass, Carrie Esposito, Wendy Fox, Victoria Maizes, Louise Marburg, and Amanda C. Niehaus.

Erika Krouse and Deborah Jayne, developmental editors whose wisdom I relied on.

My friends, bibliophiles all, who read the manuscript and encouraged me to keep going: Cathy Hawley, Heidi Pate, Josh Rapps, and Wendi Temkin—who read it twice.

Jill Marr, my agent, who believed in the project and worked hard to sell it.

The Virginia Center for the Creative Arts, which blessed me with two weeks in writerly paradise while I revised.

That one editor who insulted me but whose advice I later took.

The scientists who formulated my mental health medications.

A short PSA: Mental health medication doesn't kill creativity or at least it didn't kill mine. I've written and published three books while on it. If you need it, take it. It makes life better.

And most of all to Steve for understanding my obsession with writing and selling this book, and for bringing home cake. You have my heart.